EVEN IF WE CRY

Even if We Cry

By
Terrie Todd

Even if We Cry
Published by Mountain Brook Ink
White Salmon, WA U.S.A.

The website addresses shown in this book are not intended in any way to be or imply an endorsement on the part of Mountain Brook Ink, nor do we vouch for their content.

This story is a work of fiction. Some well-known historical figures and events are named and quoted. All other characters and events are the product of the author's imagination. Any resemblance to any person, living or dead, is coincidental.

Scripture quotations are taken from the King James Version of the Bible. Public domain.
ISBN 9781953957-49-8
© 2024 Terrie Todd

The Team: Miralee Ferrell, Tim Pietz, Kristen Johnson, Cindy Jackson and Laurel Burgess
Cover Design: Indie Cover Design, Lynnette Bonner Designer

Mountain Brook Ink is an inspirational publisher offering fiction you can believe in.

*To my children, Nathanael, Mindy, and Reuben,
without whom I couldn't begin to comprehend the unthinkable
choices faced by my characters' real-life counterparts.*

Acknowledgments

Among the many books I read while researching this novel, I'm most grateful for Geoffrey Bilson's *The Guest Children: The Story of the British Child Evacuees Sent to Canada During World War II.* Within its pages, you'll find that many of the same events experienced by my fictional characters happened to the real-life children who made this journey.

A huge thank you to my British beta reader, Sharon Hawes.

Many thanks to Miralee Ferrell and her team at Mountain Brook Ink for believing in this story enough to invest in it and in me.

Above all, my thanks are due to my Redeemer, Jesus Christ, master storyteller and main character in the greatest story ever told.

Prologue

Children's Overseas Reception Board
45 Berkeley Street, W.1.

Mr. & Mrs. Eugene Gabriel
47 Abbey Court
Middlesbrough, England

<u>CONFIDENTIAL</u>

Dear Sir (or Madam),

I am writing this personal letter on the instructions of Mr. Geoffrey Shakespeare who is the minister responsible for the administration of the Children's Overseas Reception Scheme. Mr. Shakespeare is sure that you will appreciate its reassuring nature.

You may have heard over the wireless or may have read in the press, that the government cannot take responsibility for sending children overseas under the scheme without adequate naval protection.

In the accompanying letter, you are notified that your child (or children) has (or have) been accepted for evacuation overseas. You can rest assured that arrangements will be made for naval convoy. You can also rest assured that we shall not let your child (or children) go overseas if at the last moment we find that the situation has changed and that no convoy can be provided.

In the interest of the safety of your child (or children), and others who will accompany them, we ask you to regard this information as confidential – that is to say, you should not discuss the matter even with your neighbours, and you should ask your child (or children) also not to talk about it. We know we can rely upon you in this matter.

Yours faithfully,
Arthur Mullins, Director-General
CORB

SUGGESTED OUTFIT FOR EACH CHILD
UNDERTAKING THE JOURNEY

BOYS	GIRLS
Gas Mask	Gas Mask
1 overcoat & mackintosh	1 warm coat & mackintosh
(if possible)	(if possible)
1 suit	1 cardigan or woollen jumper
1 pullover	1 hat or beret
1 hat or school cap	1 pair warm gloves
2 shirts (coloured)	1 warm dress or skirt & jumper
2 pairs stockings	2 pairs stockings
2 undervests	1 change of underclothes,
2 pairs pants	including vests, knickers, etc.
2 pairs pyjamas	1 pair strong boots or shoes
1 pair boots or shoes	1 pair plimsolls
1 pair plimsolls	2 cotton dresses or overalls
6 handkerchiefs	with knickers
1 comb	2 pairs pyjamas
1 toothbrush and paste	1 towel
1 face flannel or sponge	6 handkerchiefs
1 towel	1 hairbrush and comb
1 suitcase – about 26” x 18”	1 toothbrush and paste
Stationery and pencil	1 face flannel or sponge
Ration card	Sanitary towels
Identity card	1 linen bag
Birth Certificate (if possible)	1 suitcase – about 26” x 18”
Bible or New Testament	1 attaché case or haversack
	Sewing outfit
	Stationery and pencil
	Ration card
	Identity card
	Birth Certificate (if possible)
	Bible or New Testament

NO trunk will be permitted. All clothing should be clearly
marked in indelible ink.

Chapter One

Margaret Gabriel to the Wrights

24 June 1940

Mr. & Mrs. Harold Wright
PO Box 26
Cedar Bluff, Manitoba
Canada

Dear Mr. & Mrs. Wright,

You are no doubt wondering who in their right mind would send their own children across the Atlantic to live with strangers, and I don't blame you.

I'm sure you've heard by now of the bombing here in Middlesbrough last month, courtesy of Mr. Hitler. As parents yourselves, you can understand the great anguish my husband Eugene and I experienced as we made the difficult decision to apply for the evacuation of our children overseas, and the tremendous relief and gratitude we felt when we received your cable. Immediately, we completed the application forms— nominating you as hosts, based on your cousin Melvin's hearty recommendation and your agreement. (I think he mentioned to you that he and my husband worked together for nearly a decade.) I cannot thank you enough. While we've never met, it puts our hearts at ease to know we have at least a remote connection with you. I simply could not bear it otherwise.

As you can imagine, the evacuation scheme of both our governments (we refer to it as CORB, and I suspect you do as well) has been met with many mixed feelings and concerns—not the least of which is the question of whether it's safe to attempt the crossing given the Nazi battleships, air bombers, and submarines on full alert. But when we were assured that the ships would travel in convoys, and with the fall of France to the Germans and the assumption that Britain is next in line for invasion, Eugene and I immediately agreed that we would never forgive ourselves if we didn't at least try. We've purchased the clothing and other items on CORB's recommended list and packed the children's suitcases in the event of last-minute notification. The children agree with the plan, although we are required to keep everything quiet even from friends and neighbors. For that reason, we've not mentioned anything to our youngest. She is not the best secret keeper.

We've just received word our three will be among the youngsters selected.

I thought I would write to tell you a little about our children to better prepare you, and perhaps you can write back and tell us all about your family and your community of Cedar Bluff. With such a name, it already sounds like a lovely and safe place— although at this point, anywhere our children won't be subjected to nightly disturbances by air raids sounds heavenly.

Our firstborn is Nina, who turned fourteen on 05 March. You'll find she brings her best energy to everything she puts her heart to. I confess I often wish she would give her heart more to her studies and to rising at the appointed time in the mornings. While Nina does not consider arriving on time to be essential to a healthy life, she does take excellent care of her siblings, and I am trusting her to watch over them on the voyage and during their stay in Canada. She will be a great help with your little one as well.

Next is our ten-year-old, Geoffrey. For someone so young, he and trouble are old friends. He is an easy boy to have around when he's unwell, since he takes to his bed and quietly sleeps it out. He's been unwell only the one time. I pray that Geoffrey resists the urge to climb things he ought not to climb or to dig holes in Canadian soil that need not be dug.

Our youngest is Hazel, age seven. I worry she'll be homesick. You'll quickly see how she clings to Nina for comfort, which is why I'm so grateful to know our children will stay together in your home. Hazel does try very hard to be good and kind. It just doesn't always come naturally.

It may interest you to know my husband and I are both employed by the ministry, working for the war effort—Eugene in the aircraft industry while I work in radio manufacturing. We also serve as air raid wardens in our neighborhood, ensuring that blackout regulations are adhered to and folks are off the streets during a raid. Of course, we are trusting this Canadian adventure, as we're calling it, will be a short-lived holiday that all the children will remember with fondness and that they will be sailing home to us again in safety and victory before the school year ends. God bless you for your hospitality and your commitment to care for our children as though they were your own. I sincerely hope to visit Canada one day.

Yours most sincerely,

Mrs. Margaret Gabriel
47 Abbey Court
Middlesbrough, England

Nina Gabriel held her gag reflex in check as she wiped vomit from Hazel's hair. "Try to lie still. Here, put your head on my lap."

"But everything stinks!"

Hazel's whining did nothing to make Nina's job easier. She wished she had something to plug her nose. "I know. We'll clean you up properly in the tub once your stomach settles."

Hazel moved only slightly, her face the same shade of gray as the sky above the Atlantic on a cloudy day.

"I'll read you the letter I've started to Mummy and Daddy. Concentrate. It will help you forget your tummy." Nina stroked Hazel's silky curls with one hand, unfolded the letter with the other, and then began to read.

"'Dear Mum and Dad.'"

"Wait. You have to put the date first." Even in her seasickness, Hazel was ever the diligent scholar.

"I did. I just skipped over that part."

"But I want to hear all of it."

"All right. '24 July 1940. Dear Mum and Dad—'"

Hazel raised her head and scowled. "But you have to put the address too."

"I did."

"I want to hear it *all*." She lay down and folded her hands on her chest. "I want to picture Mummy and Daddy in the house, reading the letter when they get it."

Nina resisted the urge to let out a frustrated growl and made do with a sigh. "Fine. 'Mr. and Mrs. Eugene Gabriel, 47 Abbey Court, Middlesbrough, England. Dear Mum and Dad.'" She read it all out in one breath before pausing, expecting Hazel to interrupt again. When she did not, Nina kept reading.

"'It's our third day aboard the *SS Anselm,* and everything is fine.'"

"No, it isn't! It isn't fine at all." Hazel tried to sit up, but Nina held her head down. "Tell Mummy and Daddy I've been ever so sick."

"Sh-h. We're not to worry them. You'll be right as rain by the time they receive this letter, so there's not much point telling them anything different now, is there? Let me keep reading."

"I want to write my own letter."

"You certainly can. When you're better. May I keep reading now?"

Hazel nodded.

"'Our cabin has two sets of bunks. Hazel sleeps above me but usually ends up crawling in with me before she falls asleep. I don't mind. Our cabinmates are named Jean and Alice. They are both thirteen, and we've become fast friends, even though I was officially placed in charge as the oldest. Jean is traveling with her brother, John, who is a year older, and Alice is alone. Jean thinks Alice is a bit of a snob, but I think she's very brave. I'm sure the three of us shall be the best of chums by the time we reach Canada. I do hope they will be placed near us.'

"'There are eighty-two children on board in total. The captain tells us we'll reach Halifax in nine or ten days. Our escort, Miss Nisbet, says she remembers reading about a big explosion in the Halifax harbor in 1917 (do you recall hearing of it?) but assured us that such a disaster will not happen to us. For one thing, we're not carrying explosives—much to Geoffrey's disappointment.'

"'Geoffrey has been his usual adventuresome self, treating this as a grand holiday. He's in a cabin with five other boys and one can only imagine what they get up to since their oldest and 'in charge' boy is only eleven himself. They like to show what great sailors they are by strolling casually down the corridors with hands in their pockets as the ship rolls. They usually end up bouncing off walls, but it's great fun.'"

Hazel interrupted again. "Did you tell them about Geoffrey's big tussle?"

"No. He can tell them in his own letter."

"You know he won't."

Nina counted on it. Her parents didn't need to know Geoffrey had already got into fisticuffs with another boy. She kept reading.

"'Activities of all sorts are organized to keep the younger

ones busy, like three-legged races and the like. We've had daily drills with our life jackets for practice. Even those who are seasick are expected to participate by going on deck, putting on life jackets, and being accounted for. We're instructed on how to get into the lifeboats and asked to repeat the instructions. But don't worry, nothing is likely to happen. It feels ever so safe with the other ships surrounding us.'

"'The crew members are kind to us, and the food is tasty and plentiful—for those well enough to enjoy it. The breakfast menu includes Rice Krispies, eggs and bacon, fried tomatoes, pancakes, kippers, and oily bloaters with their heads still on— although why anyone would order those is beyond me. I think that I—'"

A loud rapping on the cabin door interrupted Nina's reading and before she could answer, a flaxen-haired boy of about twelve opened the door and stuck his head in. "Are you Nina?"

"Yes." She'd seen the boy before at meals and hanging around with Geoffrey. His older brother, Robert Kent, had caught the eye of every girl on board.

"Your brother's in trouble. Come quick!"

"Geoffrey?" Nina moved Hazel's head from her lap to a pillow and rose from the bunk.

"Yes. Follow me."

"Stay where you are, Hazel," she called back over her shoulder. She followed the boy out of the cabin and down the narrow corridor to the stairs. "What's going on?"

"He said to fetch you and not to tell any of the crew. I can't get him out."

"Out from where?"

"You'll see. I'm Peter, by the way." Peter led her down one flight of stairs to the boys' quarters and opened the door of a cabin. It wasn't even Geoffrey's cabin, but there he was, hanging halfway out the porthole, his bottom half still in the room, his legs kicking. "He's got himself stuck."

"No. No-no-no-no-no." Nina ran for the porthole and wrapped her arms around Geoffrey's hips. He'd broken a cardinal rule. "We're not to open the portholes!"

"Shall I get the matron?" Peter stayed at the door. "Or one of the crew?"

"No!" Nina stopped him. "Help me pull him back inside. You mustn't tell anyone. Do you hear me?"

Pulling Geoffrey back into the cabin would not have been difficult had he cooperated. Instead, he braced his arms against the outside wall and kept kicking his feet.

"Geoffrey. Stop mucking about or I'll..." Nina couldn't think of a threat serious enough. "I'll tell everyone you kissed Rebecca Simpson on the lips."

That did it. Peter and Nina pulled the boy through, scraping his tummy and shoulders on the porthole's edge. Nina didn't release her grasp on Geoffrey's arm until she'd marched him all the way back to her own cabin. He sat on the bunk opposite Hazel, a sheepish grin on his face and his straight brown hair sticking out in all directions.

"What have you got to say for yourself, young man?"

"They dared me."

"Oh, well then." Nina rolled her eyes. "That explains everything."

Hazel leaned over the edge of her bunk and retched into her bucket, just as their cabinmates walked in.

Alice's hand rose to her mouth. "Oh, the smell!" She turned back toward the corridor so fast that her blond hair flew around her like a flag.

"You can't have a boy in here." Jean stood frozen, staring at Geoffrey with big brown eyes as though she'd never seen a boy in her life. Suddenly, the sour odor overcame her, and she clamped a hand over her nose and mouth.

"It's all right. I'm taking him back now." Nina pulled Geoffrey to his feet. "I'm so sorry about the smell. Hazel is dreadfully seasick, I'm afraid, but she's bound to improve."

"Geoffrey opened a porthole and got himself stuck!" Hazel rallied at the opportunity to tell a good tale.

"Sh-h. He wasn't stuck." Nina delivered her most serious glare.

Jean let out a dramatic gasp. "Did you report it? You know we're supposed to tell if anybody breaks a rule."

"No." Nina steered Geoffrey toward the door. "We're not telling anyone. Everybody's safe, and he'll not do it again. I don't want this to get back to our parents. They'll only worry. They have enough to worry about."

Jean pulled her suitcase out from its place and rummaged through it. "The sun is glorious. We were hoping you could join us on the deck chairs. Get some fresh air."

"I'd love to once Hazel's better. I'll be back to look after her as soon as I see this fellow safely delivered to his own quarters." Nina stepped out of the room, dragging her brother along and lecturing him on the way. "Don't you ever do that again, Geoffrey Eugene Gabriel. You will miss your supper tonight, and you will stay in your cabin until morning. Do you understand?"

Geoffrey nodded. "Perfectly."

"Was it worth it?"

He didn't even try to hide his grin. "Perfectly."

After supper, Nina slipped quietly into Geoffrey's cabin before his cabinmates returned. He'd fallen asleep. She left the sandwich she'd brought beside his pillow.

Ann Wright to the Gabriels

July 20, 1940

Mr. & Mrs. Eugene Gabriel
47 Abbey Court
Middlesbrough, England

Dear Mr. & Mrs. Gabriel,

We received Mrs. Gabriel's informative letter and immediately realized there's been a grave misunderstanding. While your children sound delightful and we are prepared to host your older daughter, Nina, we simply cannot take more than one child. I apologize if this was not made clear to you by Harold's cousin Melvin. We desire to do our patriotic duty and support the commonwealth, and we welcome Nina with open arms. However, with deep regret, I'm writing to say we cannot take her unless you are prepared for your children to be separated. I trust this letter reaches you in time to make alternate arrangements.

Yours sincerely,

Mrs. Ann Wright
PO Box 26
Cedar Bluff, Manitoba

Chapter Two

Nina to her parents

27 July 1940
On board the *SS Anselm*

Dear Mum and Dad,

It's another sunny day on board the ship, and we are all enjoying ourselves and looking forward to our arrival in Canada. Geoffrey is convinced there will be cowboys and Indians to see despite my best efforts to explain it won't be like the Saturday afternoon movies. He insists I am daft, so I suppose we'll find out when we arrive. At the moment, I am sunning myself on deck with Jean and Alice. Both girls have been simply lovely to me, and it will be terribly difficult to say good-bye. I am praying against all odds that they go to the same town as we do, though I already suspect that won't happen. Their parents did not nominate any host family on their applications, as they have no connections in Canada. Besides, it sounds as though most of the children will be going to Ontario, not to Manitoba like us. We girls shall have to content ourselves with letters. Jean is from London, Alice from Liverpool.

We have four official escorts. Two are nurses, one is a clergyman, and Miss Nisbet is a Girl Guide officer. She is the youngest, the prettiest, and the nicest and is considered our matron. Miss Nisbet has shown us a map of Canada, and we are trying to grasp the enormous size of the country. After we dock, it will take at least three days by train to reach Manitoba from Halifax. Can you imagine? We could cross all of England and back again, and still be only halfway across this country! How is that possible, especially when they have only a quarter of the people we have? Perhaps we should bring the entire country over. There would be plenty of room to spare, and our family could stay together.

The bell just sounded for lunch, so I shall end this letter. We've heard no news, so I trust all is well at home. Please rest assured that we are fine.

Your loving daughter,
Nina

Alice's well-worn April issue of *Hollywood* magazine featured Deanna Durbin on the cover in a green swimsuit. Pages inside were dedicated to Deanna's "new spring clothes." The three girls passed it around, comparing their hair-do attempts to Deanna's.

"Not even close." Alice groaned. "Why must I have such coarse, frizzy hair?"

Jean dragged fingers through her own. "Yours looks all right. Mine won't stay put. It's too limp."

"I'd trade you in a heartbeat. I'd trade for *your* tresses too, Nina. You're so lucky." Alice pulled her hair loose and tried again. "I hope my host family doesn't have any handsome boys. I couldn't bear to be seen first thing in the morning before I've tamed down this steel wool of mine."

"I wouldn't mind having a handsome foster brother." Jean wiggled her eyebrows. "Too bad I'm taking my *real* brother along."

The girls had promised to always remain true friends no matter what. As none of the boys on board were older than fourteen, they'd quickly agreed there would be no falling in love on the trip. Still, Nina couldn't help noticing both her friends eyeballing Robert Kent. A nice boy, to be sure, and funny.

After lunch, Nina read to Hazel from a children's storybook as they lay together on Nina's bunk.

Alice and Jean burst in, arguing.

"We were not!" Alice hollered. "Don't make things up that aren't true."

"But it *is* true! I saw you." Jean whirled around, and the two girls faced each other. "You were holding hands just like this." She tried to take hold of Alice's hand, but Alice pulled away.

"Don't listen to her, Nina. I would never stoop to hold hands with a mere fourteen-year-old."

Nina smirked, knowing Alice was only thirteen. Her gaze moved from Jean to Alice and back again.

Hazel was not as polite. "Who? Robert Kent? Did you hold hands with Robert? I would hold hands with him. I think he's dreamy."

Nina shushed her. What was she going to do with such a boy-crazy little sister?

"I *didn't* though." Alice climbed to her top bunk and flopped onto her pillow.

"I'm not daft. I'm telling you, Nina." Jean turned and took Nina's hand in her own. "Just like this, they were sitting side by side on a bench on deck. Then they let go as soon as they saw me. This one jumped up like a jack-in-the-box."

"Did not."

"Did too." With a big sigh, Jean lay on her own lower bunk. She placed her feet on the underside of Alice's mattress springs and bounced her three or four times. "Did too, did too, did too."

"Stop it. You're just jealous."

Jean stopped. "You admit it."

"Anyway, so what if I did?" Alice's voice was barely above a whisper.

"Ah-ha!" Jean gave Nina a triumphant smile. "See? I told you."

Alice's face appeared over the edge of her bed. "What are you going to do about it? Kick me out and find a different cabinmate?"

"I might." Jean grinned. "I can't tolerate liars. Or flirts. You, apparently, are both."

Nina lay back with a grin and winked at Hazel, whose wide-eyed expression told Nina she was worried about the girls' friendship.

"Fine." Alice climbed down, her shoes clattering on the ladder. "I'll go find something else to do so you don't have to *tolerate* me any longer." She stepped out into the corridor and closed the cabin door.

"Such a liar. Probably off to find Robert." Jean dragged out Robert's name in a mocking singsong. She folded her hands behind her head and crossed her ankles. "See if I care. I hope they go off and get married and have a dozen lying little brats."

Nina tried to suppress a grin.

Jean would have none of it. "What? You think it's funny? We made a pact. Am I the only one who takes it seriously?"

"A packet of what?" Hazel asked.

Nina patted Hazel's hand. "Not a packet. A pact. It's an agreement. A vow between friends."

"Which, apparently, we no longer *are*." Jean flipped over to face the wall.

"Nonsense, Jean. We're all a little bored, that's all. You two will make up."

The ship's siren screamed out an alert. Mad scurrying filled the corridor. Grabbing two life vests, Nina took a firm grip on Hazel's hand and headed to their lifeboat station as they'd practiced in the drills. Off to starboard, the ominous dark outline of a submarine glimmered. Nina feared her heart would pound right out of her chest as she helped Hazel into her stiff life vest and kept an eye out for Geoffrey. If the Germans were this close, wouldn't they have torpedoed the *Anselm* by now? How long would it take to sink? Were there enough life rafts for all? She relaxed a bit when she spotted Geoffrey in his group with one of the matrons.

"Exactly like the *Titanic*," Jean whispered. "It's going to be a tragedy."

"Nonsense." Nina scowled at her friend. "Lessons were learned from that. We'll be safe."

"It's one of ours!" someone shouted.

Relief swept over the group. After what seemed ages, the children were ordered to move to the rail and wave at the submarine. Nina waved until her arms ached. The black shadow slipped below the water's surface and out of sight like a great gray whale.

Everyone talked at once as they returned to their cabins, but Nina said little. All she could think about was how on earth she would manage to keep Hazel and Geoffrey safe if they ever had to abandon ship. *Oh God, help us*, she prayed.

At supper that night, Jean and Alice, still feuding, sat as far apart as they could at their assigned table. Not wanting to appear to be taking any one side, Nina tried for a spot halfway between them. When the meal ended, Jean leaned toward Nina. "I'll take Hazel her supper if you have a chat with Alice. Try to talk some sense into her."

Nina spotted an opportunity and agreed. When Jean was out of sight, she slid over to Alice. "Want to go for a stroll with me?"

"Sure." Together, the girls left the dining hall. After a brisk walk only halfway around the upper deck, Nina clutched Alice's wrist and led her straight toward their cabin.

"Where are we going?"

"You'll see."

When they reached the cabin, Jean took one look at them and turned her face away. Alice climbed to her bunk, muttering something about bossy friends.

"Listen," Nina began. "I'm taking Hazel out for some fresh air. When we return, you two had better have things sorted out peaceably. Think about our scare this afternoon. Is this really how you want to be with each other if we end up on a sinking ship? Do whatever you must to be friends again. We made a friendship pact. I would dearly love to keep my end of it."

Nina and Hazel took their time strolling around the deck and watching the evening sunshine shimmer across the water. Hazel was finally getting her sea legs. When they approached their cabin again, melodious laughter drifted from behind the door. Nina had no idea what had transpired between her two estranged friends, but all four girls spent the rest of the night laughing and talking as though nothing had happened. Robert Kent was not spoken of again.

Overnight, the ship docked in Newfoundland. Nina's legs wobbled as she followed a line of evacuees down the gangplank and onto a bus. Their destination was a large community hall where friendly people greeted them with welcoming smiles and hilarious accents. Long tables laden with food filled the room. Nina could only stare in puzzlement at the large pitchers of milk spaced up and down the tables. How many cups of tea would they need to swallow to use all that milk?

Eventually, teenage girls not much older than Nina began filling tumblers with milk for the children. They were to drink it straight. Instead of tea, they were offered their choice of ginger ale, Orange Crush, Lime Rickey, and 7-Up. Best of all, dainty triangular sandwiches filled with sticky brown paste disappeared as quickly as they could hit the table. Though she enjoyed them, Nina had no idea what the brown stuff was until she heard one of the ladies shout, "We'll have to send out for more peanut butter!"

Once the children had eaten their fill and then some, the

Canadians came around with gifts. Each child received a shiny Newfoundland ten-cent piece.

"Something to remember your brief visit by," a plump woman announced with a smile and a nod. "I'm told it's the equivalent of five pence in Britain."

Nina stared at her dime, incredulous. It was more than she'd been given to carry with her across the ocean. Canada must be the wealthiest nation in the whole world if it could afford to be so generous. She held both hands out to her siblings. "Better give me yours for safekeeping."

"I won't lose it." Geoffrey closed his fist around his coin.

"I won't lose mine, either." The words weren't even out of Hazel's mouth before her dime hit the floor and rolled under a table. Hazel scrambled after it, scraping her back on a bench. "Ow!" She retrieved it and handed it over to Nina without another word.

Geoffrey had already run off with friends, and Nina decided the dime wasn't worth the battle.

Back on the ship, life took on a renewed energy as the ocean portion of their journey neared its end. With calmer seas, more children were out of their bunks and buzzing around getting in the crew's way and playing on the decks. Though she dreaded saying good-bye to her new friends, Nina found herself caught up in the excitement generated by the spotting of icebergs in the distance. As they neared Halifax, she prayed again for them to stay together.

"I already have the address where I'm going to be." She handed Jean and Alice each an envelope she'd self-addressed to the Wrights' home in Manitoba. "Sorry there's no stamp. Promise me you'll write as soon as you're settled so I can write back. We mustn't lose touch."

Jean accepted her envelope, and her eyes welled up. "You're breaking my heart, Nina. I feel like I've known you all my life."

"I know. Me too." The girls embraced.

Alice took her envelope without a word. She glanced at Jean but wouldn't look Nina in the eye.

"What is it?" Nina ducked her head, forcing Alice to look at her. Still, the girl said nothing. Nina turned to Jean.

"We didn't know how to tell you." Jean pressed her lips together.

"Tell me what?"

"Alice and I, and my brother John, got called into the dining hall last night with about twenty others. We're all going to Prince Edward Island."

"Prince Edward Island?"

The girls nodded, half smiling. "We don't know exactly where yet, but…it's a pretty small island. Not far from here, by Canadian measures."

"But ever so far from Manitoba." Nina let out a long sigh. "I'm happy for you two. I really am." They embraced again. "And who knows? Maybe we'll be sailing back home together in six months. How long can this stupid war last anyway?"

28 JULY 1940

CABLEGRAM TO CORB RECEPTION CENTRE
HALIFAX, NOVA SCOTIA, CANADA

ATTN: CORB ESCORTS DISEMBARKING SS ANSELM

GABRIEL CHILDREN MUST BE KEPT TOGETHER. NOMINATED HOST IN MANITOBA ONLY PREPARED TO TAKE ONE. PLEASE FIND ALTERNATE ARRANGEMENTS TO KEEP NINA, GEOFFREY, AND HAZEL GABRIEL TOGETHER.

SINCERELY, MR. & MRS. EUGENE GABRIEL,
MIDDLESBROUGH, ENGLAND

Chapter Three

Nina to her parents

4 August 1940
Dear Mum and Dad,

We have arrived in Canada! We first spotted the coast of Nova Scotia on the morning of 02 August and spent that night docked in Halifax Harbor. "Why are there so many lights?" Hazel asked. She didn't know there was such a thing as no blackout. We woke the next morning to a thick, cold fog. Officials from CORB came on board, and there was much scurrying about as they reviewed our papers with our escorts, compared them to their rolls, and placed us in groups. We were given milk and cookies while we waited. Apparently, children here drink milk by the glassful every day. Canada must be home to a lot of cows.

One girl who is going to stay with her aunt in Ontario realized she had not packed any sort of gift for her aunt, so she stole one of the ship's fish knives to give her. Can you imagine? Not that I'd be tempted to steal, but I'm so glad you gave me the tin of sweets for our host family. Geoffrey has no idea it's in my suitcase, so you needn't worry about him.

After a lot of rushing and then waiting, and then rushing again, we finally disembarked. We were placed in queues and examined by medical authorities, including X-rays. One poor little girl was held back after that, I haven't heard why. What do you suppose will become of her?

After seeing the doctor, an immigration official asked for our number (not our name) and then called out the number to another official, who called out which province we were going to and made sure everything—names, numbers, and destinations—matched up on everyone's lists. They sent Geoffrey, Hazel, and me to wait on a bench reserved for the "Manitoba" children. There are not many of us, but rumor has it more will be coming on future ships. They are no longer calling us evacuees but "guest children." That has a nice sound to it, don't you think?

We were told to keep enough supplies in our rucksacks for three days' travel. They loaded the rest of our luggage onto a train car. I truly hope it makes it to the proper destination. At this point, our British escorts officially handed us off to the Canadians. Our conductress is named Mrs. Madigan. She is not the warmest person, but I suppose that means she takes her duties very seriously. I am the oldest of our group, so she has appointed me as her assistant. I find it difficult to understand her accent, but I am trying to be polite and not ask her too often to repeat herself—while discouraging G and H from mimicking her or any of the Canadians we've encountered.

People from the Canadian Red Cross handed out packages for each of us. It was all quite wonderful, Mummy. Each of us received a cake of soap, a towel, a face flannel, some Glucose-D tablets, a toy, and a book (mine is *Anne of Green Gables*). I got a small needlework kit (a sampler to embroider) and G and H each got a tracing book. Each package also included a colorful handkerchief featuring a picture of a Canadian Mounted Police trooper. Do you suppose we will see any real ones?

By the time we boarded our train car for Winnipeg, darkness had settled in. We went straight to sleep. Now it is morning, and we are well on our way to Manitoba. I won't write again until we arrive, as the jostling of the train makes letter-writing even more challenging than it was on the ship. Rest assured we are fine, we are safe, and we are together. I'll tuck Hazie's letter in with this one.

Your loving daughter,
Nina

Nina tried to utilize the early morning daylight to read her book while her siblings still slept. What a coincidence that *Anne of Green Gables* was set on Prince Edward Island, where Jean and Alice would be. Even though it was set sixty years ago, the book helped her picture her friends in their new homes. As she got into the first few chapters, it was easy to relate to Anne—going somewhere unknown to live with strangers. At least Anne didn't have younger siblings to watch out for. Then again, Nina felt truly grateful she had two loving parents and a home to return to. Anne did not. While Nina found Anne's resilience and courage something to strive for, she thought the girl immature when it came to her flighty, melodramatic dreams. *If I were as distracted and forgetful as Anne, it would mean the death of Geoffrey and Hazel.*

Though Nina would never mention it to her parents, Hazel had cried herself to sleep their first night on the train despite Nina's holding, cuddling, and reassuring. Even though the train cars were large compared to those back home, they were far less comfortable and stifling hot. The rocking motion did little to dispel Hazel's nausea. The bare floor was dirty, and the windows appeared to not have been washed in years. Seats were upholstered with hard leather coverings, torn and stained. They opened horizontally for sleeping at night, and upper berths unfolded from above. Geoffrey slept in an upper berth while Nina and Hazel shared the bottom. Each child was issued two blankets, but no pillow. Nina rolled up one blanket for a pillow to share with Hazel. Geoffrey rolled up a jacket. Each train car had its own lavatory and sink.

As the sun rose higher and the children began to stir, Mrs. Madigan stood and commanded everyone's attention. "Good morning, boys and girls. I trust everyone was able to sleep all right. I am pleased to announce you've finished your first night of three on the train. I know it's hard for you to imagine sixteen hundred miles from Halifax to Winnipeg. But think of those children who are going all the way to the west coast, to British

Columbia. For when we arrive in Manitoba, they will be only halfway through their journey!"

The children let out appropriate gasps of awe, and Nina breathed a sigh of gratitude.

"Now you'll be happy to know that a cook has been assigned to the train. I will be going to the kitchen car to fetch your breakfasts and bring them back here for you to eat. I would like one helper to accompany me, please—someone eleven or older, please."

A girl named Betty raised her hand.

"Yes, thank you. You can come with me. While we're gone, I am placing Nina in charge. Nina, would you wave, please, so everyone knows who you are?"

Mrs. Madigan's accent was already becoming easier to understand. Nina waved and smiled at the other evacuees.

"While we're collecting your breakfast, please fold up your seats and berths. Anyone who has not already done so may use the lavatory—I suggest youngest to oldest." She glanced at Nina. "I hope you're all hungry. Our cook is working diligently to provide you with delicious and nutritious meals three times a day, so there'll be no need to hoard anything away. Come along, Betty. Everyone, we'll be back shortly."

Excited about a new routine, the children did as they were told for the most part. Nina's biggest challenge was brushing and braiding Hazel's hair while keeping an eye on Geoffrey who tried to fold up his berth with himself still in it. *If I can handle him, I can handle any of these others.*

Mrs. Madigan wasn't wrong about the food. The scent of oatmeal and bacon made Nina's tummy rumble. They enjoyed everything with milk, bread and butter, jam and marmalade, and tea. Nina made sure Geoffrey and Hazel remembered to say thank you. What Hazel couldn't finish, Geoffrey gladly did.

After everyone had eaten, Nina helped gather all the dishes, then Mrs. Madigan took them away. They spent the morning looking out the window at the rolling landscape—more trees and rivers and sprawling fields, and fewer towns than Nina had ever seen. Mrs. Madigan made a point of stopping at each seat to chat with the children individually. When she reached the Gabriels, she took the empty seat beside Geoffrey, facing Nina and Hazel.

"How's everything going here? You are all siblings, correct?"

Nina answered for them all. "Yes, ma'am. The Gabriels."

The woman flipped a page on her clipboard. "Ah yes. From Middlesbrough? Where is that in relation to London?"

"Way north. Middlesbrough's in the northeast of England. I've never actually been to London."

"Nina, thank you for the help you've been to me already." She turned to Geoffrey. "Geoffrey, age ten, correct?"

Geoffrey nodded. "Yes, but I'm practically eleven. My tenth birthday was a whole month ago."

"I see." The woman stifled a grin. "And…Hazel. You're seven? How are you enjoying your trip?"

Hazel's eyes welled up, but she managed to whisper, "It's fine."

Mrs. Madigan looked at Nina. "A little homesick, are we?"

Nina nodded. "She misses Mum."

"Perfectly understandable. You're a brave girl, Hazel. And a very lucky girl to have your big sister here to look after you." She turned toward Geoffrey. "How about you, Geoffrey?"

"I think it's grand." Geoffrey focused on his tracing book as he outlined a picture of a horse and her foal.

"Right, then. Good for you. Keep your chins up." Mrs. Madigan moved on.

Nina to Jean
6 August 1940
Dear Jean,

I'm starting a letter to you even though I don't yet have an address because I simply must describe our journey to someone, despite the rocking motion of the train car. Please forgive my handwriting. It seems we have been traveling forever already, and we still have two full days to go. It's sweltering, stuffy, and smelly with all these children on board. I can feel sweat pooling around my belt and am wondering why they kept telling us to prepare for fierce cold.

I don't know what you are seeing in Prince Edward Island, but as we travel across Canada, I am seeing water and trees, trees and water. I've never seen so much wood or so many houses made from it. Are you finding everything so very big? The trains, the cars, the homes, and other buildings. I suppose it's what people do when space is no obstacle.

We've made stops in several small towns, and it's as though we are celebrities. We've seen boys riding alongside the tracks on bicycles, waving to us. People offer sweets and fruit and words of welcome. We see Canadian soldiers at every station. It is strange to think they are probably headed to England while we are arriving here. Often, they smile at us and point one thumb in the air. I'm not certain what it means, but the younger children all return the gesture.

Several of the stops we've made had French-sounding names. Geoffrey marched right up to some boys, bold as brass, and asked if they spoke English.

"Non. Français seulement," they said. Which is about all the French I know, but clearly indicates they understood the question. I do hope people speak English in Manitoba. Well, I know our host family does. The woman who will be our foster mother, Mrs. Wright, was born in England. But what if school is in French? I shall be so lost. When we stopped in Montreal, a doctor came on board in case there were any medical issues needing attention. I can't speak for the other cars, but there were no issues in ours. Between you and me, though, I was tempted to invent an illness of my own. He was the youngest, handsomest doctor I have ever seen! Gorgeous, wavy hair and kind eyes. And he was bilingual (that's a new word I've learned), speaking

English with a most attractive French-Canadian accent.

I imagine you are already settled in your new home. Do you have your own room? Do they have any handsome sons?

Guess what? I was given a copy of *Anne of Green Gables* and have begun reading it. How lovely it would be to reach our foster home and find there's already a letter waiting there for me from you or Alice! Then I'll know right where to mail this one. Please draw me a map of PEI showing approximately where you are and where Cavendish would be in relation to it—if it actually exists. Oh, I do hope I shall be able to visit there before we return home.

All for now,
Nina

August 1940

Dear Mummy and Daddy,

I don't like Nina. She's bossy and mean. When can I come home?

Yours truly,
Hazel

Chapter Four

Geoffrey to his parents

6 August 1940

Dear Mum and Dad,

Nina is a big meanie. I know you said to obey her, but she acts like she is our mother. I want to play Mounties with Malcolm and Edward, but Nina said I must first write you a letter. So here is my letter.

The ship was grand fun. We saw a submarine and other ships and icebergs and a whale and all sorts. Lots of the kids were seasick but not me. They gave us lots of food.

The train ride was very long. They gave us lots of food.

The Canadians speak funny. I have lots of friends. I am going to be a Mountie when I grow up.

I am having a jolly time when Nina is not being so bossy. We are nearly in Winnipeg. What a funny name. Also, we saw a mother bear and two cubs running away from the train track and into the woods. I hope there are bears in Cedar Bluff.

Your loving son,
Geoffrey

Canadian train platforms were not raised up to the height of the train cars like they were at home, so Nina had to step down three steps from the car to the wide platform. The sun blistered hot from high in the sky, but at least the air moved and the ground did not—although it felt in motion. She drew a deep breath and looked around. If only she could tie a leash to Geoffrey. She watched him take off with two friends. Gripping Hazel's hand, she followed the boys inside the station only to lose sight of Geoffrey again as more children and adult passengers surrounded her. Uniformed soldiers stood in groups or hustled on and off cars, just like the other stations at which they'd stopped.

Union Station boasted a lovely, large rotunda in the center. The coolness of the room offered a wonderful contrast as Nina sank onto a high-backed wooden bench and waited for instructions. She scanned the crowd for Geoffrey. Mother should have given him a bright orange hat.

"Why is the room moving?" Hazel took a seat beside Nina.

"It's not. It only feels like it is because we've been moving for the past sixteen days." Or was it only fifteen? Nina had lost count.

Mrs. Madigan sat on the other side of Nina with a sigh. "Are you weary, dear?"

"I'm all right." She spotted Geoffrey and his friend Malcolm walking toward her.

"I wanted to thank you again for being my helper on the ride from Halifax. This is where we'll say our good-byes. I'll be continuing on with children going to Edmonton and Vancouver, and you'll be placed in charge of the Province. I imagine someone will give instructions shortly." She unfolded a paper fan from her bag and waved it in front of her face.

Mrs. Madigan had barely finished her sentence when the public address system crackled to life. "Attention, all British children. Welcome to Manitoba. For those of you who are not reboarding, we ask that you gather in the corner where Mr. Cress is waving a flag. Once everyone is assembled, you'll receive further instructions."

Nina turned to see a man with dark hair and glasses standing on a bench waving a Union Jack. She took Hazel's hand and walked across the terminal to stand near him.

"Welcome to Winnipeg, children. Everyone staying in Manitoba will be boarding a bus in just a few minutes. I'm sure you're all ready for a meal, a bath, and good sleep in a real bed, yes?"

Cheers went up, and Nina's heart soared at the idea of a bath.

"If you have good-byes to say, now's the time," Mr. Cress said. "Your luggage is being loaded into the belly of the bus, and the end of your long journey is almost here. The bus is waiting right outside those doors. Please assemble in front of it for a group photo before boarding. Once everyone is on board, we'll take a roll call."

The next several hours went past in a busy blur. Eventually, they arrived at a school for the deaf, emptied of students for the summer holiday. Nina and Hazel were assigned to a girls' dormitory and Geoffrey to a boys'. The promised bath and bed energized Nina.

The following day, volunteers herded all the children through medical offices. Nina blushed when she had to strip to her knickers. When the nurse offered her a white gown to wear throughout her examination, she took it gratefully. The nurse measured and weighed her. The doctor peered into her ears and mouth. She answered endless questions, all of which pointed to her good health—although a little underweight, according to the nurse. The doctor, though not handsome like the one on the train, set her at ease with jokes and riddles.

"Which Canadian city is full of large, wild cats?"

If it were not for his grin, Nina might have been concerned. "I don't know."

"Vancougar." He chuckled.

Nina grinned politely.

"And how are you coping with the harsh Canadian winter so far?" He laughed at Nina's shocked response. "Don't worry.

This August day is pretty much the hottest it ever gets." As he scrawled notes on Nina's form, he came to a section headed "Mental Condition."

"What shall I write here?" The doctor smiled and showed Nina the line.

"Oh. Weak." She smiled back.

The man laughed. With a flourish, he wrote one word. *Bright*.

With the medical exams out of the way, the children were treated to a tour of Winnipeg. Nina was handed her own copy of a local newspaper with their group photo on the front. She felt like a celebrity. Strangers waved and plied the children with sweets, hankies, and other gifts. They rode the bus to Assiniboine Park. Nina wished they could just live there as Geoffrey and Hazel were free to run around as much as they wanted. The park featured a zoo, which kept them entertained for an entire afternoon, as well as lovely English gardens—ironically, more beautiful than Nina had ever seen in England. They bought fruit ices for a nickel at a pavilion and enjoyed them while relaxing in the shade of beautiful oak trees.

"It's hard to imagine there's a war on back home," Nina said to Mr. Cress when he asked how she was coping. She had scanned every page of her newspaper. While a full page was dedicated to war news, the rest contained ordinary news in the life of a city—advertisements, sports, fashion, and social events.

In the evenings, they watched a film, played games, ate chocolate ice cream, and even sat around a campfire. Nina enjoyed her first taste of toasted marshmallows while Mr. Cress announced an oral quiz.

"I'll call out a word, and let's see who can be the first to yell out the Canadian term for the same thing. Ready?"

"Ready!"

"Jumper!" he called.

"Sweater!"

"Correct. Dressing gown."

Some said, "bathrobe," others said, "house coat."

"Either is correct," Mr. Cress encouraged. "Trousers."

"Pants." At this, most of the children giggled.

"Vest."

"Undershirt." More giggling ensued.

"Right you are. Here's a confusing one. Waistcoat."

"Vest."

"Well done, children. Challenging, isn't it?"

When they clamored for more, Mr. Cress tossed out one more. "All right. Just one. Ready?" Heads bobbed in anticipation. "Nappy."

The children looked around in confusion. *Nappy?* Everyone knew what nappies were, but what did Canadians call them?

"No fair, Mr. Cress." one of the bigger boys complained. "That one wasn't on our list."

Mr. Cress grinned. "The list you were issued is far from comprehensive, my friends. You'll run into all sorts of words that will make you wonder, and you will say words that make others laugh. You'll do well if you can learn to laugh with them. Don't assume they are being unkind. Anybody want to take a stab at the word *nappy*?"

Nina raised a cautious hand. Somewhere in the dim recesses of her memory, she thought she'd heard or read the word. It would be embarrassing to be wrong, though.

"Yes, Nina? Do you know it?"

"Diaper?"

"Yes. That's it. Canadian babies wear diapers. I imagine some of the homes you're going to will include babies in diapers, so it's best you know this one. Here's hoping you don't have to change them."

By the third day, local families had picked up at least half the children. Those moving to other towns within Manitoba, like Nina and her siblings, awaited the arrival of their host families to escort them to their homes. Nina had resisted making friends with anyone after saying good-bye to Jean and Alice. It was simply too hard. Geoffrey bravely shook hands with his pal Malcolm and waved as his friend rode away with his foster family. Then he turned and wiped tears on his shirt sleeve, remaining quiet until evening.

By that night, only the Gabriel children remained.

"It seems there's been some sort of mix-up, Nina." Mr. Cress tapped his clipboard with his pencil. "We were under the impression that your hosts, the Wrights, from…" he checked his board again. "Cedar Bluff … were coming to pick you up today. We are trying to reach them. They apparently live on a farm three miles from town."

"How far is it to Cedar Bluff?" Nina tried to calm her worst fear. What if the Wrights had changed their minds?

"About ninety miles northwest. Don't worry. I'm sure it's just a small miscommunication. In any case, you needn't worry. We'll not leave you stranded. Try to get a decent rest tonight, and I'm sure all will be sorted out tomorrow."

Nina spent more of her night tossing than sleeping. What had happened to the Wrights? If they were this careless or forgetful, what did the future hold for the three of them?

The next day, Mr. Cress announced he would drive the Gabriel children to Cedar Bluff himself.

"Did you ring Mr. Wright?" Nina asked.

"You mean did I *call* him."

"Yes. Did you?"

"Apparently, they don't have a telephone on the farm. I spoke with a Mrs. Jasper at the Cedar Bluff General Store who assured me the Wrights are expecting you. 'It's all Ann has talked about for weeks,' she said." Mr. Cress leaned his head toward Nina. "But Mrs. Jasper thought the Wrights were expecting you by bus or train. That must be the mix-up. They didn't know we were expecting them to come fetch you. It will all be fine."

Once they were organized, Mr. Cress loaded their bags into the boot of his car, reminding Nina that it was called a *trunk* in North America. As the one most prone to motion sickness, Hazel sat up front. Within minutes, they were out of the city and traveling down a long stretch of flat highway surrounded by fields that seemed to go on forever. Mr. Cress pointed out wheat, flax, potato, and sugar beet fields. Geoffrey asked endless questions about cowboys and Indians, to which Mr. Cress gave patient explanations about reservations and rodeos and residential schools—much to Geoffrey's disappointment. The few small towns they passed through consisted of a handful of homes, usually a church or two, a school, and a post office— often combined with a store. Some had hotels and most of those boasted pubs. None of it looked much like home to Nina. No stone buildings anywhere, and only a few of brick. Most of the buildings were made from wood. Even fences were made from wooden posts and barbed wire instead of stones.

When they pulled into Cedar Bluff, Mr. Cress stopped in front of a store identified by a large overhead sign as *Jasper Grocery*. Above the sign were two upper windows, both with curtains drawn. Mr. Cress went inside while the three siblings got out to stretch their legs and look around. The main block of town featured a dry goods store, post office, restaurant, bank, and a store with a sign that read "Seed and Feed."

"Seed and Feed?" Hazel sounded out the words. "Is that what Canadians call a grocer?"

"I don't think so." Nina shook her head. "I think it's a place for farmers to buy supplies. The feed would be for animals."

Three boys came down the sidewalk, one on a bicycle and two on foot. They stared at Geoffrey's short pants, then at Nina, then at the car. A woman came out of the post office, stared for a moment, and then walked over to them. "Good afternoon. You must be the British children."

Nina cleared her throat. "Yes, ma'am. We're the Gabriels."

"Like the angel?"

Nina nodded and smiled.

"All siblings?"

"Yes, ma'am."

"Well, I heard Ann was taking in an English child, but I certainly didn't realize there were three of you. Oh, I do hope she can handle it, poor thing." Suddenly a big smile lit her face. "Well, I'm sure she can. Welcome to Canada." She turned and continued down the sidewalk and around the corner without introducing herself.

Nina muttered a quiet "thank you." The woman was clearly misinformed.

"Tally ho!" The boy on the bike shouted in a mock English accent as he took off down the street and around the corner, the other two laughing and running after him.

Hazel waved at something up high, and Nina followed her gaze. Above the store's sign, a girl with red braids watched from one of the windows, but she didn't wave back. When she caught Nina's eye, she let the curtain drop.

Mr. Cress came out of the store carrying three bottles of Orange Crush which he distributed to the children. "I've got directions to the Wrights' farm. Anyone need a bathroom before we head off again?"

They settled into their seats with the refreshing drinks. Should she relay the conversation with the woman on the street to Mr. Cress? Probably better not to. She'd find out what was going on soon enough.

Hazel to her parents
9 August 1940
Dear Mummy and Daddy,

We are in Canada now. Did you know they have lions and monkeys and zebras and giraffes? But guess what? They all live in the zoo. Do you like my joke?

Soon, we are going to our new foster family. What will we call them?

I miss you, but Nina says we must not let our new family know if we get lonely because that will make them wish we didn't come, and we want them to be glad we are here. Nina says we must be helpful and kind. Nina is bossy. But if I can't be with you, I'm glad I can be with Nina. I will write another letter when we reach our new home.

Love and kisses,
Hazel

Chapter Five

10 AUGUST 1940

TELEGRAM FROM CORB RECEPTION CENTER
HALIFAX, NOVA SCOTIA, CANADA

TO DISTRIBUTION CENTER, WINNIPEG

ATTN: MR. D. CRESS

RECEIVED CABLE FROM MR. EUGENE GABRIEL, MIDDLESBROUGH, ENGLAND, REQUESTING CHILDREN BE KEPT TOGETHER. CHILDREN ALREADY EN-ROUTE TO MANITOBA. NOMINATED HOST IN MANITOBA ONLY PREPARED TO TAKE ONE CHILD. NO ALTERNATE ARRANGEMENTS FOUND AT THIS TIME FOR NINA, GEOFFREY, AND HAZEL GABRIEL. PLEASE MAKE EVERY ATTEMPT TO KEEP CHILDREN IN SAME COMMUNITY IF NOT SAME HOME.

Mr. Cress turned down a dusty gravel road and instructed the children to roll up their windows despite the heat. "Each intersection is one mile." He pointed to a corner fence post. "Although some of the 'intersections' are merely a dirt road… or maybe just a road allowance at this point. You can count off the miles, though, by the fence lines or the change in crops."

Nina counted one mile before she saw a white farmhouse in dire need of paint. A large barn and several other smaller outbuildings, a vast vegetable garden, and a dozen or more roaming chickens completed the picture. Would the Wright farm look similar?

At the second intersection, a small building with a peaked roof bore a large sign on its front. DERRYLINE SCHOOL NO. 1421. *A school?* Oddest-looking school Nina had ever seen. Rows of tall evergreen trees flanked the area on the north and west sides. Two tiny outhouses and a stable with a metal roof and half-walls stood behind the main building. A set of swings and a something like a cricket field rounded out the deserted schoolyard.

"This is where you'll go to school, I imagine," Mr. Cress said. "At least, Geoffrey and Hazel will. These country schools generally go from Grades One through Eight."

"In such a small building?" Nina craned her neck to view it from the other side as they passed.

"Yes, well … there might only be twenty children. Are you ready for high school, Nina?"

"I finished year nine in June."

"Then you will most likely attend high school in town."

Nina wished she'd looked around more for a high school while they'd been in town.

Another farmyard appeared at the next corner on the opposite side of the road as the school. "That should be the Wright place up ahead," Mr. Cress pointed with his chin. "Only a one mile walk to school."

A larger, two-story house with a more recent paint job than the one they had passed greeted them. A wide porch wrapped around three sides, and red geraniums grew from window boxes. Orange marigolds formed a row in front of the porch railing and a massive vegetable garden filled the space south of the house. A big red barn rose on a small hill, overshadowing nearly everything. A woman hung clothes on a line. A boy and a dog ran around in another part of the yard.

"Look, Nina. Pigs!" Hazel pointed.

Sure enough, a pen on one side of the barn held half a dozen large black and pink pigs. *Oh, dear.* She'd seen pigs on visits to a friend's farm back home. Did Canadian pigs smell as awful? On the opposite side of the barn stood a chicken coop with a wire enclosure on one side. Dozens of hens wandered inside the pen, some white, some the same reddish-brown as the dog that began barking as soon as Mr. Cress pulled into the yard. By the time the car stopped, it was surrounded by the boy, the dog, and the woman from the clothesline, a baby on one hip. This must be Daddy's friend's cousin, Ann Wright. Tired lines around her eyes revealed the face of a worn and weary woman. She did not appear happy to see them.

Mr. Cress rolled down his window and addressed the boy. "Is this the Wright place?"

"Yes, sir." The boy looked around Nina's age.

"Does your dog bite?"

"Naw." The boy scratched the dog between the ears as she stood beside him, tail wagging. "Rosie won't hurt anybody, just skunks and raccoons."

Mr. Cress opened his door and stepped out, removing his hat. "Ma'am, I'm from CORB. My name is Donald Cress. I'm here to deliver your guest children."

The woman's jaw dropped, but she quickly recovered. "Children? But—what about my letter?"

"Letter?"

Geoffrey had his door open and was getting out of the car. "Geoffrey!" Nina lunged for him. "Get back in here." But she was too late. Geoffrey had closed the door and stood, hands on hips, facing the Wright family with a glare that dared them to mock anything about him.

"I wanna get out too!" Hazel fumbled with her door handle as Nina reached forward and grabbed the back of her collar and hushed her. She was missing whatever Mrs. Wright was saying.

"...I explained to their parents we can only take one, the oldest girl, or none at all. I assumed alternate arrangements had been made by now. We haven't heard a thing."

"Well, that explains why you weren't in Winnipeg to pick

them up." Mr. Cress scratched his head, replaced his hat, and looked around. "Girls, you might as well get out too."

Hazel wasted no time hopping out of the car and making a beeline for the dog. Nina climbed out, unsure what to do with her hands or where to look.

"This is Nina." Mr. Cress waved a hand in Nina's direction. "That's Geoffrey and that's Hazel. Gabriel. Your cousins, I believe?"

The woman shook her head. "No. Their father knows my husband's cousin is all. Hello, children. I'm Ann Wright." She nodded toward the boy. "That's Jim." She shifted the baby to her other hip. "And this is Daniel. Six months old."

Was this why the Wrights wanted a teenage girl around—to babysit the little one? Nina turned to Mr. Cress and delivered her most imploring look.

He wasn't looking at her. "Well, ain't he a cutie?"

"This isn't all of us," Jim piped up. "Dad's in the field. Carol's working for Miss Filmon."

Mrs. Wright stepped forward. "Our daughter has a summer job at the dress shop in town. Mr. Cress, I'm terribly sorry for the misunderstanding, but I wrote to Mrs. Gabriel and explained. I thought someone would have cabled you about it. We can only take Nina."

Nina's insides began to protest. She took a deep breath and tried to appear as tall as possible. "That's quite impossible. My siblings and I are not to be separated. No matter what. I'm sorry for your trouble, Mr. Cress, but you'll have to take us back to Winnipeg with you and find another home where we can be together. All three of us. C'mon, Hazel. Geoffrey." She turned and climbed back into the car before anyone had a chance to protest. The Orange Crush had reached her bladder. It screamed for relief, but she'd promised her parents, and she couldn't let them down.

"No need to be so hasty, Nina." Mr. Cress leaned into his open window. "Let's at least stay long enough for a proper conversation. See if we can't sort this out."

"Yes, of course," Mrs. Wright said. "You all must be tired from your drive. Jim, please go fetch your father. Quickly now." She turned toward the house. "Come have a cold drink and use the facilities. We can talk on the shady porch."

Nina climbed out of the car again only to see Geoffrey already making himself quite at home. After greeting the dog, he approached a tire swing hanging by a thick rope to an oak tree and threaded himself through its center, much as he'd done with the ship's porthole.

"Outhouse is around back," Mrs. Wright said to Nina.

"Thank you." Nina took Hazel's hand. "C'mon, Hazel. Let's use the loo." Nina led her past the corner of the house and spotted the outhouse.

"But why aren't we using the loo in the house?" Hazel spoke loud enough for all to hear.

"Sh-h. It isn't inside." Nina lowered her voice even more. "They must not have indoor plumbing."

Maybe it wasn't so bad that the Wrights couldn't take all three of them. Nina didn't want to stay. She wanted Mr. Cress to take them back to the city and find a lovely home with running water and a proper school nearby and cinemas and parks and that wonderful zoo. Did these people even have a wireless?

Hazel used the outhouse first and then waited outside for Nina. Just as Nina was finishing, Hazel began to scream. Nina threw open the door and stepped out. Hazel clamored to hide behind her. A horribly loud *honnkkk,* followed by hissing, grabbed Nina's attention just in time. An enormous white gander ran toward them, neck stretched out and wings spread wide. Nina reached back inside the outhouse and grabbed the straw broom she'd seen leaning in the corner. She waved it wildly, keeping the goose back. Hazel remained glued to Nina's backside as she walked sideways, trying to fend off the bird while making her way toward the house. She was vaguely aware of laughter coming from the direction of the porch.

"Atta girl! Don't worry about Adolf. You just need to show him who's boss."

Nina took her eyes off the goose long enough to look at the speaker. Walking toward her came the most handsome fellow she had ever laid eyes on. He wore denim overalls with no shirt underneath, providing Nina with a full view of tanned and muscled arms. Broad shoulders. When he reached up to remove his hat, he revealed thick, almost black hair. He wiped one arm across his forehead and returned the hat to his head. He was looking straight at Nina and smiling—revealing a friendly row of straight, white teeth.

"*Adolf?* As in—?"

He nodded. "The same. The Wrights plan to eat him for Christmas dinner."

The Wrights? Who was he, then?

The gander gave up the game, strutting off when the dog approached.

"Hey, Rosie." The boy crouched to rub the dog's ears and looked up at Nina. "I'm David Cain. I work for Mr. Wright."

Nina's heart raced. Maybe staying here would not be such a bad idea after all. "I'm Nina." Oh, she must look frightful. "This is my sister, Hazel."

"Welcome to Canada." David stood.

"You're very tall," Hazel said, her eyes scanning from David's feet to his face. "How tall are you?"

He laughed. "Not sure. Last time Mother measured, six-four, I think. I like your accent."

"I don't have an accent. You have an accent."

"Hazel," Nina warned.

David only laughed as he took the broom from her and returned it to its place.

When they reached the porch, Mrs. Wright handed out cool glasses of water. Another man had joined them.

"Nina, Hazel, this is Mr. Wright. He's the real reason you're here," Mr. Cress said.

"Welcome to Canada, girls. I met Geoffrey already." He nodded toward where Geoffrey now swung atop the old tire, looking up into the tree as though contemplating how tricky it might be to climb while Jim pushed the swing. "Sorry about Adolf. David's right. Just show him who's boss, and you'll be fine."

Nina sat on a bench on the porch, but Hazel ran off to join Geoffrey and Jim. Baby Daniel lay on a blanket on the porch floor, playing with his bare toes.

"I do apologize for the mix-up." Mr. Wright turned to Mr. Cress. "The CORB people called the community together and gave a presentation in town. I know of two other families for sure who signed up when we did."

Mr. Cress released a low hum. "Their guest children must be coming on the next ship."

"Maybe one of the other families would take these three instead."

"Are you able to give me their names?" Mr. Cress pulled a pencil and notepad from his pocket. "Perhaps I could pay them a visit while I'm here and see what we can arrange."

The thump of an ax hitting a log rang through the air, drawing Nina's attention toward the barn. David raised an ax high above his head and brought it down, splitting wood with apparent ease. She tried to stay focused on the adult conversation.

"Well, I'm sorry if you've come all this way for nothing." Mr. Wright sat on one of the chairs and leaned his elbows across his knees, hat in hand. "My fault, really. When we got the request from the Gabriels and saw the ages of the children, I thought it would be a perfect fit for us. I should have consulted my wife. You see, we—"

He stopped abruptly. Nina looked away from David in time to see a look exchanged between Mr. Wright and his wife. Mrs. Wright shook her head almost imperceptibly, but her panic-stricken eyes communicated clearly. She did not want him to finish his sentence, whatever it was.

"—I mean, we'd love to keep Nina if the other families can take the two younger ones."

Thud! Another log split into two.

"No!" Nina hadn't meant to speak so loudly. Now all eyes were on her. "My parents were assured—"

"Settle down. Nina." Mr. Cress pressed his lips together. "No one is separating you yet."

Nina gritted her teeth. Her mother's words came back to her. *Always be polite and respectful.* Another thud of the axe drew her attention. How old was David? Seventeen, eighteen? With his good looks and charm, he no doubt already had numerous girls vying for his affection. Only a few feet away, Hazel now sat cross-legged on the ground, staring adoringly and without reservation straight at David.

By the time the adults ended their conversation, all had agreed that the three Gabriel children would stay the night with the Wright family while Mr. Cress visited the other host homes to see what he could arrange.

Perhaps Nina's best course of action would be to impress Mrs. Wright so she'd change her mind and let all three of them stay. She worked hard to make herself useful, bringing in laundry, peeling potatoes for supper, and even changing the baby. She engaged Hazel to entertain little Daniel while she set the table, hoping and praying that Geoffrey would not only stay out of trouble but somehow endear himself to the Wright family.

Just as they were sitting down for supper, a teenage girl walked through the kitchen door. Her flawless face was framed with luxurious auburn hair. Her dress mirrored one Nina had seen Deanna Durbin wearing in Alice's magazine. Could this be Carol? Only *sixteen*? She looked eighteen, at least. She captured everyone's attention as she stood taking in the scene. Her eyes roamed from Nina to Geoffrey to Hazel and then back to Nina.

"Right on time, Carol," Mr. Wright broke the awkward silence and pulled out the chair next to his where a place had been set for his daughter. "Say hello to Nina, Geoffrey, and Hazel Gabriel. All the way from England."

Carol didn't sit. "I thought the whole thing was called off."

"Well, now, not the whole thing. We were prepared to take one child, but there's been a little mix-up and the family's not prepared to separate. They're with us just for tonight, until things can be sorted out."

"Where will they sleep?"

"Well, I believe Geoffrey is bunking in with Jim—"

Jim put a hand on Geoffrey's shoulder and beamed at him. "It'll be nice to have a roommate again, even if it's only for one night."

Who had Jim's other roommate been? Oh well, after the mockery he'd endured in town, it was nice to see Geoffrey smiling.

"—and Nina and Hazel can share the bed in my sewing room," Mrs. Wright finished. "Now sit down and join us. Your father was just about to say grace."

Carol scowled at her mother and took her seat. "I suppose David's gone home for the night?"

Nina had wondered the same thing when she'd asked Mrs. Wright how many places to set but hadn't dared come right out and ask.

"Don't worry. You'll see him tomorrow. Now let's pray." Mr. Wright delivered a simple prayer of thanksgiving.

Throughout the meal, Nina did her best to politely answer questions about England and the trip, relieved that her siblings remained quiet. Whether they were too tired or too hungry, Nina wasn't sure. Probably both.

Jim was the first to rise from the table when they were done. "Would you all like to come watch me milk the cows? There are some kittens in the barn too."

"Kittens?" Hazel's face lit up.

Nina turned toward Mrs. Wright. "I'll stay and help with dishes, but I'm sure Geoffrey and Hazel would love to go."

"Nonsense." Mrs. Wright stood and began stacking plates. "Carol can help me. You go on ahead."

Hazel to her parents
12 August 1940
Dear Mummy and Daddy,

Our new family doesn't want me or Geoffrey. Only Nina.

But Nina said we must stay together. They let us all stay for just one night while Mr. Cress finds us a new family. They don't have any little girls to play with, but there is a pretty dog named Rosie and some baby kitties in the barn with their mama. My eyes got itchy, and the big sister said it must be from the hay, and Nina said it was from the cats. I don't think the sister liked that Nina didn't agree with her. I can't remember her name. The big brother is Jim and the baby brother is Daniel.

Nina and me had a nice room to sleep in last night. I wetted the bed in the night, and Nina had to wash the sheets. I think this is why I can't stay. But I don't know why Geoffrey can't stay. Also, I don't like Adolf. He is a big, ugly goose and he's mean. I want to come home.

David is the hired man. He lives down the road with his own family. He is dreamy. When I am twenty, I am going to come back to Canada and marry him.

Love and kisses,
Hazel

Chapter Six

Nina to Alice

12 August 1940
Dear Alice,

I was overjoyed when your letter arrived this morning. Now I know where to send this. I'm glad you like your new home and family. I have not heard from Jean yet. I miss you both.

We've arrived at the Wright farm in Cedar Bluff, but there was a nasty misunderstanding, and they apparently only want me. That is, the adults do. I don't think their daughter Carol (16) wants any of us. She has not stopped glaring at me. Her brother Jim is fourteen. He's all right for a kid. And the baby is just six months old, so there's quite a spread between them. Daniel is a darling. In fact, I am watching him for Mrs. Wright now, while Hazel writes to Mum and Dad.

I'm not sure why they want only me, but I explained to Mr. Cress that this is not acceptable.

"Nina," he said. "We'll do what we can, but you must understand you are a war refugee. You may not get to choose."

I wanted to smack him. I must keep us together, Alice. I promised my parents I'd look after Geoffrey and Hazel. How can I if they don't live with me? It will be bad enough when school begins next month, as we'll be in separate schools.

But I must tell you a secret. I know we agreed there would be no falling in love on the trip, but our journey is over, and I am completely in love. David Cain is the Wrights' hired man from up the road. He is seventeen. It was love at first sight for me. You'll think I'm silly—especially since he probably thinks of me as a child, same as Hazel—but trust me, Alice, if you could meet him, you would feel the same. Cary Grant has nothing on David in the looks department. Dark hair, eyes like chocolate. So tall. But he is also sweet and kind and brave and smart and hard-working and generous. How can I tell all this so soon? Because I've seen his patience with Jim and his respect for the adults and the way he helps out, like splitting wood for the kitchen stove (can you believe they cook with wood?). And while I was peeling potatoes for supper I could see and hear through the window as Mr. Wright and David discussed their plans for today before he went home for the night. I don't even know what they said, I was just enjoying the sound of his deep voice. This morning, though we rose early, he and Mr. Wright were already gone to the field. Even Hazel is smitten with him.

Don't worry, though. It will never amount to anything. How could it? He is not only too old but way out of my league. Except for telling you—and Jean, in my next letter—I'll hide my love safely away in my heart and admire David from afar.

And it truly will be "from afar" because we'll be going to a new home today. It will break my heart, but I know it must happen. Now I sound like the melodramatic Anne Shirley from Green Gables.

Love always,
Nina

Nina was on the porch watching Daniel when Mr. Cress's car pulled up, accompanied by Rosie's barking and Adolf's honking.

Mrs. Wright stepped out of the house, wiped her hands on her apron, and picked up Daniel. "Let's hope he's got good news for us."

Nina followed her to the car, crystal clear on what the woman would consider good news. During the previous evening's devotional time before bed, Mrs. Wright had prayed aloud. She asked God to help Mr. Cress find a home for Geoffrey and Hazel so that Nina could stay. The nerve. How dare she invoke God's help for something that was clearly the opposite of God's will?

Being less helpful might have better served Nina's purposes. Then again, Mum and Dad would be horribly disappointed if they knew she even entertained such manipulative ideas.

Mr. Cress was all smiles as he exited his car. "Good news."

Geoffrey joined Nina and Mrs. Wright at the car, but Hazel clung to the tire swing, studying the dirt beneath her feet.

Mr. Cress leaned against his car door. "I visited the two other host families who've already been approved by CORB. Mr. and Mrs. Cooper are prepared to take Geoffrey. They are lovely people." He waved a hand in the direction of the swing. "And Miss Filmon is delighted at the idea of hosting a seven-year-old girl. It's exactly what she applied for."

"That's wonderful!" Mrs. Wright smiled at Nina. "You can all be in the same community."

Nina shook her head.

Mrs. Wright wasn't done. "Miss Filmon runs a little dress shop in town, the one where Carol works. And the Coopers have a farm just a couple of miles the other side of Cedar Bluff. Lovely people."

"Well, it's five miles from town to be exact," Mr. Cress was still grinning broadly. "But yes, theirs will be a fine home for Geoffrey, Nina. Their own two sons are grown and gone, so Geoffrey will have plenty of space. You needn't worry."

Nina stopped chewing her bottom lip and took a deep breath. "It won't work, Mr. Cress. I promised my parents I'd look out for Geoffrey and Hazel. We need to stay together. You must understand."

"I do understand, Nina, and we'll keep working toward a more acceptable solution. But for now, you're all in the same tightly knit community with five adults looking out for the three of you. Isn't that better? It really isn't your responsibility to take care of your siblings when you're still a child yourself."

"No!" Nina marched over to where Hazel twirled on the swing. "My sister needs me."

Mr. Cress sighed. "It will have to work for now. I'm due back in Winnipeg this afternoon to greet the next shipment of children from England. Please. Think of *them*. If I spent this much time on every child, why—it would simply be impossible. I've already taken much more time than I should have for your family. I'm prepared to deliver your siblings to their new homes before I head back to the city."

Nina stared at the house. Carol stood in her bedroom window, holding the curtain open with one hand and glaring down with the same surly face she'd given Nina from the start. Maybe if Nina could win Carol over, Mrs. Wright might be convinced too. But how on earth could she do that? The girl had clearly made up her mind she hated Nina and didn't want her around. Maybe she could start with Jim since he already seemed glad to have them.

"Jim is so good with Geoffrey, and Geoffrey's really taken to him. And Hazel won't be any trouble, she loves all your animals—"

"No, I don't." A grumpy little voice rang out. "I don't like Adolf at all."

Mrs. Wright and Mr. Cress exchanged a look.

"What if you rode along with Mr. Cress, Nina?" Mrs. Wright said. "That way you can see for yourself that your siblings are in good hands. After you've been to the Cooper farm, you can stay a few hours with Hazel at Miss Filmon's. Get her settled. Mr. Cress can head back to the city, and we'll have David fetch you with the truck this evening."

David? Nina's heart did a little flip. For one brief moment, she imagined herself riding in an automobile with David, just the two of them. But no, this was still not acceptable.

She bit her lip again. "My parents never would have agreed to send us if they hadn't been assured we'd stay together."

Mr. Cress let out a long sigh. "Nina, your parents are four thousand miles away. We are doing the best we can here. Your concern for your siblings is admirable, but I need you to be a big girl about this. Your parents sent you here to be safe, above all else. We all have the same goal for you. Surely, you can see that."

"Your parents will understand, Nina. I'll write to them myself." Mrs. Wright turned toward the house. "Let's gather Geoffrey's and Hazel's things." It was as though she couldn't wait to get rid of them.

"Fine, but I'm going along." Maybe she could buy some time to formulate a plan.

"That's fine." Mrs. Wright called back over her shoulder.

Geoffrey ran past Nina into the house, ready for his next adventure, but Hazel let out a wail and hurled herself into Nina. "I don't want to leave you, Nina!"

Nina dislodged herself from Hazel's skinny arms and spoke softly. "It'll be fine, Hazie. I won't let them separate us. I'll figure out something." She ran to catch up with Mrs. Wright on the porch. "How can you be so heartless? Can't you see my sister needs me?"

Mrs. Wright turned slowly around and gazed at Hazel. To Nina's surprise, tears glimmered from the woman's lashes.

"Please just do as she asks, Nina," Mr. Cress said quietly. "It will be better for everyone."

Half an hour later, Mrs. Cooper welcomed them, explaining that her husband was at work in the gypsum mine and wouldn't return until evening. "But we're delighted to have you, Geoffrey." Her short stature put her eye-to-eye with Geoffrey. "Your bed is at the top of the ladder there."

Geoffrey scrambled up a ladder nailed to the wall which divided the Coopers' living space from their bedroom in the little cottage. Nina and Hazel followed. Geoffrey's "room" was a loft. Plenty of space, but no windows. Had the Coopers' two sons shared this?

When they returned, Mrs. Cooper provided a brief tour of the farmyard with its compulsory outhouse. Nina tried to memorize every building, tree, and clump of grass as she silently strategized.

Mr. Cress's impatience was clearly growing. "Time to go."

Less than an hour after they'd arrived, Hazel hugged Geoffrey goodbye and climbed into Mr. Cress's car. When it was Nina's turn, she hugged Geoffrey at length and whispered her scheme into his ear. He nodded somberly and waved the whole time they drove down the long driveway.

Nina studied every inch of the journey back, noting they did not meet a single vehicle the whole five miles to Cedar Bluff.

The next stop was a tiny house in town. Painted bright yellow, it boasted a neat yard with pink peonies and rose bushes all around the house. An older woman in a blue printed dress and white apron met them at the door with twinkly eyes and a smile. She focused directly on Hazel while Nina hung back.

"Miss Filmon, this is Hazel Gabriel," Mr. Cress said.

"Gabriel?" The woman asked. "Not Jewish, I hope."

Hazel looked up at Mr. Cress and frowned.

Mr. Cress shook his head.

"Well then, welcome, welcome!" Miss Filmon reached out a hand to stroke Hazel's hair. "How are you, dear?"

Hazel whispered, "Fine, thank you," and followed the woman into the house.

"Oh, aren't you a polite little thing." Miss Filmon waved a hand toward a paisley sofa. "Come sit."

The pungent smell of mothballs met Nina's nostrils. A long-haired tabby cat rubbed up against Hazel's leg.

"That's Herman. He'll warm up to you in no time. Did I tell you my mother's name was Hazel? I do believe God chose you especially to stay here with me. Isn't it wonderful?"

"Cats make Hazel sneeze," Nina said.

Miss Filmon looked up at Nina. "Who's this?"

"This is Nina," Mr. Cress said. "Remember, I told you Hazel has an older sister and brother?"

The woman stiffened. "Well, I can't take *her* too!"

"No, no. I understand. She's come to meet you and see where her sister will be staying. David Cain will be by this evening to take her back to the Wrights. Now, I really need to get going. I'm already much too late." He turned to Nina. "I'm sorry this hasn't gone the way you hoped, but I'm confident everything will turn out fine. I'll be back 'round to check on everyone in a month or so."

"A month! But Mr. Cress. You said you'd find us—"

"Nina, I will do what I can, but I cannot promise you anything. Try to be grateful you have a roof over your head and food to eat." He hastened toward the door. "Thank you again, Miss Filmon. You know where to reach me if you have any problems."

Just like that, he was gone.

"Come, dears, you must be hungry." Miss Filmon led them to a kitchen with a tiny table and two chairs. She puttered around the room and kept up a running monologue about the war as the girls ate tomato and cheese sandwiches. "Oh, it's terrible what's happening over there. I do hope your parents survive it."

Hazel looked up at Nina, fear in her eyes.

"Of course, they will," Nina said quickly. "Tell us about Cedar Bluff."

Miss Filmon launched into a history of the area and how she ran the dress shop previously owned by her mother. "I don't spend much time there anymore since I've got such good help, but I'm not ready to give it up yet."

When the girls finished their food, Miss Filmon showed them to a little room off the kitchen. "This will be yours, Hazel dear."

A toddler-sized bed, covered with a pretty lavender quilt, nearly filled the room. White lace curtains covered a narrow window.

"Why don't we go ahead and get you unpacked?" Miss Filmon opened the top drawer of a four-drawer bureau beside the bed.

"I can do that." Nina placed Hazel's suitcase on the bed and opened it. "Why don't you get acquainted with Hazel while I'm still around? That way, if any questions come to mind, I can help answer them. She loves to be read to."

"Oh, that's wonderful because I love to read." Miss Filmon took Hazel's hand. "Come along, Hazel. I'll show you my books, and you can pick one out."

As soon as they left the room, Nina closed the suitcase and stepped over to the window to examine it. Instead of opening outward on hinges like windows back home, she'd already observed that most Canadian windows slid up. She waited until she heard Miss Filmon reading aloud. Then she carefully inched the windowpane up far enough to ease the suitcase through. It was a tight fit, and Nina cringed as the case scraped the ledge. Reaching as far down on the outside of the window as she could, she let the suitcase drop the last several inches into the peonies below. She slowly lowered the window and began opening and closing dresser drawers. When she figured enough time had elapsed, she came out, brushing her hands together, to join Hazel and Miss Filmon.

"All done already?" Miss Filmon smiled up at her.

Nina nodded. "Do you need to use the outhouse, Hazel?"

"Oh, I have indoor plumbing. Right this way, Hazel, I'll show you."

Nina's heart sank. The one time she needed an outhouse to make her plan work. She'd need a new strategy.

While Hazel used the bathroom, Nina leaned toward their hostess with a conspiratorial voice. "Do you have a rubber sheet? Sometimes Hazel wets the bed."

The woman's eyebrows rose. "At the age of seven?"

"Especially if she's in a strange place. It might happen tonight. If you can find something that will work, I'll gladly put it on the bed for you."

Miss Filmon pursed her lips and slowly let air out through them. "I know. Mrs. Kindersley across the street will have something I can use. She's got five children. Let me just step over there and ask. I'll be right back."

Even better. As soon as Miss Filmon closed the front door, Nina opened the bathroom door. Hazel was washing her hands, and Nina grabbed one of them. "Come on!"

"But I have to dry my hands."

"No time. Come on. Run!"

"Where are we going, Nina?"

"We're going to get Geoffrey." She pulled Hazel through the kitchen, out the back door, and then ran as fast as she could without letting go of Hazel.

"But it's so far!"

"It's not that far. Let's pretend we're going to the beach and can't wait to get there." Making their way behind homes and outbuildings, it was easy to find the edge of the small town and the road that had brought them to it. When they were well out of sight of Miss Filmon's house, they stopped running, but Nina urged Hazel on at a brisk pace.

"What about my suitcase?"

"We can pick it up later. I set it outside the window at Miss Filmon's."

The girls walked at a good clip for the first mile, and Nina welcomed the sight of an intersection in the gravel road. On the next mile, they passed a farm. Although they couldn't spot any people, a dog barked. "Let's cross the road." She took Hazel's hand and crossed to the other side, down into the ditch opposite the farmyard. What she hadn't reckoned on was the long grass or the mosquitoes that swarmed up to feast. Slapping themselves, both girls ran as far as they could before returning to the road.

"I'm thirsty," Hazel whined.

"I know. Me too. Remember, we're headed for the beach.

Think how lovely and cool that water's going to feel."

"Can we buy Orange Crush at the canteen?"

"Sure. But we must hurry, or they'll close before we get there."

"My feet hurt."

"I know. Try to think about that Orange Crush."

A stench rose up to meet them, like something dead but much worse. On the road ahead, two crows pulled trailing bits from a bloody mass of fur. They flew off as the girls approached.

"Yuck! What is that?" Hazel stopped short, not wanting to get any closer to the smelly mess.

"I don't know, but we must go around it to keep going. If we run, we'll pass it faster." They held their hands over their noses but as they skirted the roadkill, Nina's curiosity got the best of her. She stopped for a closer look. What she at first thought was a black and white cat had too pointy a face and too bushy a tail. "I think it's a skunk, Hazel."

"Eww. I've only ever seen one in pictures."

"Me too. Now I know what all the fuss is about." They ran until they couldn't smell it anymore.

At the third mile marker sat a schoolhouse similar to the one on the Wrights' road, complete with two matching outhouses. Mr. Cress had pointed it out to Geoffrey earlier as the one he would attend. A well with a water pump stood a few yards from the school building, though Nina would not have known what it was if she hadn't seen David pumping water from one just like it at the Wrights' home the previous day. *God bless David Cain.* "Look, Hazel. Water."

A dipper for drinking even hung from the handle. Nina began pumping like she'd seen David do. Nothing happened. She pumped some more. Harder, faster. Nothing. Exhausted and thirsty, she slumped to the base of the well and sat with her chin in her hands.

"Why won't it work?" Hazel put her face under the spout and tried to look up into it. Her face and arms were covered with red blotches from mosquito bites.

"I don't know." Nina sighed. Was she making a terrible mistake? How upset would Mum and Dad be when they found out she'd let Hazel go thirsty? What choice did she have? Hazel wandered over to the swings and slumped onto one, too tired to swing or even ask for a push.

A thought came, seemingly from nowhere. *Prime the pump.*

Prime the pump? Of course. Somewhere, she'd read or heard that you had to pour water into a pump to get it to pump more. But where could she find water? The door to the school was locked with a big padlock, and even if she could get in, she'd be unlikely to find water. She grabbed the dipper hanging from the pump and headed for the ditch.

"Where are you going?" Hazel followed.

"Let's see if there's water in the bottom of the ditch."

"Don't be daft. We can't drink that."

Nina tried to ignore the mosquitoes as she parted some tall reeds. Sure enough, a trickle of greenish water reflected the sunlight. She filled the dipper. "We're not going to drink it." She carried it back to the pump. She could find only one place to put it. With one hand, she let the water pour out of the dipper into the top of the pump. With the other, she began pumping the handle up and down. Sure enough, a teensy trickle came out of the spout. She kept pumping until water gushed.

"Hooray!" Hazel held her hands under the spout and splashed herself all over. Both girls drank their fill using the dipper, and Nina poured some over her head. Never had water tasted so good. They pulled off their shoes and stockings to discover painful blisters on the backs of their heels. Hazel's had bled a little. They cooled their feet under the spout and let them dry before putting their stockings and shoes back on. Then they used the outhouse marked "Girls" and carried on down the gravel road.

By mile four, the sun was going down. "Almost there," Nina tried to encourage Hazel along.

"Then what?"

"Well, then we're going to get Geoffrey."

"And then what?"

Nina had no answer. "Just keep walking. And keep a lookout for cars." She dared not voice her more worrisome fear. *Keep a lookout for bears.*

TO CORB RECEPTION CENTER WINNIPEG, MANITOBA, CANADA

12 AUGUST 1940

ATTN: MR. DONALD CRESS

WE HAVE NOT RECEIVED A REPLY TO OUR PREVIOUS CABLE REGARDING A CHANGE IN OUR CHILDREN'S HOST HOME. RECEIVED LETTER FROM NINA MAILED FROM WINNIPEG, AT WHICH TIME SHE WAS STILL ANTICIPATING STAYING AT THE WRIGHT HOME IN CEDAR BLUFF, ALONG WITH HER SIBLINGS GEOFFREY AND HAZEL. PLEASE CONFIRM ASAP. BEYOND WORRIED.

SINCERELY, MR. & MRS. EUGENE GABRIEL, MIDDLESBROUGH, ENGLAND

Chapter Seven

Mr. Cress to the Gabriels

August 12, 1940

Mr. & Mrs. Eugene Gabriel
47 Abbey Court
Middlesbrough, England

Dear Mr. & Mrs. Gabriel,

We are in receipt of your cable from early this morning.

I have only just returned from delivering your children to Cedar Bluff myself. While Nina is in the care of the Wright family as planned, we placed Geoffrey with Mr. and Mrs. Lawrence Cooper whom you can reach at Post Office Box 14, Cedar Bluff, Manitoba. Hazel is with a lovely lady named Miss Bernice Filmon, Post Office Box 89 of the same town. Please understand that this is a temporary arrangement since I know you wish to have your children together and understandably so. As you can imagine, the administrative work involved with placing all these children can be challenging at times, but I assure you we are making every effort to find a suitable solution. In the meantime, please rest assured your children are perfectly safe and lovingly cared for.

I trust you are safe as well, and I apologize for the confusion with the Wrights. I trust you will hear from Nina again very soon with a happy report.
Sincerely,
Mr. Donald Cress

The mosquitoes came out in full force after dark. By the time Nina and Hazel reached the Cooper farm, they'd been driven half-mad by the constant biting, itching, and high-pitched buzzing. Only one vehicle had passed while they crouched in the ditch, a gray pick-up truck that now sat next to the Coopers' barn. No lights shone from the windows of the house.

"Did you see a dog when we were here before?" Nina whispered.

"No. No goose, either."

"Me, either. Follow me." Nina led the way to the outhouse. If Geoffrey had followed her instructions, he might already be there, waiting. Though they didn't spot him, Hazel nearly tripped on something as they went around to the far side of the outhouse, away from the house.

"That's Geoffrey's suitcase."

"Sh-h!" Nina smiled. Geoffrey must have found his chance to leave it there. A stack of firewood sat nearby. She rolled two pieces away from the pile and stood them on end for stools. It felt good to sit.

"I'm hungry."

Nina had expected Hazel's complaint much earlier when she first began hearing her own stomach growl. "I know. Me, too. Try to ignore it."

A moment later, a scraping sound from the direction of the house lifted Nina from her seat. She peered around the corner of the outhouse. Geoffrey stepped out the back door. He wasn't being particularly quiet, but if the Coopers heard him, they would most likely assume he needed the outhouse. He ran straight for it.

"Nina?"

"We're here."

Geoffrey hugged them both. "C'mon, let's go." He grabbed his suitcase.

A breeze had picked up, cooling the air and keeping the mosquitoes to a minimum. Nina breathed a prayer of thanks as they headed down the road. It was a long way back to town, and another long way to the Wrights' farm. Would they get there by daylight? She didn't even know if that was where they should go, but that was where her belongings were. Once they had her things, maybe they could somehow catch a train to the city and … and … one step at a time.

"I'm thirsty and tired." Hazel's plodding grew slower.

"We can have a nice drink at the school like we did before."

"Maybe we can get inside and sleep there," Geoffrey suggested.

Nina didn't argue. That might not be a bad plan.

A set of headlights appeared over the crest of the next hill.

"Quick! In the ditch." The three of them crouched in the long, wet grass, once again stirring up hungry hordes of insects.

The vehicle moved painfully slow. Had it stopped?

"Nina." Geoffrey elbowed her and pointed. A set of glowing gold eyes peered at them from about eight feet away. "It's a bear."

"Sh-h. No, it's not. It's not a bear." Nina wished she were as certain as she sounded. Her heart pounded.

"What is it?" Hazel asked.

The doctor's joke about cougars came to mind. "I don't know. But hold still. The car will likely scare it away."

Suddenly, the animal jumped up and ran across the road. The oncoming headlights revealed a young deer. It crossed to the other side and leaped over a barbed-wire fence, its white tail flagging as it bounded across the field on the other side. The vehicle stopped and then slowly carried on.

"Wait 'til it's out of sight." The scare had energized Nina, and the promise of a drink pulled her forward. By the time they neared the schoolhouse, they'd seen a porcupine, heard an owl, and spotted some unidentified creature rustling through the long grass in the ditch.

Once again, Nina pumped water from the well. The three of

them drank deeply, until the lights of a vehicle shone directly on them.

Nina regretted her mistake. She should have kept watch. No chance to hide now.

"It's Mr. Wright." Trust Geoffrey to recognize the truck first. "That was him on the road before too. I just realized it."

"Nina?" Mr. Wright stepped out. "What on earth are you children doing here? You had us worried half to death."

Nina stood frozen, not knowing what to do or say. Even Geoffrey had probably never been in as deep a trouble as she surely was now.

"Mr. Wright, I can explain," she began.

"Oh, you'll explain all right. You'll explain to me and to the Coopers and to Miss Filmon and to David Cain—"

"David?" Nina squinted toward the truck's cab to see whether anyone else was inside but saw no one. In her determination to escape, she'd forgotten about the promised ride with David.

"Come on. Climb in. All of you." Mr. Wright picked up Geoffrey's suitcase and placed it in the back of his truck.

Without a word, the three children climbed inside, squeezing together with Nina nearest the window.

"But I haven't got my suitcase." Hazel cried.

"Your suitcase is in the back." Mr. Wright huffed. "That's the least of our worries."

He turned the truck around and headed toward the Coopers' place. "By the time David arrived at Miss Filmon's to pick you up, Nina, the poor woman was frantic. She'd found the packed suitcase outside the window and claimed the two of you vanished. David came all the way back to our place, and from his report, I put two and two together. Then I nearly hit a deer coming out here. When I arrived at the Coopers, they were still asleep and blissfully unaware. They fully expected to find Geoffrey in his bed. You can imagine their shock. Our first stop is their house."

"Are you going to make me stay there?" Geoffrey's voice trembled.

"Please don't, Mr. Wright." Nina cleared her throat and tried to stop her own tears. "Please."

The man let out a long sigh. "I reckon we'll keep you together at least one more night. But the Coopers need to know you're all right, and I think you're the one who oughtta tell 'em, Geoffrey."

Nina and Hazel waited in the truck while Mr. Wright accompanied Geoffrey to the Coopers' steps where he stood with his head appropriately bowed. They talked at the door for five minutes before returning to the vehicle.

Everyone rode along in silence. By the time they reached town, Hazel had fallen asleep. Mr. Wright stopped in front of Miss Filmon's house. He studied the sleeping little girl for a moment. "No point in waking her. Since I suspect you're the instigator, it's really you who should apologize, Nina. Come on."

Nina followed him to the front door which opened before they reached it. Miss Filmon stood wringing her hands.

"Everyone's safe, Miss Filmon." Mr. Wright cleared his throat. "I think it's best if I take them all home with me at least for tonight. But Nina here has something she'd like to say to you."

Nina looked at Miss Filmon's feet, clad in pink bedroom slippers. What could she truthfully say she was sorry for? She did regret not coming up with a better plan, but she didn't regret the attempt to rescue her siblings.

"Nina?" Mr. Wright prompted.

"I'm sorry for causing you to worry, Miss Filmon." It was true, though there was a lot more truth she'd love to add. Like how none of this would have been necessary if adults only did what they said they were going to do. Or if they didn't start wars to begin with.

When she heard no response, Nina finally looked at the woman's face.

Miss Filmon stared at Mr. Wright, her lips pressed together. "You shouldn't have let this one come along in the first place."

Mr. Wright opened his mouth as though he was about to

argue. He let out a long sigh as he ran the back of his hand across his weathered forehead. "I suppose you're right. It's much too late, and everyone's too upset to figure this all out tonight. I hope you can get some sleep."

Miss Filmon nodded. "Let me know. I'm still more than happy to take Hazel, but I'll not be tolerating runaways."

They returned to the truck. The final stop—back at the Wrights'—might be the most humiliating yet. Rosie greeted them without judgment, her tail wagging as they climbed out of the truck. Mr. Wright carried Hazel, resting her head on his shoulder. Nina carried both suitcases. By the time she reached the porch, Mrs. Wright, still fully clothed, stood holding the door.

Best to get it over with. "I'm sorry, Mrs. Wright." Nina crossed the threshold and set the suitcases at the foot of the stairs, not daring to look the woman in the eye. She waited for her scolding.

"You must be hungry. Come into the kitchen."

Had she heard correctly? Geoffrey followed Mrs. Wright into the kitchen. Mr. Wright started up the stairs but didn't make it halfway before Hazel woke up.

"Nina? Where's Nina?"

"I'm right here, Hazie. We're back at the Wrights.'"

Hazel looked around, blinking. "You mean we ran away for nothing?"

Mr. Wright chuckled and set her down. The girls joined Geoffrey in the kitchen where the sizzle of eggs in a frying pan and the welcoming aroma of toast enveloped them like a hug. Mrs. Wright poured warm water into a basin near the back door so they could wash up. The clock in the living room struck midnight as the Gabriel children polished off their food and mugs of hot tea.

As they made their way to the same beds they'd used the night before, Mrs. Wright handed Nina a tube of ointment. "For the mosquito bites."

Nina lay awake despite her deep fatigue and aching feet. The Wright family wouldn't want to keep any of them now.

Word of what she'd done would get back to Mum and Dad, and then what? Would they arrange passage for the children to return home?

The long, hot day had left her dehydrated. When the clock struck two, she rose from her bed to tiptoe downstairs for a drink of water. As she neared Mr. and Mr. Wright's bedroom, she could hear their voices and stopped.

"I just don't think I can do it, Harry. It's too soon. Please don't ask me if I've prayed about it. I have."

A long pause ensued and then Mr. Wright answered. "All right. I'm sorry I pushed you. It seemed like a good plan for all of us, but I see now I was wrong. Please forgive me."

Nina crept back to her bed without a drink.

Carol to her diary
August 12, 1940
Dear Diary,

No end of drama here tonight. The English kids all left this morning and good riddance. Nina was supposed to come back here after the younger ones were settled. When I found out Mum was sending David to fetch her, I asked to go along. "She'll feel awkward with David," I said.

"Nobody could ever feel awkward with David," Mum said. "I need you to stay here and help me get supper on the table."

I could scream about that.

When David came back without Nina, he said the two girls disappeared from Miss Filmon's. Hours later, Dad showed up with all three kids. I didn't bother going down but heard enough from up here to know they were trying to run away. Nina's name should be *Ninny*. That's obviously what she is. I don't know what they think is going to happen now. That we'll welcome them with open arms? I'm so mad at Dad for ever thinking this could fill the gaping holes in our lives. That it would be good for me to have her here. At least now David will be sure to see what a little ninny she is. I hope we'll be putting all three of them on the train for Winnipeg in the morning.

Carol

Chapter Eight

Ann Wright to Mr. Cress

August 13, 1940

Mr. Donald Cress
CORB Distribution Center
Winnipeg, Manitoba

Dear Mr. Cress,

You may have already heard about the runaway attempt by the Gabriel children. No need to go into details except to let you know that all three children are safe and are back in our home. I don't mind telling you I was fully prepared to put all three on a train out of here as soon as I saw my husband's truck pull into the yard late last night with those three dirty and bedraggled hooligans.

But I am a woman of prayer, Mr. Cress. As they crossed the threshold into my home, the only thing the Lord would allow me to think of was their mother, Mrs. Gabriel, and what it must have cost her to send them here. I did not sleep a wink.

I know my husband shared with you some of our troubles of the last eighteen months and how difficult it's been for us all, particularly for our daughter, Carol. When the request came from England to take the Gabriel children, and we learned they included a boy of ten and a girl of seven, Harold believed it was a direct answer from God. He thought Nina would be a bonus, a friend for Carol perhaps, and a way for the younger children to adjust more easily to our family. He quickly offered to take them in, thinking the rest of the family would agree with the idea. But we did not.

Wishing to do my patriotic duty, I agreed to take Nina only—for Carol's sake. Once the Gabriels arrived, it became apparent that was probably a mistake too.

In my prayers over the past month, I have repeatedly explained to God why it is too difficult to have the ten and seven-year-olds here. Surely, I thought, God understands why I can't do it. Surely, He would not ask such a thing of me. But in my prayers last night, as I imagined the relief of sending them away, I realized the burden of guilt would be far greater than the burden of letting them stay. God's only answer to my pleading was Philippians 4:13. "I can do all things through Christ which strengtheneth me."

So I'm writing to tell you I have had a change of heart. I cannot speak for our daughter, but I am willing to concede that perhaps my husband was not wrong. Even if he was, none of this has been fair to the Gabriel family. I apologize for taking so long to reach this conclusion and for the inconvenience my hesitancy caused you. Please know that all three children may stay as long as needed, and we shall do our best to meet their needs and make them feel at home. Miss Filmon and the Coopers are now free to host whichever children were originally assigned to them.

I look forward to your checkup visit, by which time the children will be in school.

Sincerely,
Mrs. Ann Wright

Nina woke to the warm glow of sunlight streaming through sheer yellow curtains and Hazel's morning breath as she whispered, "Nina, wake up."

Nina pushed herself onto her elbows and squinted at her sister. Somewhere in the house, baby Daniel squawked.

"Are we running away again today?" Hazel sat cross-legged on top of the blankets, taking up the middle of the bed. Her face was covered in red blotches, her hair still a disgraceful tangle. "Because my feet have blisters."

Nina had no idea how to answer or what today held in store. Surely, the Wrights would send all of them away, but to where? Her only mission had been to keep the family together, to protect her siblings. She'd failed miserably. They might be under the same roof for now, but she had not managed to protect them from the simplest of perils found in the Canadian countryside in August. How could she possibly see them through a winter? She needed to write home, but what could she say?

She flung the covers off and examined her own insect bites, scratches, blisters, and sunburned arms. She walked over to the mirror to find her freckles on full display and her hair in as rough a shape as Hazel's. "I don't know what's going to happen today, Hazie, but we better get ourselves fixed up as best we can. We're a fright."

A knock on the door, and Geoffrey poked his head in. "You up? It's ten o'clock already. The family's been up for hours!"

Ten o'clock?

Geoffrey stepped into the room. He was dressed, but his hair stood out in all directions, and his face looked like it had been dragged through a slough. "We're all supposed to come downstairs right away for an announcement."

Nina could imagine the announcement. She leaped into action, finding clothing and a hairbrush.

"No time for that. Come on." Geoffrey pulled on her arm.

"Mr. Wright needs to get back to work. We've already kept them waiting."

Oh no. What more could go wrong? She and her siblings had not only foolishly tried to run away, they'd gotten everyone worried and disrupted the whole family late at night. Now they'd kept them waiting, and they were about to show up looking like swamp creatures. Mum would die of embarrassment, and it was all Nina's fault. *God, please don't let David be here.*

Mrs. Wright's voice floated up the stairwell, reiterating Geoffrey's message. "Nina? Hazel? Come on down, girls. Don't worry about dressing. You can do that later."

Nina grabbed her dressing gown to cover her nightie and tied the belt as she followed Geoffrey. While he took the stairs two at a time, she plodded slowly down each one, dread growing heavier with every step. Hazel followed in her cotton nightie, unusually quiet.

The kitchen smelled of warm oatmeal and toast. Carol was washing dishes, Mrs. Wright drying. Mr. Wright and Jim sat at the table, heads bent over a Farmer's Almanac. Daniel sat in a wooden highchair, trying out various syllables to accompany the clatter of his spoon hitting the tray. No sign of David, for which Nina breathed a sigh of relief. All eyes except Carol's turned toward Nina.

"Help yourself to some breakfast." Mrs. Wright waved a hand in the direction of the stove where a pot of oatmeal still bubbled. Geoffrey filled a bowl for himself and carried it to the table, oblivious to the awkwardness in the room.

Nina wasn't sure she could eat but filled bowls for herself and Hazel, then took a seat. A dish of brown sugar and a pitcher of milk sat on the table, waiting to be used. Guilt tore at the edges of Nina's heart. She didn't deserve a hot breakfast, a warm bed, a single grain of the family's rationed sugar. Surely, the Wrights were performing one last duty before putting them on a train. But wasn't that what she had wanted only yesterday? Why did it feel like such a heavy failure now?

"Did you rest all right?" Mr. Wright raised his kind eyes

toward the girls.

Nina nodded. "Very well, thank you." She should apologize for the previous day but could not coax out the words.

Mrs. Wright hung up her dish towel and joined them at the table. "I'm glad you're all here because we need to tell you we've reached a decision."

Here it comes. Nina moved only her eyes as she tried to interpret the expressions on the faces around her. She swallowed a mouthful of oatmeal and felt it inch its way down. Carol turned to face the room and leaned against the counter, drying her hands and then folding one arm over the other.

"First, I need to apologize to you children," Mrs. Wright began.

Nina's eyes grew wide, but she focused on the tabletop.

"Especially to you, Nina."

This drew her head up. Were those tears in Mrs. Wright's eyes?

"I put you in the horrible position of trying to keep a promise to your parents without having the authority to fulfill that promise."

"Mrs. Wright, I can see now that I—"

The woman held up one finger. "Please. Let me finish first. I'm sorry I wasn't more hospitable to all of you. Nina, you've demonstrated a ferocious desire to protect your younger siblings, and I find that admirable. You've helped me see that I've been selfish. Please don't blame Mr. Wright. He wanted all of you here from the start. Now, I do too. We want you to know that all three of you can stay, however long you need to."

Had she heard wrong? Nina looked around the table.

"Hooray!" Geoffrey smiled up at Jim, who rewarded him with a big grin and a hair-ruffling.

"We can stay?" Hazel's blue eyes sparkled. "Can I have one of the kittens for my very own? When are we going to eat Adolf?" She climbed down from her seat. "Can I go tell Rosie we're staying?"

"Not so fast, young lady." Mr. Wright pointed to Hazel's

cereal bowl even as his eyes twinkled. "Finish your breakfast. We have some rules to go over."

"Rules?" Geoffrey yanked his elbow off the table.

Mr. Wright rested his own elbows on the table and clasped his fingers together. "That's right. If you're going to live with us, we want you to feel like you're part of the family, with all the rules and privileges that go along with that." He looked at Nina, though she had still not spoken a word. "All three of you will attend school, do your homework, and so on. That's your number one responsibility. It should go without saying, but I'll put it out there so we're clear. Next, you'll each write to your parents at least once a week."

The organizers at CORB had already delivered that instruction.

"You'll come to church with us on Sundays and participate in scripture reading and prayer time each evening."

Nina's family had attended their Anglican church regularly at home. The rest was pretty hit-or-miss. Mostly miss.

"And you'll each have your own chores." Mr. Wright looked at his wife. "Ann?"

Mrs. Wright cleared her throat and smiled at Hazel. "Hazel, your job will be feeding the chickens and gathering eggs each day. Carol or Jim will do it with you until you're comfortable doing it on your own."

"I'm already comf'table," Hazel announced.

"Well, just in case." Mrs. Wright failed to stifle a grin.

"Geoffrey, you're big enough to handle the cows. Your job will be to milk Greta while Jim milks Nancy. Twice a day. That includes bringing her into the barn, giving her fresh hay, letting her out again, cleaning up after her, bringing the milk inside—all of that. Jim will teach you."

She may as well have pinned a medal on Geoffrey's chest, the way he grinned.

"You'll also help Jim feed the pigs."

His face fell. "Oh."

"It's not so bad, Geoffrey," Jim chimed in. "Wait 'til you

see 'em come running when they see you carrying Mum's slop bucket."

Geoffrey wrinkled his nose. Nina glanced at Carol and then at Mrs. Wright, waiting to hear what her assignment would be.

"Nina, I'll be calling on you for all the same things I ask of Carol. Cleaning the milk separator is a twice-daily necessity. It's usually my job, but we'll be showing you how to do it too. This time of year, the garden takes priority. Dishes, food preparation, minding Daniel now and then…" She pulled the baby out of his highchair and wiped his face with the edge of her apron. "I usually manage to do laundry on Mondays while everyone's in school, but you can help bring it in from the line when you come home. House cleaning on Saturday mornings. But don't worry, there will be plenty of time for fun too."

Carol let out a snort. "When do we ever have time for fun?"

"Hey, now. You have plenty of fun." Mr. Wright peered at his daughter over the top of his glasses. "Any more free time and you'd only find ways to make trouble."

"Dad." Carol tilted her head to one side. "Be truthful. The dance last week?"

Mr. Wright shook his head. "We're not discussing that. It's already been discussed to death. Now, do you Gabriel children have any questions before we get on with our day and all its chores?"

Hazel's hand shot into the air.

"You don't have to raise your hand, Hazel." Mr. Wright smiled. "What's your question?"

"What should we call you?"

The man looked at his wife with eyebrows raised. "Well now, that's a good question. What do you think, Mother?"

"Oh. That *is* a good question. I don't know. What do you call your parents?"

"Mummy and Daddy," Hazel answered solemnly. "I don't think we should call you that."

"No, that wouldn't do, would it? Our children call us Mum and Dad. We'd be fine with that, but if you'd rather … Aunty and Uncle?"

"But you're not our aunty and uncle," Geoffrey reasoned.

"Mum and Dad Wright?" Mr. Wright suggested.

Jim grinned. "Why not Harold and Ann?"

"Absolutely not." Mrs. Wright scowled at her son. "You'll be flicked on the ear if I ever hear you calling any adults by their first names, and you know it." She turned to Nina. "Nina, you've been pretty quiet. What do you think?"

Nina hesitated just long enough for Carol to break in. "I think they should call you Mr. Wright and Mrs. Wright, and they should address me as Miss Wright." She hung her towel on a peg and headed for the door.

Jim let out a hoot. "You want 'em to curtsy too, your highness?"

"Carol, don't be silly," her father sighed. "Where are you off to?"

"I'm due at work at eleven." She walked out the back door without another word. The crunch of bicycle tires on gravel carried through the open window. The kitchen grew silent except for Daniel's babbling.

"Nina?" Mrs. Wright coaxed.

Nina was still trying to grasp the idea that they were being allowed to stay after all that had transpired. "Maybe … maybe Carol's right. Maybe we should keep calling you Mr. and Mrs. Wright. At least for now."

"Well, whatever you're comfortable with, as long as it's not just to appease Carol."

"And under no circumstance will you call her Miss Wright." Mr. Wright stood. "C'mon, boys. We've got work to do."

Nina watched Geoffrey happily follow along after Jim.

"Did you have more questions, girls?" Mrs. Wright asked.

Nina pressed her lips together before she spoke. "Shall I write Mr. Cress to let him know?"

"I've already written him. I think your first order of business—as soon as you're dressed—should be a letter to your parents. The chicken chores were done while you slept in, Hazel, but from now on it will be your job. Understand?"

Hazel nodded. "I can do it." She slipped from her chair and scampered upstairs. "C'mon, Nina. You did it. We get to stay together. Well done, you."

Embarrassed by what her sister implied, Nina began clearing their dishes.

Mrs. Wright placed a hand on her forearm. "Leave them, Nina. Just this once."

Nina looked up into kind, blue eyes. She wanted to ask what had changed the woman's mind, but the words would not come. "Thank you."

She hoped the simple words conveyed a fraction of all she felt.

Nina to her parents
13 August 1940
Cedar Bluff, Manitoba

Dear Mum and Dad,

I'm sorry it's taken me so long to write. We've arrived, safe and sound, at the Wrights' farm and have been so busy I've hardly had time to think. Yesterday, we went for a long walk through the lovely Canadian countryside. We saw various wildlife, wheat fields as large as a town, lovely wildflowers of all kinds, and a gorgeous sunset. The room Hazel and I share is wallpapered in a sunny yellow with a white bureau and bed frame. Geoffrey shares with Jim, age fourteen. Their daughter Carol is sixteen—a beautiful girl, and I'm sure we will be fast friends. And the baby, Daniel, is simply charming.

We've been welcomed as part of the family, and we each have our own assigned tasks. You'll be pleased and proud to know Geoffrey and Hazel are learning how to care for livestock and poultry. We are all enjoying the abundant produce from their enormous garden. There's even a funny fat goose who wanders freely.

I am looking forward to starting school soon and making lots of new friends.

I hope you are well and not missing us too much. If you see Sharon or Donna—or any of the old gang, really—please tell them I say hello and offer them my address as I would love to hear from anyone.

Please rest at ease knowing all is well with your children.

Your loving daughter,
Nina

Chapter Nine

Mrs. Gabriel to her children

25 August 1940
My darling children,

What a relief to finally receive word that you are all, indeed, safely established at the Wrights' home. Your father and I were sick with worry and regret when we first learned of the mix-up. Now, we are glad to know you're being well cared for and treated as part of the Wright family.

Shortly after you left us, Prime Minister Churchill visited Middlesbrough to inspect the damages of that awful night. Daddy and I caught only a glimpse of him. Daddy says the man won't back down. Now it's official. Our air force has bombed Berlin. If I could be satisfied that such actions would put a stop to things, it would be wonderful. But retaliation is certain, and we don't know where or when they might strike. Don't worry about us—the air raid sirens are working, and the shelters are safe enough. We're thankful you are not here, forced to live this way. Our rations have been further cut with only the two of us here.

Nina, I know you will continue to make sure Geoffrey and Hazel behave so that the Wrights will be glad they agreed to host you.

Geoffrey, you must mind Nina and the Wrights even when you don't want to. They will keep you from undue harm.

Hazel dear, you are so very young to be so far from home, but we're thankful you're with a loving family. I saw your friend Connie yesterday. Her mother is still waiting for word as to whether Connie will be included in the evacuations to come.

May God give you pleasant days filled with fresh air and sunshine. May He grace you with precious friendships and plenty of good food. And may you soon be on your way home to us again in peace and safety. I pray for you every day.

Love and hugs,
Mummy

Sunday morning, Nina pulled on her church dress and brushed her hair with extra care before assisting Hazel with hers. CORB tried to place children with families of the same faith, but since Cedar Bluff had no Anglican Church, Nina and her siblings would attend the nondenominational community church that had, according to Mrs. Wright, been the church of her husband's family for generations.

A heavy-set woman at a small organ pumped out strains of "Onward, Christian Soldiers" as the Wrights and the Gabriels made their way inside and quickly filled a pew. This church felt nothing like her church back home. No candles, no stained-glass windows. No tall pipes running up the wall from the organ. No somber sense of reverence. Folks chatted cheerfully with one another.

To her delight, Nina found herself directly behind none other than David Cain, whose entire row was filled with family members who looked much like he did. Nina counted ten heads of curly dark hair, including the parents.

The girl beside David turned around and smiled. "Are you Nina?"

"Yes."

"Hi. I'm Emma Cain. David's sister. Welcome to Canada."

"Oh, thank you."

David turned around too. "Hi, Nina."

Nina gave him her warmest smile. "You didn't tell me you had so many siblings."

"You didn't ask." He chuckled and waved a hand down the row. "You just met Emma. Next is Julia, Jessie, Matthew, Nellie, Edna, and the little one on Dad's knee is Tommy."

Emma put one hand to the side of her mouth and whispered, "And Mum's got another on the way." The girl's smile was so contagious that Nina couldn't help but like her instantly.

David shushed his sister.

"What? It's not like people don't know."

"I don't mean that. The service is about to start. Turn around."

Nina checked to make sure her own siblings were properly seated. Hazel perched between Nina and Mrs. Wright, who held baby Daniel on her lap. She'd placed Geoffrey between herself and Mr. Wright—strategically, no doubt. On the other side of him sat Carol and Jim.

For the next hour, Nina's head filled with questions. The pastor was dressed the same as everyone else—not even a clerical collar. He stood behind a rustic wooden pulpit and spoke in plain, ordinary Canadian English. No robes or choirboys. Even the hymns were different.

"Today, I'm calling on David Cain for the scripture reading," the pastor announced. David left his row and hurried to the front, a large black Bible in his left hand, one finger stuck inside to mark his place. "You can follow along with David if you turn to Isaiah, chapter two, the first four verses."

Pages rustled all around. David waited a moment and then began to read. Though the King James English was familiar, the words went straight over Nina's head while she stared at David's beautiful eyes and listened to his deep voice. Could there be a more appealing young man on the face of the earth? Yet here he was, right in front of her. He read with eloquence and confidence, making eye contact with members of the congregation—though not with her. He seemed familiar with the passage, as though he'd made it his own. She squeezed her eyes shut and forced herself to listen to what he was reading. "… And he shall judge among the nations, and shall rebuke many people: and they shall beat their swords into plowshares, and their spears into pruning hooks: nation shall not lift up sword against nation, neither shall they learn war anymore."

She opened her eyes in time to see David close his Bible and return to his seat. She tried to resist staring at his dark curls, imagining how they'd feel between her fingers, as the pastor preached about how all war would one day cease. How we needed to trust God and stay true to His call. Repeatedly, her thoughts drifted back to the young man right in front of her. She'd have to keep writing about him to Jean and Alice, or she'd explode with admiration.

Her attention was drawn back to the moment. The pastor had finished his sermon and shifted his style.

"I'd like to offer a warm welcome to the newest members of our Cedar Bluff community. All the way from Great Britain, it's our privilege to have—" he looked down at a note on his pulpit— "Nina, Geoffrey, and Hazel Gabriel with us for the duration of the war. They're staying with the Harold Wright family. Welcome, children. We hope you'll feel very much at home here, and please know that we are all praying for a swift end to the conflict."

Nina's face grew hot as people around her smiled and nodded. She did her best to smile back and then focused on Hazel, running a hand through her fine curls. Geoffrey stood and turned a complete circle as he waved to the congregation.

When the service officially ended, the small pump organ in the corner started up again and the pastor hurried up the aisle to wait at the back door. Nina stood when others did.

"Beautiful job reading scripture today, David." Carol spoke behind her.

"Thanks."

How good would it feel to see David's winning smile aimed at her instead of Carol? If only Nina had worked up the nerve to compliment him first. To say something now would make her look like a copycat.

Eager members of the congregation, mostly women, soon surrounded Nina. They welcomed her warmly, commented on her lovely accent, and then shifted their attention to the little showman, Geoffrey, and the little cutie, Hazel. Nina felt a hand at her elbow and turned to see Emma Cain smiling back at her.

"Jim tells me you're starting high school with us."

"Yes. I'm looking forward to it." As an afterthought, she added, "But also a little nervous." No point denying it.

"Don't worry. I'll introduce you around. It's not like there are very many of us."

When Nina turned to check on Hazel, she found David crouched down, introducing one of his little sisters to Hazel. The scene endeared him to Nina even more.

On the ride home, Hazel spoke of nothing but her new best friend, Nellie Cain. How she would see Nellie again at school and they would spend every recess together and maybe sleep over at each other's homes too.

"How about you, Geoffrey?" Mrs. Wright prompted. "Did you make a friend today?"

The boy nodded. "Jessie Cain. But not his twin sister. She's a girl."

That night, Nina went to sleep with visions of David's tender actions toward Hazel, his lovely voice, and those beautiful chocolate-colored eyes. Clearly, the Cain family was going to be a big part of the Gabriel children's adventure in Canada.

Nina picked up the bushel basket of freshly picked tomatoes and carried it toward the house, keeping an eye out for Adolf. The angry gander had kept his distance since their original meeting, but Nina's wariness had not dimmed. It was her third day of assisting Mrs. Wright with canning. She'd never learned the skill back home but was assured by Mrs. Wright it was something "all girls need to know." Nina didn't mind the work or even the way the tomatoes stained her fingers orange by the end of the day, but her mind was often on her parents.

Inside, sandwiches waited on the table. "Eat quickly, girls." Mrs. Wright stood at the counter packing food into a box. "Carol and Nina, as soon as you're finished, I want you to take lunch to the men."

"Oh, can I go?" Geoffrey bounced in his chair.

"Me too?" Hazel spoke around a mouthful.

"Not today. I need you two to entertain Daniel while I finish up these tomatoes."

The arrangement made no sense unless Mrs. Wright was trying to force a friendship between Nina and Carol. Nina suspected that was the case. She helped Carol load the food into the truck and climbed into the passenger seat for the bumpy but quiet ride.

Carol parked the truck under a shady elm at one end of the field where she opened the tailgate and handed Nina two old blankets. "Spread these on the ground."

Nina did as she was told. Five minutes later, Mr. Wright, David, and Jim were enjoying roast beef sandwiches on homemade bread and taking long draughts of cool well water from canning jars.

"Hot enough for ya?" David aimed his question in the girls' general direction.

Carol nodded and rewarded him with a pretty smile.

"It's lovely to have the shade trees," Nina said.

"Smart farmers leave at least one good tree on the edge of every field they clear," Mr. Wright waved a finger around. "Provides shade on a day like today or a bit of shelter in a storm if you can't make it home on time."

Carol pulled out a newspaper. "Mum sent this along."

"She went to town this morning?" Mr. Wright took the paper and glanced at the headlines.

"No. I think Mr. Feenie dropped it off."

Her father handed it back. "I don't suppose she sent along my reading glasses. Read it to me while I eat." He shoved a sandwich toward Nina. "Want one?"

"No, thank you. We ate before we came." She dared a shy glance at David who had removed his hat and lain back on the blanket. He raked a hand through his thick curls and laid one arm across his eyes.

Carol unfolded the paper and read the front-page headline. "'A THOUSAND PLANES ATTACK ENGLAND. Nazis Launch Terrific Assault Against Britain.'"

Nina's eyes grew wide. She stared at the ground by her feet as Carol continued.

"'London, August 15. Sky-clouding waves of Nazi warplanes, estimated upward of a thousand, with a single armada flying in a thirty-mile-wide formation, stormed the British Isles in a maelstrom of fierce new raids, apparently the biggest onslaught since Chancellor Hitler turned on the full violence of his aerial might one week ago. The British government said—'"

"That'll do." Mr. Wright glanced at Nina and then away. "Anything local in there?"

Carol turned the page and scanned it.

"It's all right." Nina folded her hands. "I know you want to spare my feelings, but I need to know what's happening over there."

David sat up and took another sandwich. "How far from London is your home?"

"Around two hundred and fifty miles. North."

"Have you been there? To London?" Jim asked.

"No. When we launched out of Liverpool to come here, that was the farthest I'd ever traveled from Middlesbrough."

"I'm sure your parents are safe." Mr. Wright sounded as though he was trying to convince himself as much as Nina.

Nina nodded. "Yes. I'm sure they are."

"What was it like, at home?" Jim asked.

Nina closed her eyes and heard the soft twittering of birds. "Very different than here."

"Different how?"

"Jimbo—" Mr. Wright's tone sounded like a warning.

"No, it's all right." Nina took a deep breath and let it out. "It's much quieter here. No air raid sirens or public address systems. And no blackouts. It's lovely."

Jim frowned. "What's a blackout?"

Nina looked with envy on the boy who had no experience with such threats. "After dark we put black drapes on all the windows. Lights off. Candles or torches only."

"Torches?" Jim's eyebrows rose.

"She means flashlights." David looked at Nina. "Right?"

"Um. Yes, flashlights. Streetlights were always off. Always. That's what we noticed first when we arrived in Halifax, and in every city and town we came through after that. All the lights! Remarkable, really. Lovely."

"Funny what you can grow used to." Mr. Wright nodded his head.

"Did you fight?" Nina asked him. "In the last war?"

"I did. I was seventeen when it began in 'fourteen. Went off to France in 'fifteen. Feel very blessed to have survived."

"Glad ya did, Dad." Jim flashed his father a smile.

"Me too. I pray every day our local boys make it home in one piece like I did."

David appeared in deep thought as he studied his boss's face. No more was said about war or the newspaper as they cleaned up their lunch.

"Thanks for lunch," Mr. Wright said. "Are you girls helping your mother with the canning today?"

Carol answered. "Yes. We are helping *my* mother."

Geoffrey to his parents

01 September 1940
Dear Mummy and Daddy,

I like Canada. I only got in trouble three times so far since we got to the Wrights'. One time was for riding one of the pigs. I don't think the pig minded. One time was for climbing too high in the crab apple tree. I also got a tummy ache from eating too many crab apples, but I didn't get in trouble for that. And one time was for putting a frog in Carol's room.

I am really good at milking cows now. I get most of the milk into the pail.

We are starting school soon, but I'm not scared or anything. I already have a friend, Jessie Cain. He is David's little brother. He lives just up the road. He said maybe I can come to his place soon.

Oh yes, and I got in trouble after church too, but it wasn't my fault. It was Jessie's idea to climb on the headstones.

Jessie has a twin sister named Julia. And then they have a bunch more little kids, but I don't know all their names yet.

I will write again next week.

Yours truly,
Geoffrey

Chapter Ten

Nina to Jean

01 September 1940
Dear Jean,

Please write as soon as you can and tell me all about life in PEI. I finished *Anne of Green Gables,* and now I want to know if your life is like hers. I'm starting school in just two days. Mrs. Wright took me along when she registered me for school last week. The principal, Mr. Gordon, gushed about my accent and provided a short tour. The school is nothing like ours back home. The main floor has two classrooms, washrooms, and the school office which doubles as a staff room. Upstairs are two more classrooms and a tiny science lab. That's it.

If that seems small, you should see where my brother and sister will go. It's a wee building in the corner of a farmer's field. The farms here are so far apart that the kids come from a three-mile radius and still fit eight years (they call them "grades," here, but you probably know that) into one room, with one teacher. I can't imagine how they're going to learn a blessed thing—especially Geoffrey. I don't think I'll bother telling my parents how it is. The adults here all seem to know how to read and write, and I suppose most of them attended this sort of school so perhaps I should reserve judgment.

On to more interesting things. I am in love with David Cain. Not only is he devastatingly handsome, but he's kind and smart and articulate and a hard worker and a solid Christian. Sadly, he barely knows I'm alive. I'm simply "one of those English kids the Wrights took in."

I'm being called to set the table. Will write more later.

Nina

On Tuesday, September third, the first day after Labor Day, Geoffrey and Hazel walked to the one-room school a mile down the road while Nina, Carol, and Jim rode bikes the three miles to town to attend high school. Come winter, Jim told Nina, they would walk as far as the country school with the younger kids and from there, ride the additional two miles to town with other high school students from their area.

Glad for the physical exercise to help ward off nerves, Nina had no trouble keeping up with Jim and Carol. She'd taken a few rides alone on the weekend to get used to peddling on a gravel road. Until the week before, she'd been expecting David to be returning to school too, only to be disappointed to learn that he'd be staying home and helping on his father's farm while he continued to work for Mr. Wright.

"Did David graduate last year then?" she asked as they peddled along.

Jim laughed. "Graduate? No. Hardly anybody graduates. Maybe the town kids."

"Whyever not?"

"No reason to graduate unless you plan to go on to university. No need for university if you're just going to stay on the farm or become a housewife. Like my sister."

"Really?" Nina looked at Carol, expecting her to argue.

Carol answered without taking her eyes off the horizon. "I'll be marrying David in a couple of years."

So that's how it was.

"Oh yeah? When ya gonna tell David?" Jim's front tire began to wobble in some loose gravel, and he expertly corrected it as he laughed. His sister chose to ignore him, increasing her speed to get ahead of them both.

It didn't appear to bother Jim. "I might graduate. Depends what happens with the war, I guess."

Nina pulled alongside him. "What do you hope to do?"

"I'd sure love to be a pilot someday. I figure if I enlist in the Air Force, I could learn to fly for free."

"Don't you have to be eighteen to enlist?"

"Yes. But lots of fellas sneak in at seventeen. That's only two and a half years."

Two and a half years? Nina would be seventeen herself and long gone from Canada. "The war will be over by then."

"Yeah. But I could still join the service probably. Suppose they'll be fussier about who they take after the war is over?"

Nina laughed. "I'm sure they'll be happy to have you. Are you nervous about starting high school?"

"Naw. My pals Billy and George are starting too. I know my way around the school from going to concerts and stuff. Plus, when you have an older sister, you already know who the good teachers are and who to watch out for."

Nina laughed. "Enlighten me."

"Well, mostly Miss Simms is the tough one. Right, Carol?" He raised his voice to make sure his sister heard.

Carol slowed enough to join the conversation. "She's a beast. You'll have her for English, grammar, literature, all those things."

That was a relief. Nina's favorite subjects. "What about maths and science?"

Carol let out a snort. "Maths."

Jim explained. "We just call it math. Not maths."

One more thing to learn. "Oh. Thanks. I wonder why? You do have different types of maths, right? Algebra, geometry …?"

"Oh, sure. I don't know why, but it's just math."

"Thanks. I'll try to remember." Like she'd try to remember

that *sport* was *sports* here. Nothing was logical.

They reached Cedar Bluff High School and placed their bikes in the bicycle rack outside the main doors. Nina followed Jim upstairs to the Grade Nine classroom, where they discovered desks had been assigned to them in alphabetical order. With so few students in each grade, Nina found her spot behind a desk labeled "Emma Cain" and breathed a prayer of gratitude. The desk behind her said, "Irene Jasper." Her heart pounded as she took her seat. Students looked at her and then glanced away to carry on conversations with kids they knew. If only Jim's last name was closer to hers in the alphabet. He was two rows over near the back and already connecting with friends. She focused on placing her supplies inside the desk.

"Hello, Nina." The beautiful Emma smiled down at her.

"Hi, Emma. I can't believe my luck to get right behind you."

"No students between Cain and Gabriel." Emma flopped into her seat and turned around to face Nina. "Bet you're used to a bigger school."

"Yes."

Emma's smile, thick hair, and brown eyes resembled David's so much. "It must be hard to be so far from home."

Nina nodded, uncertain her voice would remain steady if she answered verbally.

Another girl approached, taking the seat behind Nina.

"Hello, Irene." Emma waved. "Meet Nina—all the way from England!"

"Hello, Nina." Irene appeared younger than the rest of the class with her red hair still in two French braids. "I saw you the day you arrived in town."

"You did?"

"At the grocery store. You didn't come inside, but I saw you through the window."

"Oh. Yes. Hi." The girl in the upstairs window who'd dropped the curtain so abruptly.

"Don't worry. My rash isn't contagious."

Confused, Nina glanced at Emma and then back at Irene. "Your rash?"

Irene pulled her hands out from under her desk briefly, exposing red, itchy-looking blotches on the backs. She quickly returned them to her lap. "It's eczema."

"I hadn't noticed." Nina felt sorry for someone who felt she had to keep her hands hidden.

Emma picked up the conversation. "Irene and I have known each other forever, from church and from the store."

Irene placed her school supplies inside the desk. "My parents own the store. We live above it."

"Irene's always gone to town school, but I went to Derryline, of course," Emma added.

Nina nodded. "Yes, my sister and brother are starting at Derryline today. It will be very different from what they're used to. All the classes in one room together with one teacher?"

Emma shrugged. "It works. Nearly all the kids at Derryline are either Wrights or Cains … cousins, if not siblings. Lots of big families around here."

"Well, I'm glad the Wrights have only three." Nina said it in a lighthearted way, but Emma's face turned serious. She glanced at Irene, so Nina did too. Irene's face had adopted a somber expression as well, but before anything more could be said, a tall, slim woman in a gray suit walked into the room.

She pulled down a window blind against the bright morning sun streaming across her desk. "Good morning, class. Welcome to Grade Nine and your first year at Cedar Bluff High. My name is Mrs. Strong"—she wrote it on the board in beautiful penmanship— "and I'll be your homeroom teacher, as well as social studies, history, and geography.

"Speaking of geography, I'm excited that we have a student all the way from England in our class this year. Nina Gabriel, welcome to Canada and to Cedar Bluff. I'll let you introduce yourself a bit more when it's your turn. Right now, let's start at the front." She indicated a girl in the first desk nearest the windows. "I want each of you to say your name and in one or two sentences, tell me the highlight of your summer holidays."

Nina pulled a notebook and pencil out so she could jot down students' names as, one by one, they stood to introduce themselves. It quickly became evident that they all knew one another already, and most had similar highlights to share— swimming at the lake or playing baseball.

When her turn came, Nina stood and clasped her hands together to quell the shaking. "I'm Nina Gabriel. I suppose my highlight was finding out in early July that my siblings and I were going to Canada. Then… making the trip over on a ship, and the long train ride, and finally coming here to—"

"Is it true you tried to run away?" a boy at the back called out.

Nina froze.

"Didn't get very far." Another boy guffawed.

Giggling and outright chuckling filled the air as Mrs. Strong wrapped her knuckles on the desk. "Class, settle down! Arnie, one more crack out of you, and you'll be sent to the principal's office. Now apologize to Nina."

"Sorry," the boy muttered.

"Properly." Mrs. Strong glared at him.

"I'm sorry, Nina."

"Better. No more out of you until it's your turn." The teacher turned toward Nina. "Did you have more you wanted to add, Nina?"

Nina slid into her seat, refusing to turn around to see who had heckled her. "No, ma'am." So the whole community knew about her attempt to rescue her siblings. If only she could disappear.

"All right. Well, we're delighted to have you with us, and I look forward to hearing more from you in the weeks to come. Next up? Irene?"

Nina continued jotting down the names of each student but refused to turn around so she could match names with faces. When the heckler introduced himself as Arnie Strong, Irene leaned forward and whispered, "His mom's the teacher. He likes to rile her up, so don't worry about him."

Nina dared turn her head just enough to see the boy. It wouldn't be hard to remember his straw-colored hair that reminded her of the African porcupine they'd seen at the zoo. He grinned back. Nina quickly focused her attention on the next person and kept writing down names and making personal notes about their appearance so she could remember them. When the introductions were out of the way, Mrs. Strong instructed them to pull out their history books.

At recess, the students flocked outside, and Nina found herself surrounded by girls wanting to ask questions and hear her accent. In every class, teachers called on her to describe life in England. In Mr. Gordon's class, he asked the name of her hometown.

"Middlesbrough."

"Oh dear. The first to be bombed."

Nina nodded, feeling all eyes on her.

"Can you tell us what that was like?"

Nina glanced around. "Well, we went to the shelter and … and waited until the all-clear sounded. Then we came out." How could she begin to describe the paralyzing vibrations of the Luftwaffe planes overhead, the thirteen bombs dropping one after the other, wondering if it would ever stop? She shivered.

"Mr. Gordon?" Emma raised her hand.

"Yes, Emma?"

"How are bombs made?"

"Well now, that's a good question for science class. Bombs are all about explosives, and explosives are all about chemistry…"

Nina could have hugged Emma. The class turned their attention back to the teacher, and Mr. Gordon was happy to share all he knew about the creation of various bombs, answering questions that arose—mostly from the boys.

By the end of the first week, the novelty of her Britishness had begun to wear off, and Nina was thankful to feel more like just one of the seventeen Grade Nine students at Cedar Bluff High.

Hazel to her parents
07 September 1940
Dear Mummy and Daddy,

When can I come home? I miss you.

I started school. Nellie Cain is my bestest friend. She is teaching me to speak Canadian. Mr. Fuller is our teacher. He is old. The regular teacher is gone to fight in the war, so Mr. Fuller came out of retirement. That's what Mrs. Wright said. What is retirement? I think it might be like a cave or a bomb shelter since he had to come out of it. I hope the war is over soon and the regular teacher comes back. The kids like him better than Mr. Fuller.

We play hopscotch at recess. Some of the girls have skipping ropes, but Nellie doesn't have one. Mrs. Wright found one for me to use, and I share it with Nellie. I like to skip. I'm having fun. I'm doing my chores. Jim showed me how to gather eggs from under the chickens so they don't peck, but I still got pecked a little bit. I don't like Adolf at all. He chases me with his nasty honking and hissing.

If I can't come home, can you please come visit us in Canada? I miss you very much. You could come at Christmas and eat Adolf with us.

Hugs and kisses,
Hazel

Chapter Eleven

12 September 1940
Dear Nina,

How lovely to hear from you! I am doing fine. PEI is wonderful, filled with color everywhere—the houses, the flowers, the fields. I've started school as well. Ours is bigger than yours but still very different from home.

And Manitoba isn't the only place with gallant young men. RCAF Station Charlottetown is very near, in Sherwood, and we see the pilots and trainees all around, so handsome in their uniforms!

Jean may have already told you—our homes are only about twenty blocks apart. A little far to walk, but I have the use of a bicycle and have visited her several times already. I think her brother John is having a harder time adjusting than Jean. Their host family is not as nice as mine. They have one daughter, Clara, age seventeen, who is serious and studious like her parents. My family, on the other hand, is boisterous and great fun. Besides Mr. and Mrs. Perkins, there's Ronald, Patricia, and Nickolas, ages fifteen, twelve, and nine. The dinner table is always a time of joking and laughter so that I can sometimes forget how far away my family is or what's going on back home.

I got a letter from my mother. My best friend from back home, Elizabeth, is scheduled to sail to Canada very soon, and I am dearly hoping she'll be staying somewhere near enough to visit. I still cannot fathom the size of this country though, can you?

Please write again and tell me all about everything.

Your friend forever,
Alice

Nina plunged the last pot into the basin of dishwater and started scrubbing. The potatoes had stuck to the bottom, scorched in spots, and it was all her doing. Would she ever get the hang of cooking—especially with wood?

"Why don't you let that one soak awhile, Nina?" Mrs. Wright hung her apron on its hook and lifted Daniel to her hip. "I can finish it later. I know you have homework."

"I don't mind." Nina kept scraping the steel wool across the bottom of the pan until she felt a hand on her upper arm.

"You'll scrub a hole right through it. Go on, now. I don't want to have to write to your parents that your schoolwork is slipping."

Nina pulled her hands from the water and took the towel from Mrs. Wright. "No worry of that. I'm at the top of the class. Though I suspect that will change when the novelty wears off."

"Novelty?"

"I think my teachers are being extra generous. Everyone seems enamored right now with my accent and all." Well, almost everyone. Carol still behaved as though she'd gladly throw Nina on a bomb, given the chance, but Nina could hardly say that to Carol's mother. Or to her own.

Mrs. Wright smiled. "And you think that will wear off?"

"I certainly hope so." Nina laughed and settled herself at one end of the kitchen table with her textbooks and notebooks.

"You know you can study in your room like Carol does, right? It would be quieter."

"Oh, yes. I know." Nina turned her gaze to the screen door, beyond which she could see Hazel emerging from the barn with a basket of eggs. Jim and Geoffrey would be following shortly with the evening milk. "It's easier to keep an eye on those two from here is all."

Mrs. Wright said nothing, opening the screen door to let Hazel through.

"I found ten!" Hazel was all smiles. "And I didn't get pecked once. Would you like to know which hens these are from? Betty, Olivia, Paulette, Rosalind—" She'd named all the hens after movie stars, and the lone rooster was Tyrone, after Tyrone Powers.

"That's fine, dear." Mrs. Wright neither discouraged nor encouraged the naming scheme. "Get them washed up and put away now, and you'll be free to listen to *Amos 'n Andy* with us."

Hazel opened her mouth to speak again, but Nina caught her eye just in time. She knew exactly what Hazel was about to say. The girls had listened to the comedy radio program with the family on a few occasions. Hazel couldn't understand a word the American actors rattled off. Nina didn't blame her. She had a tough time understanding them herself, but she played along, laughing when the others laughed, hoping in time she'd pick up the lines. She gave Hazel a glare that she hoped communicated *never mind, just do your chores.* That language, Hazel understood perfectly. She closed her mouth, carried the eggs to the wash basin, and began cleaning them with the care Mrs. Wright had taught her.

Mrs. Wright closed the door and pulled out a chair next to Nina's. "Nina …" She took a seat, Daniel bouncing restlessly on her lap. She seemed uncertain about what she wanted to say. "You know you're not responsible for your siblings, don't you?"

Of course I'm responsible for them. Nina knew better than to argue.

"I mean, it's admirable how you want to look after them,

but … your parents asked us to take you in because they trusted us, as adults, to provide and parent them. And you."

"I promised them I'd look after Hazel and Geoffrey."

"Did they ask that of you?"

Nina wanted to jump in with an immediate *yes* but stopped herself. Had they actually asked? "Well … Mum told me to take charge on the trip."

"Are you still on the trip?"

"I suppose not. I suppose I just got used to being in charge."

"Perfectly understandable. Still, I think it would sadden your parents if they thought you were taking the responsibility too seriously—if your schoolwork was suffering or if you were sacrificing your youth. At least some of these days should be happy and carefree for you."

Carefree? What did that even mean? "I don't want us to be a burden to you. And these two—well … how many eggs did Hazel break the first week?"

"Hey!" Hazel turned to scowl at Nina just as a large brown egg slipped from her hand and fell to the floor. "Oh no. Nina, look what you made me do."

Nina jumped to her feet and grabbed a rag and a cup to start cleaning up the broken egg. Mrs. Wright would want the inside part in the pigs' slop bucket and the shell in her compost pail.

"Girls." Mrs. Wright set Daniel on the floor and came over to them. "A broken egg is not the end of the world, but the eggs are Hazel's job, and Hazel knows how to clean them up. Don't you, Hazel?"

"I made her drop it, though." Nina got down on her knees to wipe the mess.

Hazel's curls bobbed. "That's right. She did."

Mrs. Wright crouched beside Nina and held out her hands for the cup and the rag. Nina reluctantly surrendered them. "Not really, Hazel. Nina can't force you to drop an egg from across the room." She held the items out to Hazel. "The eggs are your responsibility, and you're doing a great job. I want you to keep getting better at it. Now be sure to wipe up all of it. Egg white gets really sticky."

Hazel made a face but obediently went to work.

Nina returned to her homework. She'd just read the first paragraph of her reading assignment when the boys came in with the milk. Their conversation and the clatter of setting up the milk separator really did make it difficult to concentrate. Maybe she should take Mrs. Wright's advice and work in her room. Carol had certainly disappeared into hers right after supper, claiming a test tomorrow.

Just as she closed the book and stacked it with the others, Mr. Wright and David pulled into the yard. With harvest in full swing, they worked until dark and ate supper late. The two plates of food Mrs. Wright had set aside meant that David would be having supper here. Nina tried to appear casual as she reopened her book and put her face closer to the page than necessary, resting her elbows on the table and her forehead on both hands.

The two men came inside, washed up, and sat at the opposite end of the table where Mr. Wright said a quick prayer, and they dug into the food his wife had pulled from the oven. Carol suddenly appeared and took a seat at the table too. A fresh spritz of lilac scent filled the room.

"I'm putting this guy to bed." Mrs. Wright picked up Daniel and headed for the stairs.

"I'll warm up the radio," Jim announced when the last of the milk had run through the separator. He disappeared into the living room. The kitchen ruckus continued as everyone finished their tasks and Mr. Wright reported on the day's accomplishments.

The theme music from the *Amos 'n Andy Show* drifted in from the living room.

"You staying to listen with us?" Carol asked David.

"Thought I might." David stood and carried his plate to the washbasin.

"Might as well," Mr. Wright followed suit. "It'll be nearly over when you get home if you leave now."

The whole group moved to the living room and gathered

around the wireless. Hazel snuggled against Nina, and Nina tried hard to catch all the words the comedy team said. In the middle of a joke, a shrill whistle erupted from the wireless.

"We interrupt this program to bring you dire war news. Near midnight on September seventeenth, a German U-boat torpedoed and sank the British steamship, the *SS City of Benares*. In addition to the crew and paying passengers, she carried ninety child evacuee passengers on their way to Canada."

Nina leaned forward, staring at the wireless and straining to hear every word.

"The full extent of lost lives is unknown at this time, but of the four hundred and seven total people on board, only one hundred and five have been rescued alive so far—ten of them children. One hundred and five survivors were picked up from lifeboats by the *HMS Hurricane* and taken to Greenock, Scotland. The *City of Benares* left Liverpool on September thirteenth, bound for the Canadian ports of Quebec and Montreal, under the command of her Master, Landles Nicoll. It's been confirmed that Captain Nicoll went down with the ship."

Nina took her eyes off the wireless long enough to glance around the room. Mrs. Wright stared at the radio as well, one hand stretched across her open mouth.

"That could have been us!" Geoffrey piped up.

"Shh." Nina hushed him so they didn't miss anything.

But little more was said, and Nina couldn't focus on it anyway. The image of the submarine that was spotted on their own journey—though it turned out to be American—was etched in her heart. If the Germans attacked at midnight, the children would have all been asleep in their cabins, forced to climb into lifeboats in their pajamas. If they made it to lifeboats at all.

"CBC Radio will continue to bring up-to-date news as more information becomes available. For now, this network wishes to express its deepest condolences to the families who have lost loved ones, especially to the parents of the lost children. We now return you to your regular programming."

"Oh, how awful." Mrs. Wright snapped off the radio.

"Filthy Nazis." Mr. Wright rose from his seat. "What do ya bet they knew that ship was full of kids?"

"Harold. We can't know that."

"Well, it makes no difference to their families. That's heartbreaking. Just heartbreaking." With a sigh, he moved to the stairs. "I'm gonna turn in. Morning's coming earlier every day it seems."

"Geoffrey, Hazel. C'mon. Let's get you two tucked into bed too." Mrs. Wright started up the stairs.

Hazel had grown dozy. With any luck, she hadn't grasped the magnitude of the news. Nina took her hand and headed for the stairs.

"I guess I'll be on my way too." David rested a hand ever so briefly on Nina's shoulder as she passed. "I'm sorry, Nina."

Nina pressed her lips together and nodded, not trusting her voice.

"Good night, David. Want me to walk you home?" Carol asked.

David's answer drifted up the stairs as Nina turned the corner halfway up. "Silly girl. I'd only have to walk you home again."

Hazel snuggled close to Nina in bed that night. "I'm scared. Will the Nazis come here?"

Nina wrapped an arm around her and enclosed Hazel's little hand in her own. "No. They won't find us here."

If only she could be as certain as she sounded.

Donna to Nina

11 September 1940
Dear Nina,

This will be the first letter you've received from me since

you arrived in Canada, but it is not the first I've written. You can be glad I didn't mail that first one. The day I went to your house to share my latest issue of *Girl's Own* with you, only to learn from your mother that you were gone—I went home in tears and didn't stop crying for three days. That's how hurt I felt. Then I just got angry. I wrote you a scathing letter declaring we were over. I felt betrayed. Shocked, completely shocked. Why didn't you tell me you were leaving? We didn't even get to say goodbye! Your mum explained that you had to keep everything hush-hush, but you could have confided in me. I wouldn't have told anyone.

But I got over it when I received your letter, complete with your apology for not telling me. I understand better now because guess what? I'm coming too!

I'm going to a town called Sudbury, Ontario. How close is that to where you are? Can we bicycle?

I'm so excited, Nina. I'm already packed and can hardly sleep for the excitement. We'll be leaving from Liverpool in just two days on the *SS City of Benares* and our escort is going to be Mary Cornish, an accomplished classical pianist. Can you believe it?

I'll write again as soon as I reach my new home. Let's make plans to see each other. Perhaps we can travel home together when this is all over.

Love,
Donna

Chapter Twelve

Nina to Donna's parents

10 October 1940
Dear Mr. & Mrs. Cutting,

I cannot begin to tell you how sorry I was to hear the news of Donna's passing. I received her letter the day after we heard the awful news about the *City of Benares*. That's how I learned she'd been aboard, and I hoped and prayed with all my might that she was one of the few survivors. When the names were released in the days to follow, I knew she was not among those who made it, and I have been crying for days.

I'm sure you know Donna was a dear friend since we started school together. She was so funny and so faithful. She helped me through many difficult days and made me laugh. She was generous and caring, and I know she loved you very much. Thank you for being good parents to her. Thank you for putting her first by arranging for her to come to Canada. You could not have known what would happen, and this is not your fault. I wish I could tell you in person how sorry I am. That's not possible, but I am sending my deepest condolences with this letter.

My foster father, Mr. Wright, gave me a young oak sapling to plant in the yard here in memory of Donna. He says a tree planted in the autumn will be stronger and more resilient than any other. I will think about her every day, and I promise to keep praying for you and the whole family. May God bring you comfort.

Sincerely,
Nina Gabriel

In the days and weeks following the sinking of the *City of Benares*, headlines broadcast controversy about the CORB program. The British seemed angrier at their own government and their navy than they were at the Germans. Prime Minister Churchill, who'd been opposed to the plan all along, announced an end to overseas evacuation.

Everywhere she went, adults wanted to engage Nina in a discussion about it, as though she had some sort of inside information. While most people gently expressed their sympathy and their thankfulness that the Gabriel children had not been aboard, others proved more vocal. Mrs. Jasper, Irene's mother and the proprietor of the general store, declared her opinion boldly one Sunday morning before church. "What's wrong with those Brits? Have they no hearts? No loving parent could send their child across an ocean teeming with Nazi submarines. It's unthinkable!"

Nina felt dozens of eyes turn in her direction. She wanted to clamp her hands over her siblings' ears. If only she had enough hands. Instead, she herded Geoffrey and Hazel to their pew and tried to stifle her tears. Though she'd told no one about Donna except the Wrights, one of them must have shared that piece of information—probably with David. Emma Cain slid into the row beside Nina and gave her a quick hug and a homemade sympathy card before moving to her own family's pew.

Monday morning between classes, Emma invited Nina for an overnight stay in their home for the following Friday. "I already asked my parents, and they said, 'What's one more?' We can camp out on the living room floor. We'll have gobs of fun."

"Oh, I'd love to, but I couldn't leave Hazel overnight. Thank you, though."

"Maybe Hazel could come too."

Nina tried to imagine it. "Wouldn't that spoil the whole thing?"

Emma shrugged. "I suppose. But she and Nellie are tight chums now."

Nina shifted the books in her arms. "Maybe I can invite you over sometime. I just don't feel comfortable asking yet."

"That's okay. I understand."

Today was the day Miss Simms, their English teacher, would announce roles for the Christmas play. She'd written a half-hour play called "Home for Christmas" to be performed by the high school students and elementary children combined. Those not in the play would provide the music and the whole concert would be held at the community hall right before Christmas break. Nina was hoping for the role of Miss Mirabelle Lipton, one of two young teachers who become stranded in the school with their students through a horrible blizzard over Christmas.

"You'll get the part," Emma said as they walked together to the assembly. "You read so beautifully."

"I won't, though. They'll give it to one of the older girls—I'm too young to be convincing as a teacher." Nina sighed. "Carol tried for it too, you know."

"I hope she doesn't get it. She got the lead role last year, and she was horrible."

"I sort of hope she *does*. I wouldn't have even tried for it if I'd known Carol wanted it. Even though I do want it very much."

Emma shook her head. "Don't be silly. You've got as much right and a hundred times more talent."

Nina chuckled. "I don't know about that, but I know one thing. If I do get it, Carol will make my life miserable. If *she* gets it, I'm going to do everything in *my* power to encourage her and help her if she'll let me. It might be my chance to win her over."

"Who says you need to?"

Nina laughed. "Life would be a lot more comfortable without her constant glares and put-downs."

Since none of the school's classrooms were large enough to hold all the students and staff, assemblies took place either in the main hallway, or outdoors, or at the community hall a short walk from the school. Today it was warm enough to meet outside, and the students gathered around the flagpole. The principal, Mr. Gordon, stood with Miss Simms on the top step of the main entrance and commanded the students' attention.

"Good afternoon, everyone. It may seem early to be preparing for our Christmas concert, but as you know, it takes many weeks of hard work and rehearsals. The elementary students who are going to be acting in the play received their parts and their scripts this morning. I'll turn things over to Miss Simms who will announce the high school roles."

Miss Simms, a tiny forty-something-year-old woman who taught with strict sincerity, cleared her throat. Her brown curls moved in the October breeze under a blue felt hat as she held tightly to a stack of play scripts and a clipboard. Her big voice belied her small stature.

"Thank you to each and every one who signed up to help with this play. It's going to be our best yet. I'll be announcing the names of the crew first, then the cast. While I'll be your staff adviser, I'm pleased to announce the play will be directed by Grade Twelve student Martha Henning. She and I have decided together who would be best in each of the parts."

She consulted her clipboard. "If I call your name, please stop for a copy of the script on your way back to class. On the first page is the cast list so you can see who all the children will be, I won't bother reading them out. Rehearsals start tomorrow afternoon." She cleared her throat and then began reading out the roles for the characters with fewer lines—a janitor, a police officer, a soldier who makes it home for Christmas, some parents who arrive near the end. "Now for the main two parts. The role of Mr. Joseph Kimble will be played by Arnie Strong."

A cheer went up from the area where Carol and her classmates stood. One voice rose above the others, "Atta boy, Arnie!"

Two boys thumped Arnie on the back while another shouted, "He's the only one who tried out for it."

This brought a round of laughter, and Mr. Gordon had to settle everyone down again before Miss Simms could continue.

"And the role of Miss Mirabelle Lipton will be played by…" she paused for effect. "Nina Gabriel."

"Yahoo!" Emma's voice rang out as she hugged Nina. "I knew you'd get it."

Nina couldn't help smiling, already mentally composing a letter to her parents. If only they could be here to see her on stage. As the students filed back into the building, she paused to receive her script from Miss Simms.

"Thank you so much." She gave the teacher her biggest smile.

"It was really no contest, Nina." Miss Simms handed her the stapled pages of dialog. "Even with five contenders, Martha and I both agreed immediately we wanted you for the part."

When Nina turned, tucking the script between her textbooks, Carol and her friends were entering the school.

"I'm glad I didn't get it." Carol tossed her head. "Once I read the script, I could see what a childish play it is."

"She'll botch it with that stupid accent. The audience won't catch half her lines." The words from Carol's friend were barely discernible but stung all the same. Nina turned to Emma with a "see what I mean" look.

"Pay no attention." Emma took her elbow and steered her into the school and up the stairs to their homeroom. "They're completely jealous. Their problem, not yours."

That night at supper, Jim began the announcement to the family. "I'm going to help with the lighting for the play. Just what I signed up for."

Mrs. Wright's eyebrows went up. "Oh? They've announced the parts? And—?"

"Nina's got the lead role." Jim smiled broadly. "She'll be great!"

"Yay!" Hazel and Geoffrey cried out in unison.

"You did?" Mrs. Wright turned her attention to Nina. "Well, congratulations." She glanced at Carol and then at her husband.

"Well done, Nina." Mr. Wright chimed in. "We'll look forward to seeing you in it. What about you, Carol? You in it this year?"

"No." Carol took a bite of her bread and chewed, appearing nonchalant. "Didn't want to be."

Jim spoke around a mouthful. "Yes, you did. You wanted Nina's part."

Carol swallowed, giving her brother a dismissive glance. "At first, I did. But after I read the actual script, I asked Miss Simms to take my name off the list. It's a stupid play."

Mr. Wright looked around the table at all three teenagers. "Didn't you say Miss Simms wrote it? I certainly hope you didn't tell her it's stupid."

Carol shook her head. "No. I told her I've got plenty to do with my schoolwork and my job on Saturdays and chores around here."

"When did that happen?" Mrs. Wright looked confused. "This morning you still sounded excited about doing it."

"She's lying." Jim shrugged as though Carol's deceitfulness was a normal event.

"No, I'm not."

Mr. Wright cleared his throat. "It doesn't matter. Sounds like everyone got what they wanted in the end. So we can all be happy about it."

"Our school's doing a concert too," Geoffrey announced. "I'm going to be in the choir. It's a living Christmas tree."

"I'm going to be one of the presents under the tree." Hazel sat up straighter. "I already know my line."

"That's wonderful. Sounds like two great concerts already." Mr. Wright smiled at Hazel and tucked away another forkful of food.

"Want to hear my line?" Hazel looked around the table.

At that moment, Daniel began to babble at the top of his little lungs as though he had an audience of hundreds. Everybody laughed, causing the baby's eyes to grow wide.

"Why don't you save it for the night of the concert, Hazel?" Mr. Wright leaned toward her. "I hate to spoil a good surprise, don't you?"

"Besides," Mrs. Wright added, "if you reveal your line, little Daniel here might steal it right out from under you."

"Babies are good at stealing parts away from others more worthy," Carol muttered as she rose from the table. "May I be excused?"

"Only if it's to go straight upstairs to do homework." Mrs. Wright stood as well, pulling Daniel from his highchair.

"It is." Carol carried her dishes to the sink and hurried upstairs.

"You're all excused." Mr. Wright pushed his chair back. "C'mon, boys. Hazel. Critters are waiting."

Nina rose to help clear the remaining dishes while Mrs. Wright poured hot water from the kettle into the dish pan, cooled it with cold water from the hand pump beside the sink, and added washing soda.

"Some of the rehearsals will be after school." Nina plunged her hands into the water and began cleaning glasses. "I hope I won't be inconveniencing you all too much."

"It's fine, Nina. Carol's been in the play every year, so we know what to expect." She paused only a moment. "Don't worry about her. She'll get over it."

Nina to Alice
01 November 1940
Dear Alice,

I've not heard from Jean. I hope that means she's too busy with fun things. Is she doing all right?

Guess what? I've got the lead role in the school play! We rehearse three times a week, sometimes during the school day and sometimes after school. I play a teacher who becomes stranded in the school with a bunch of little kids through a blizzard over Christmas. The boy who plays the other teacher, Mr. Kimble, is named Arnie. He's in my class and rather cocky. In the play, the two of us get into constant spats about how to keep our students warm and fed. You can tell it was written by a woman. His character thinks he knows best because he's the man (typecasting if you ask me) and my character keeps coming up with solutions that work better most of the time. By the end, as you might guess, there is a spark of romance between the two of us (but don't worry, no kissing or anything so embarrassing) but then, at the end when the storm is over and the parents come to rescue their children, Mr. Kimble learns he's been drafted and will be leaving New Year's Day. Miss Simms had to write it that way, because there can't be any hint of romance between teachers. This way, the audience is left imagining the relationship will continue blossoming while they're apart.

Even if Arnie's rather arrogant, I am having so much fun in rehearsals that I don't want it to ever end. Of course, the other students are teasing both of us about being boyfriend/girlfriend in real life. I think Arnie might be okay with that idea judging by the way he flirts. I would not. My heart belongs to David Cain. I still get to see him at the house a couple of times a week, at church on Sundays, and the handful of times I've been to the Cain home with Emma. She's guessed how I feel about her brother. She has not given me any reason to hope that his feelings might be mutual, but she has assured me that Carol, my foster sister, doesn't have a chance with him no matter how much she assumes otherwise. I suppose time will tell.

In other news, Geoffrey continues to be Geoffrey. Some days I fear the Wrights will have had enough and change their minds about us. He fractured his collarbone after falling from a swinging rope from the hayloft, so now his arm's in a sling. The doctor said he was lucky he didn't break his arm or worse. Mrs.

Wright has had to meet with G's teacher at least twice to discuss his distracting behavior in the classroom. Despite all that, he's a favorite on the playground and seems happy.

Hazel is adjusting well but still clings to me at night or in any new situation. It's probably best that we're in separate schools. She's become best chums with Emma's little sister, Nellie, so that works out well. Emma and Nellie have come over to the Wrights' home, but I haven't the nerve to ask if we might do an overnight. I suspect the adults would deem it entirely too impractical.

My friend from back home, Donna, was aboard the *City of Benares*. She didn't make it. I am heartsick, but so grateful for this play to keep me busy and give my mind other things to think of than those poor children drowning or dying of exposure in lifeboats on a cold, dark ocean. Or their families back home, dealing with grief and guilt and anger and blame. It's all too awful. How can anyone bear it? How can anyone not be eaten up with hatred for the Nazis or for Germans in general? There are kids at school here whose parents came from Germany, and they are not always treated kindly. One of them found a swastika painted on the side of their home.

Does your school put on a Christmas play or concert? Are you in it? Please write soon and fill me in on everything. I miss you.

Affectionately,
Nina

Chapter Thirteen

Hazel to her parents

25 December 1940
Dear Mummy and Daddy,

It is Christmas Day. I have so much to tell. We did our concert at school on Friday afternoon. I wore a big red ribbon around me. It was tied in a bow at the top of my head. I said my line perfectly. "I am a present, so straight and so tall—to stand for God's gift to one and to all." Nellie was the star at the top of the tree! I know her line too. Do you want to hear it? "I am the star, see its bright shining light—that shone on the manger that first Christmas night." We each got a bag of nuts with some candy and an orange too. That was our last day of school. Now we are on Christmas holidays.

That night, we went to the concert in town. Nina was the star of the play! She looked so beautiful and grown up, Mummy, you should have seen her. Everyone clapped and clapped at the end. Except Carol.

Last night we went to a carol service at church. I thought Carol was going to be at the front talking or something like that. But it means Christmas carols, like "Joy to the World" and "Silent Night" and like that. They turned all the lights off. Then they lit lots and lots of candles. It was so pretty. They spent a long time praying about the war and the soldiers who can't come home for Christmas. I fell asleep. Mr. Wright carried me to the truck after.

This morning was very exciting. Jim woke us early. We gathered around the Christmas tree. I miss you very much, but I would rather have you here with us than go home because Nina says the bombs are still falling. Are they? We opened presents. Santa brought me a doll. Mrs. Wright said he would find me here and he did. Thank you for the beautiful red sweater. It fits just fine. I also got a bracelet from Nina and Geoffrey. I got some doll clothes from the Wrights. It's almost as though they knew what Santa was bringing me. The clothes fit my new dolly perfectly. I can't decide what to name her. I like *Nancy* but that's one of the Wrights' cows. Maybe *Rebekkah.* Or *Rachel.* Those are nice names from the Bible.

Geoffrey will write you his own letter, so I won't tell you what he got. He sure was excited about the baseball from Santa. I guess Santa doesn't know Geoffrey will likely put the ball through a window. His collarbone is healed now. He doesn't have to wear the sling anymore. But I will let him tell you.

It's very cold here. We all went to the Cains' house in the afternoon. They have a pond. There weren't enough skates for all to skate at the same time. Nellie shared hers with me so I could try it. It's very hard. I fell down a lot. Nina tried it too. She thought the skates were supposed to go over the top of her shoes and the other kids laughed. Especially Carol. I laughed too, at first, but I stopped when I saw Nina's face was all red. David was kind to her. He helped her tie her skates up nice and tight. She fell some too, but not as much as me.

When we came back home, we had roast goose for supper. It was Adolf. I didn't feel even a little bit sad. Adolf was delicious.

Merry Christmas. I love you and miss you.

Hazel

How was it possible for the world to be so cold? Mountains of snow had fallen over the Christmas break. At first, Nina had great fun making snow angels and snowmen, learning to skate on the Cains' pond, and sledding down the hill beside the Cains' barn. Any time spent with their large family was always filled with laughter. Being in David's presence helped Nina forget how far from her parents she was and that a war was going on back home.

After Christmas, the temperature dropped to thirty below zero and keeping warm seemed like a full-time job. Nina, Geoffrey, and Hazel learned to bundle in layers of long underwear, outerwear, hats, scarves, mittens, and boots. The girls wore pants under their dresses until they got to school, then stashed the pants in their desks until it was time to go out into the cold again and return home at the end of the day.

For the most part, the success of the Christmas play had only increased the number of friends Nina made among the families of Cedar Bluff. The exception was Miss Filmon. No other British children had arrived in the community as planned, probably due to the sinking of *The City of Benares* and the end of the program. When Miss Filmon came to the concert, she spotted Hazel and paused for a warm chat. To Nina, she delivered only a grudge-filled glare.

"I have no regrets," Nina confided to Emma.

"Why should you?" Emma agreed. "You've kept your family together like you promised your parents. You're earning top marks at school. Making friends."

Plus, I found the man I want to marry. Nina wouldn't admit it to Emma, let alone her parents. After news came of a major bombing blitz in London, she focused even harder on her tasks.

When Emma begged again for Nina to come for an overnight stay, it was the thought of seeing more of David that motivated Nina to finally ask the Wrights. "Hazel's invited too," she added. "If you think that's a good idea."

"I can't imagine why the Cains would want two extra kids around with that passel they've already got," Mr. Wright observed, "but it makes no difference to me. What do you think, Mother?"

"I'll allow it." Mrs. Wright bit off a piece of the thread she was using to mend a shirt. "That said, if you don't get enough sleep and end up too tired to do your chores around here the next day, it won't happen again."

"I won't. I mean, I will." Nina smiled.

"Take Hazel too." Carol chimed in. "Nobody wants to have to come fetch you in the middle of the night to settle her down."

"Carol." Mr. Wright looked at her over the top of his glasses. "It's not up to you."

"That probably would be best, though," Mrs. Wright added.

"Okay." Nina didn't mind. Hazel and Nellie were as thick as thieves and would not likely bother Nina and Emma. This way, Nina could avoid the guilt she'd feel if she left Hazel behind. The Gabriel girls would go home with the Cain girls after school and were to return by noon on Saturday.

Overjoyed at the prospect, Hazel threw together pajamas, a toothbrush, and more books and toys than she could possibly share in the allotted hours. Nina prayed Geoffrey would stay out of trouble in her absence.

Though she shared a bedroom with her sister Julia, Emma had worked out a barter whereby the room was exclusively hers and Nina's until bedtime. Emma and Nina closed themselves in as soon as they got home from school so they could talk, do each other's hair, and look at the latest issue of *Chatelaine* Emma had borrowed from Irene Jasper. They didn't emerge until suppertime when the regular din of the Cain household reached its peak. The family gathered around the huge table laden with fresh bread and a hearty soup made from beef stock and at least half a dozen different vegetables. Mr. Cain said grace. Bread, butter, and strawberry jam began circulating in all directions. David stood to fill bowls from the pot in the middle of the table.

"What's so interesting in your room, Emma?" David ladled out soup for the youngest sibling first. "Sounded like a hen house in there. I thought you must have brought in some chickens."

"David," his mother chided softly.

"Wouldn't you like to know." Emma buttered her bread. "We sure weren't talking about *you,* if that's what you're wondering."

It wasn't true. Nina had peppered Emma with so many questions about her big brother that Emma had finally grown exasperated enough for Nina to stop. But she now knew David's birthday, February twenty-eighth. Favorite meal, roast beef. Favorite color, red. Favorite Bible story, David and Goliath. It stood to reason he'd love that, given that his parents named him David.

Nina held her tongue at the supper table.

Not that there was room to sneak in any words edgewise. If she'd thought meals at the Wrights' home had ever been lively affairs, the ruckus around the Cain kitchen was on an entirely new plain. Mrs. Cain, appearing ready to deliver her next baby any day, merely watched in amusement while she fed two-year-old Tommy. Four-year-old Edna competed with Nellie for their parents' attention while the twins, Julia and Jessie, showed off for Hazel's sake. Only Matthew was quiet. At age eight, he merely observed the others when they were around and buried his nose in a book when they weren't.

As the meal ended, David tapped his butter knife against his water glass. "Can I have everyone's attention?"

It took a couple of tries, but eventually, all eyes were on David.

"I have an announcement." His eyes were twinkling. Nina couldn't help grinning. She had no idea what news he had to share, but she sure enjoyed looking at him.

His mother tilted her head. "David. Are you sure now's the

best time?" Her eyes darted between Nina and Hazel and then back to David.

"Oh, Nina and Hazel are part of the family. Practically. Right, girls?"

"I … hope so," Nina stammered. She had every hope in the world of being part of this family one day, but not as David's sister.

"Yes, we are!" Hazel shouted, making everyone laugh.

Nina slanted her head as she observed her little sister. Was Hazel picking up a Canadian accent?

"Get on with it already." Emma sat back in her chair. "Some of us have things to do. What's your big announcement?"

"Mom and Dad probably suspect what's coming because I've talked about it." David stood as he glanced at both his parents. "Today it's official. I've enlisted."

Nina's heart sank. Jaws dropped around her. Emma's. Julia's. Jessie's. If not for Tommy's jabbering, the room would have grown quiet enough to hear the clock tick.

"What's *enlisted* mean?" Nellie asked.

"Which branch?" Mr. Cain wanted to know.

Julia turned to Nellie. "It means he's going to go fight in the war."

"But I don't want him to fight in the war!" Edna began to cry, which gave Tommy all the incentive he needed to start too.

I don't want him to fight in the war, either. Nina felt tears welling and choked them back.

"The Air Force." David beamed. "I start training at the end of the month."

"But you're only seventeen." Mrs. Cain protested.

"I'll have my birthday before the training is over. I didn't lie, Mum."

Mrs. Cain rose awkwardly from her chair, supporting her large belly. She moved to the window and stood staring out, supporting her back with one hand.

"Isn't anyone but me excited?" David looked around the table. "What's with all the long faces? Don't you know the Nazis dropped ten thousand bombs on London in one night? Just a couple of weeks ago?" He unrolled a newspaper Nina hadn't noticed in his hand until now. "Listen to what Churchill said in Parliament. 'The gratitude of every home in our island, in our Empire, and indeed throughout the world goes out to the British airmen who, undaunted by odds, unweakened by their constant challenge and mortal danger, are turning the tide of world war by their prowess and their devotion. Never in the field of human conflict was so much owed by so many to so few.'" He handed the paper to his father.

Mr. Cain patted his arm. "Good for you, Son. You'll make us proud."

"Thanks, Dad." David sat down again. "I'll expect letters from all of you. Even you, squirt." He tickled Edna under her chin.

She pulled away, giggling. "But I don't know how to make letters yet."

"I do!" Hazel beamed up at David. "Can I write to you?"

"Of course, you can. You too, Nina. If I end up in England, I'll have gobs of questions for you."

Nina's face grew warm. She wanted to say, "I'll write you every day." Instead, she merely nodded.

Emma jumped up from her seat. "How could you, David?" She glared at her dad. "How could you allow this? We need David here."

"I would get drafted eventually, Em." David spoke softly. "This way, I get to pick which branch I want to serve in. I'll learn to fly. How great is that?"

A shudder escaped Mrs. Cain's body, but she held her tongue.

"I want to fly." Jessie slid his chair away from the table and raised his arms to form a gun. "Better yet, I want to be the gunner in the back." This was followed by sound effects and a round of blasts at the floor.

"Stop it." Without turning around, Mrs. Cain busied herself filling a kettle with water. "Emma and Nina, I'd like you girls to do the dishes, please. After that, you're free for the evening. The rest of you know what you're supposed to be doing. I don't want to hear any bickering."

David's announcement completely changed the atmosphere in the household. Even if the younger children didn't understand what it all meant, they picked up on the seriousness of the situation and behaved accordingly. Emma was too angry to be much fun. Nina tried in vain to comfort her, to assure her that David was doing a good thing. After they settled down to sleep, she lay awake a long time, already composing letters in her head. Writing to David might provide better opportunities to build a relationship with him than if he stayed home. She'd focus on that rather than the danger. If she dwelled on the danger, she'd never be able to bear it.

Mrs. Gabriel to her children
20 January 1941
Dear Nina, Geoffrey, and Hazel,

How are my darling children? Your father and I miss you horribly, but we are so thankful you are safe and well. By now you'll have heard of the endless raids and bombings but try not to worry. We are all right, and the travesties only serve to convince us we did the right thing in sending you to Canada.

We have the most exciting news. You have a baby brother! Sullivan George Gabriel was born 18 January, weighing six pounds, eight ounces. We will call him "Sully." He is perfectly healthy. We are still in the hospital, but we are both doing well despite the blackouts. I hope and pray all the conflict is over soon and you three will be able to come home to meet Sully before he is old enough to ever remember your being away.

I'm pleased to hear how well you are all doing, and that G's collarbone has healed. Keep up the good work. I will try to send a photograph of Sully as soon as possible. Please tell Mrs. Wright I will write soon and that I do appreciate her letters and all she and her family are doing for us. May we be able to make it up to them one day.

Lovingly,
Mother

Chapter Fourteen

Carol to her diary

January 1941
Dear Diary,

I'm so mad I could spit. David has enlisted. That's not even the worst part. The worst part is, he didn't tell me. Instead, I had to find out from the stupid ninny who happened to be at the Cains' house with Emma when David decided to tell his whole family. She came home the next day just gloating with the news. Well, actually, it was Hazel who blasted it out as soon as Mr. Cain dropped the two of them off on his way to town, but it was the ninny who answered Mum and Dad's questions. David will be gone by the end of the month. He's joining the Air Force even though he won't turn eighteen until the end of February.

I can't stand it. Why didn't he tell me? I should have been the first to know. I should have had the opportunity to well up with tears, for him to see how much I care about him. How much I'll miss him. Maybe he'll ask for a private conversation with me today. Or tomorrow. Maybe he'll ask me to write. To wait for him. Of course, I will gladly do both.

Maybe I should join up myself, after graduation. I suppose I'd have to go to nursing school first. I don't really want to be a nurse, but I don't know what else I could do. Maybe I'll look into it. Miss Simms said women are lobbying for Ottawa to form a Canadian women's army corps, that a woman named Joan Kennedy is the driving force. Maybe I'll write to her. I don't suppose Mum and Dad would be too happy with me.

In any case, I guess I can't afford to stay mad at David for long. I couldn't bear to be, anyway, any more than I'll be able to bear his being away. I'll just have to direct all my anger at the ninny. Oh, how I'd love to ship her and her bratty brother and sister back to England. Lord, let this stupid war end soon.

All for this time,
Carol

Nina stared at the letter in her hands. It couldn't be true, it just couldn't. How could Mum have had another baby? How on earth could she even think about bringing another child into the world after sending her surviving children away? And how was Nina supposed to break the news to Hazel and Geoffrey? They'd be devastated. Maybe it was best if she didn't tell them at all. But eventually, they'd receive their own letters from Mum or Dad. The letters would mention Sully, and they would wonder who he was. Nina shook her head. It had to be some sort of prank. She'd already read it three times, but she started over at the beginning to see if there was some hint of a joke she'd somehow missed. Her intent was to fold it back into its envelope as soon as she reached the end and not tell anyone—at least not yet.

But Geoffrey skipped over and saw the salutation before Nina could hide it. "Hey, that's for all three of us. Read it out loud, Nina."

"Let *me* see." Hazel moved in close.

Nina stuffed it into the envelope. "It's just the same old news. Nothing really—"

Geoffrey snatched it out of her hand. "I don't care. I want to read it."

"Me too."

"Geoffrey." Nina tried to take it back, but Geoffrey dashed under the kitchen table and surrounded himself with chair legs.

Hazel sat cross-legged on the floor, waiting. It wasn't worth the effort. They'd find out eventually. At least this way, Nina wouldn't be forced to break the news. The horrible, senseless news. She moved to the window and stared out while Geoffrey unfolded the letter and read in a loud voice.

"We have the most exciting news. You have a baby brother."

"We have a baby brother?" Hazel's excitement pulled her to all fours, and she tried to crawl to Geoffrey to see the letter for herself.

Nina turned around but kept leaning on the kitchen counter, her arms crossed.

Geoffrey kept reading through to the end. "We have a little brother." He crawled out from under the table and waved the letter around. "At last, I have a little brother of my very own."

"Yay!" Hazel began dancing around the room. "C'mon, Nina. We have a baby brother! Oh, I bet he's so cute." She grabbed Nina's hand and tried to pull her into the dance. Nina shrugged her off. Undaunted, Hazel grabbed both of Geoffrey's hands in hers. He submitted to one circle with her.

Mrs. Wright entered from upstairs. "What's all the excitement?"

"We have a baby brother named Sully," Geoffrey hollered.

"Aww, Sully. I love him already." Hazel rocked her arms as though holding a newborn. "I'm going to cuddle him and help Mum feed him and change his little clothes—"

"Not me. I'm going to teach him how to swing a bat and catch a ball and skip stones and—"

"Congratulations." Mrs. Wright's face held a knowing grin, igniting Nina's suspicion.

"You knew about this?"

Mrs. Wright smiled. "Your mother mentioned it in a letter. She asked me to keep it a secret. I didn't know the baby had arrived—"

Nina stomped out of the room and flew up the stairs and into her room, slamming the door. Her actions might be childish, but if she stayed around people, she'd be sure to say something she'd regret. What were her parents thinking? Why did they tell Mrs. Wright and not her? Did they really expect her to be happy about this? Geoffrey and Hazel might not know any better, but Nina was no child. She understood the dangers all too well. Did they plan to send Sully to Canada too? She'd read that some private groups were still evacuating their children. Would she be expected to take care of him? Then what? Would Mum keep having more babies, like Mrs. Cain, even while bombs kept falling all around?

Nina grabbed Hazel's doll and flung it at the door. At the last second, the door opened and the doll struck Carol in the stomach. Somehow, she had the reflexes to catch it. She stepped into the room, holding the doll, and closed the door. "What's going on? You nearly broke the door, slamming it like that."

Carol was the last person Nina wanted to confide in. But it was all she had at the moment, and the words tumbled out of her faster than she could think. When she had no more to say, she sank to the edge of the bed.

Carol stood there, holding the doll and staring at Nina. Slowly, she began to shake her head. "You child. You are an absolute child, you know that? How could you not know?"

Nina stared back. "What do you mean?"

"Don't you know how long it takes to make a baby?"

Nina scanned the floor. Of course she knew. It took—

"Nine months. It takes nine months to make a baby, Nina. How long have you been here?"

Nina counted backward. She'd arrived in late August. It was now early February. "Five months?"

"Your mother was pregnant long before you ever left England. How did you not know?"

This was not helping. Nina stared at the floor, feeling stupid. Carol was right. Mum must have known she was expecting a baby before Nina even left home. Had she already known when the evacuation plans were made?

"No wonder your mother wanted the three of you out of her hair."

The back of Nina's neck tingled as she stood. "She did not want us 'out of her hair' She cried while we packed. She cried when we said good-bye. Oh, she tried to hide it, but I could tell she was torn. She and Dad did what they thought best for us, to keep us safe."

"Well, that clearly can't be true. Now she's got a brand-new baby to replace you."

"Don't be ridiculous. You have no idea what it's like over there." Nina blinked hard to keep the tears at bay.

Carol stared at her a moment. Instead of leaving, she laid Hazel's doll in the toy cradle that had once been her own. Then she took a seat on the chair in the corner and studied Nina some more.

"And you have no idea what it's been like *here* for the last few years. Your parents are not the only ones who think they can replace their children, you know."

Nina's gaze roamed from the doll to Carol. What was she talking about? "I don't know what you mean."

Carol let out a big sigh. "Haven't you noticed that my mother visits the cemetery nearly every Sunday after church?"

Nina thought about it. She had seen Mrs. Wright wander over there a few times, but a lot of people did. The graves were right next to the church. Like the building itself, everything seemed more rustic than the churches and cemeteries back home. "I guess I didn't give it much thought."

Carol stared another moment and then rose. "Wait here."

Too weak from her outburst to argue or even move, Nina did as she was told. In seconds, Carol returned with a framed photograph in her hands. She sat beside Nina on the bed and handed her the picture without a word. Nina studied it.

A family portrait. Mr. Wright stood in the back, a much younger Carol on one side and Jim on the other. In front of them, Mrs. Wright was posed on a chair, a little girl in her lap. Standing beside her was a little boy of five or six, one hand on his mother's arm.

"When … when was this taken?" Nina's voice came out almost a whisper.

"In 1934."

Carol would have been ten. Jim, eight. Daniel not yet born. Nina gently traced a finger around the faces of the two younger children. "What are their names?"

"Bart and Violet." Carol took the picture from Nina's hands.

Fragments of comments Nina had heard around school and the community floated to the forefront and began to make a glimmer of sense. "What happened to them?"

Carol stood and headed for the door. Was she not going to answer? She flung open the door, pausing long enough to glance Nina's way. "They died."

She closed the door firmly behind her.

Nina to her parents
February 1941
Dear Mum and Dad,

I know I will never mail this letter. I'll write something polite and encouraging instead. I'll tell you the truth about how G and H danced around the kitchen when we received the news of Sully's arrival. I'll tell you how Mrs. Wright is teaching me to knit and how I'm going to make a little blanket for Sully—not a sweater because a sweater would have to fit. How Mrs. Wright will probably need to finish the blanket for me. Otherwise, I'll be too slow and by the time I finish it, he'll be off to school. I'll lie and tell you how pleased I am and how I can't wait to meet him. I'll be nice. And funny. And kind.

But for now, I really hate you both for this. How could you? Sending us away made sense until I knew about the baby. But YOU knew, didn't you? You knew there was another one coming and you sent us away anyway, without saying anything. You even told Mrs. Wright! A stranger to you. How could you keep this from your children, your own nearly grown daughter? I'm not a baby, you know. I understand there are ways to keep babies from coming. After what happened the last time, I never dreamed you'd have another. What were you thinking? How could you add this new child? Were you trying to replace that other one? Are you trying to replace us now? Are you going to have two more to even things up? Then you'll be back to three, and we won't need to bother coming home. Is that what you're planning? Will G and H be my responsibility forever?

How can Sully possibly be safe there if we were not? What if something should happen to him?

What if something should happen to *you*?

I truly hate you for this.

Nina

Chapter Fifteen

Nina to David

March 1941
Dear David,

Your mother has encouraged all of us to write. I understand if you're too busy to write back, but I hope you receive lots of letters and that they encourage you on tough days. At least I assume you have tough days. Who doesn't?

By now you'll have heard about the big blizzard. I've never experienced anything like it, and you can be thankful you weren't around. Saturday, March fifteenth dawned a beautiful, warm day hinting at the approach of spring. Finally, I thought. After the coldest winter of my life. Everybody was so happy to be outdoors. Jim, Geoff, and Hazel were tearing around outside, making drainage ditches with your mother's garden tools and watching the water flow from puddle to puddle. I hung clothes on the line, taking my time, soaking up the beautiful sunshine.

It came out of nowhere in the middle of the afternoon. We all worked together to bring in the laundry, the high winds nearly ripping the clothes from our hands and making it almost impossible to reach the house. Once we were all safely inside, we tried the radio. It was on and off through the rest of that day and the next. The wind sounded like a freight train hitting the house. We read books and did jigsaw puzzles, thankful to be warm and safe. Mr. Wright finished all the outside chores alone, using a rope to guide him back and forth from the barn. He even allowed Rosie into the kitchen.

When we finally got the news on the radio, we heard the devastating report of deaths because people were not dressed for a winter storm. Many were trapped in cars, or worse—abandoned their vehicles and tried to walk to safety but succumbed to the elements. Terribly sad. Last report said five Canadians died and many more in North Dakota and Minnesota.

Sorry. I suppose that's not very happy news. The younger kids were thrilled to again have mountains of snow to play in, although it disappeared much more quickly this time. The Wrights tell me this isn't necessarily the end of it, either—that they've seen snow dumps as late as May. I can't imagine.

In other news, my parents wrote to tell us we have a new baby brother—Sullivan George Gabriel, or "Sully" was born in January. Geoffrey and Hazel are over the moon. Can I tell you a secret? I am not over the moon. In fact, I was quite angry at first—for all kinds of reasons that I'm still sorting out. Of course, I can't tell Mum and Dad that. But it feels good to say it to someone. I hope you can understand and not think me perfectly wicked.

Do you have any idea where you'll be posted once basic training ends? Are you flying planes yet? Maybe you're not even allowed to tell us. Rest assured, prayers are going up on your behalf at every meal around our table and, of course, at your own family's home. I've visited twice since you left. It's not quite the same, but everyone is doing well. They miss you. Your newest little sister is adorable.

I would love to hear from you. If you ever need to confide in someone who knows how it feels to be far from home, I hope you'll think of me. Take care and write if you can.

Your friend,
Nina

Nina reread her first letter to David, agonizing over it. Was inviting him to confide in her crossing a line? Being too obvious? She quickly sealed and addressed the envelope before she could rethink it. Carol, of course, was composing letters of her own, and Nina could only imagine how she signed hers. *Yours forever? Your one and only? All my love?*

Since Carol's revelation about the deceased Wright children, the two girls had barely spoken outside of the mundane, practical conversations about school or chores.

By the first Sunday in April, the blizzard's snow had disappeared and a warm breeze compelled Mrs. Wright to go around opening windows before they left for church. After the service, Nina ventured toward the graveyard. The two small graves, side by side, were not difficult to find. Their headstones revealed that Bartholomew and Violet Wright, aged ten and seven, had died on the same day—July 14, 1938. Nina stood staring at the engravings, doing the math. Just two years before the Gabriel children arrived, and they'd been the same age as Geoffrey and Hazel were now. No wonder Mrs. Wright hadn't wanted them. What a difficult reminder, day in and day out.

Nina returned to the family and rode home in silence, feeling horrible for what she'd put the Wrights through when she tried to run away. If only they'd have told her up front, maybe she could have behaved in a more understanding way—but why did they agree to take Nina at all? Was it merely to be patriotic or was there more to it? Why did adults keep everything so secret, everything that truly mattered?

By late afternoon, she had more pressing things to worry about than her parents or her new brother or even David. She was at the kitchen table, focused on math homework when Hazel hurried by. "Going outside," she announced.

Nina might not have even looked up, but the distinct smell of lilac perfume followed Hazel, filling the room. The fragrance pulled Nina's focus from her Algebra just in time to glimpse Hazel's face as she grabbed a warm sweater and ran out the door. Was that lipstick?

"Hazel!" Nina jumped from her seat, but the little rotter had let the screen door slap shut behind her. Without grabbing a sweater or jacket, Nina ran after Hazel, catching up to her near the tire swing. She grabbed an arm and swung her around.

Hazel's face was matted with beige powder and pink rouge, her lips bright red. "What on earth have you done?"

"Ow! Let me go. You're hurting me." Hazel yanked her arm away.

"I am not. Whose makeup did you get into?"

Hazel grabbed the swing and started slipping her feet through the tire. "Nobody's."

"Don't lie to me, I can plainly see it all over your face. You look ridiculous. Were you in Mrs. Wright's room?"

Hazel didn't need to answer. At that moment, a scream let loose from an upstairs bedroom. There was no mistaking Carol's voice, even if Nina couldn't make out the words. *Oh no.* She turned back to Hazel.

"You got into Carol's makeup?"

Hazel already had the swing pumping. Nina reached out to grab it but misjudged its force. Hazel's outstretched foot struck Nina on the shoulder, pushing her to the ground. She got up, ran around to Hazel's back side and caught a firm grip on the inside rim of the tire. Hanging on with determination until the swing's momentum stopped, she wrapped her arms around Hazel's waist and began to pull. Hazel kicked her feet in protest.

"We have to get that off your face. Come on. I'll clean you up before you get into big, big trouble."

Carol's shouts and Mrs. Wright's calmer voice both continued to drift out the open windows and into the yard below.

Hazel kept kicking. "You can't make me go with you!"

"Yes. I. Can." Nina kept pulling until Hazel was free of the swing, her arms and legs still flailing. Now what? She couldn't very well take Hazel inside. Could she wrestle her over to the water pump and try to clean off the makeup with nothing for a wash rag? Not likely. What was the point? Maybe it was best to let her face the music. Before Nina could decide, the screen door opened again.

Mrs. Wright stepped out and quickly closed the door on Carol. "Stay inside and calm down. Let me handle this." She headed toward Nina and Hazel. "What's going on over there, Nina?"

"I knew it." Carol disregarded her mother's directive and stepped outside, carrying something. She marched past her mother and held out her hands. "Look what your precious sister did! Just look at it!"

Hazel finally stopped wiggling and dropped to the ground in a heap. Nina stared at the remains of Carol's makeup. A small pot of pink rouge, its lid missing, looked like someone had sprinkled it liberally with dirt from the driveway. The mirror in her powder compact had cracked into at least three sections, one of them gone altogether. Worst of all, her cherry red lipstick lay broken in two halves.

"I could strangle you, you little brat!" Carol yelled at Hazel.

"Carol!" Her mother gripped her arm above the elbow.

Carol unleashed her fury on Nina next. "Why don't you watch your little sister? Do you have any idea how much this cost me? How long I saved or how hard I had to work for it? It's completely ruined."

"I'm sorry, Carol." Nina stepped back. "I'm so sorry. Hazel knows better, don't you, Hazie?"

Hazel only sulked.

"Girls. We need to work this out in a peaceful fashion." Mrs. Wright kept her voice even and subdued.

"Peaceful? She had no business even going into my room, let alone—"

"I know. I know. Settle down." Mrs. Wright focused her attention on her daughter until Carol pressed her lips tightly together. She turned toward Hazel. "Hazel. Tell us what you've done."

Carol's composure didn't last. "Isn't it obvious?"

Her mother held up one finger. "I want Hazel to tell us. Truthfully, Hazel."

Hazel glanced around the farmyard without raising her head. Finally, in a voice little more than a whisper, she spoke. "I wanted to be pretty like Carol."

Carol let out a huff and turned her back.

"Okay. So … what did you do to make yourself pretty like Carol?"

Hazel stared at her shoes in silence.

Nina couldn't stand it. "I'm so sorry, Mrs. Wright. I should have been watching her. I'll make sure it never happens—"

"Nina. Stop." Mrs. Wright spoke firmly. "I've told you before. It is not your job to watch your siblings every moment, and it is certainly not your responsibility to discipline them. Now Hazel, I need you to say what you did, and I need you to apologize to Carol."

Still without looking at anyone, Hazel took a deep breath and let it all out with the words, "I put on some of Carol's makeup, and I'm sorry."

"Thank you. Now—"

"That's it?" Carol whirled around, her face nearly as red as the lipstick in her hand. "No consequences? Just one little 'I'm sorry' and she's scot-free?"

"No." Mrs. Wright placed one hand on Carol's arm. "Let me finish. Hazel, do you understand that you used something that didn't belong to you—without permission?"

Hazel nodded.

"And do you understand that you've ruined it?"

Another nod.

"Now here's what's going to happen. You will need to earn enough money to replace the items."

Nina gasped. How on earth could Hazel manage that? "But Mrs. Wright, she doesn't have any—"

Mrs. Wright held up a finger again. "We'll help you find ways to earn it."

"Maybe our parents can—"

"Nina!" This time, Mrs. Wright's voice was sharp. "In this family, we teach our children to take responsibility for their own actions. How will Hazel learn if you or your parents bail her out? Now if you really want to help, you can supervise while she cleans off that makeup. *All* of it. Then we'll come up with a plan. And *you*." She turned to her daughter. "Get rid of that broken mirror before someone gets hurt. Figure out how much replacing all this will cost. I think you can salvage at least some of the rouge and lipstick, can't you?"

Carol let out a growl and stomped back to the house mumbling about it taking years for Hazel to ever earn enough money. Nina took Hazel to the wash basin in the corner of the kitchen and cleaned the makeup from her face, although her lips remained brightly tinged for the rest of the day. By supper time, Mrs. Wright had helped Hazel work out a payment plan and a list of extra chores she could do to earn some money.

"I can take her and Geoffrey with me collecting pop bottles and digging Seneca root," Jim offered. "We get two cents apiece for the bottles and twenty cents a pound for the roots."

"That's kind of you, Jim." His mother ran a hand over his hair. "Just be sure you teach them how to leave part of the root for regrowth."

"I know."

After Hazel fell asleep that night, Nina crept downstairs where she hoped to have another conversation with Mrs. Wright about the makeup. She paused on the stairs when she heard Mr. Wright's deep chuckle.

"You gotta admit, it's kind of funny. I wish I'd seen it."

Mrs. Wright's knitting needles clacked together in a steady rhythm. "Oh, she looked like a little clown. I honestly had a hard time not laughing. Carol would have had a conniption if I had."

"Sounds like she had one anyway."

"Well, yes. She'll survive. I'm pretty sure she's got close to enough money squirreled away to replace most of that stuff much sooner than Hazel can earn it."

"Hard to believe she'll soon graduate. I'd like to see a little more maturity." The snap of a newspaper opening punctuated Mr. Wright's words.

"Mmm. Well, regardless. I'm sure Hazel won't try that stunt again. Do we tell their folks?"

"Good question."

"I hate to bring such a trivial thing to their attention when they have so much hardship, but one of the kids might mention it to them."

"You probably should. Keep it light."

A sigh. "It's Nina I worry about."

"Oh?"

"She seems to feel she's completely responsible for the other two. It's not right."

"I know. I haven't even told her half the antics Geoffrey's gotten into out in the barn. Unless he tells her himself, I figure it's better she doesn't know."

"Agreed."

Geoffrey to his parents
May 1941
Dear Mum and Dad,

None of the ten-year-olds here call their parents Mummy and Daddy. Just the little kids do. And the girls. So I shall call you Mum and Dad from now on. That's what Jessie calls his parents. He's my very best chum. His big brother David has gone to war. He is going to be a pilot. I know you already heard of David because Hazie is smitten with him. So is Carol and every other girl in Cedar Bluff, I think. Even Nina. She won't admit it, but I can tell. I want to be a pilot too.

Thank you for sending the photograph of Sully. It's strange to think I have a little brother. Daniel Wright feels more like a little brother to me than Sully. He had his first birthday, and we had a special supper, but no cake. Mr. Wright said cake would be a waste for a kid who's so little he doesn't even know it's his birthday. I told him the rest of us could enjoy it, and then he asked when my birthday is. So I hope that means there will be cake for mine next week. I will be eleven on the twenty-fourth in case you've forgotten.

Nina pretends to be happy about Sully and everything, but I don't think she is. I heard her crying in her room when she thought she was the only one in the house. She's worried about you. She misses David too. I can tell. I think she writes to him more than she writes to you.

Summer is almost here and then no school for two whole months. Do you think we'll go home before school starts again in September?

Your loving son,
Geoffrey

Chapter Sixteen

Carol to David

July 5, 1941
Dear David,

Graduation was lovely, despite everything. The war, of course, places a damper on everything … except for the boys who are excited to be going off and having an adventure. Larry Nickels dropped out in March to join up—much to his mom's horror, not to mention Tina L. who has been carrying a torch for Larry forever (even though we all know Larry loves Emma). So that left just five of us in our graduating class—two boys, three girls. Martha Henning delivered the valedictory address. We had our banquet at the community hall as usual but this year, only grads, their dates, and their parents were invited. No siblings. Nina and Emma helped serve. Lots of funny speeches and silly awards. I was declared "most likely to marry first." (I suppose that depends on how soon I'm asked.)

It feels good to be done. I've been working as many hours at the store as Miss Filmon will offer me and helping Mother at home. I've gone with her to the Women's Institute meetings a few times. The W.I. is doing various projects to help with the war effort. Dad says he misses your good work around here, but Jim has stepped it up a notch. He misses you too.

The English kids continue to delight.

I have a secret. I have been closely following the campaign

to form a Canadian Women's Army Corps, and I intend to enlist as soon as possible. British Columbia already has a Women's Corps begun by Joan Kennedy. They train women for first aid, motor mechanics, and clerical duties. Maybe more. Across the country, women are volunteering for things like Morse code signaling and map reading … some are even doing infantry drills! And why shouldn't they be taken seriously? The British have had official women's auxiliary services for years.

I still need to inform my parents of my plans. They have some pretty old-fashioned ideas, so it will be a challenge to convince them. In my very best calligraphy, I printed out a Churchill quote and put it up in the kitchen, hoping it would influence their thinking. "To each, there comes in their lifetime a special moment when they are figuratively tapped on the shoulder and offered the chance to do a very special thing, unique to them and fitted to their talents. What a tragedy if that moment finds them unprepared or unqualified for that which could have been their finest hour."

So, I hope by my next letter I'll have even bigger news, because the opportunity to prepare for my finest hour will be real. How wonderful would it be if you and I were eventually stationed together somewhere? I hope and pray for it. I miss you terribly.

Lovingly,
Carol

Nina stood staring at the calendar on the kitchen wall. One year. One entire year had passed since she first stepped into this house. She'd arrived believing she would be returning home six or eight months later. Now, the end of the war seemed nowhere in sight. While so much remained the same, a lot had changed. All three of the Gabriels had grown taller and put on weight to the point where Mrs. Wright had spent long hours at her sewing machine. CORB's rules did not allow for Mum and Dad to send the Wrights money, but they could send parcels. Mum wrote that she longed to put together care packages of socks and underwear, fabric and wool—if only there was any to be had. Store-bought clothing was out of the question for both families—except for Carol, who earned her own money and was entitled to an employee discount at Miss Filmon's shop.

With a sigh, Nina picked up an empty bushel basket. "Hazie? Geoffrey? You coming? It's only going to get hotter out there."

"Coming." Hazel tromped down the stairs followed by her brother. They each grabbed a basket and followed Nina to the garden where tomatoes awaited picking.

The siblings worked together, filling their baskets. "Do you realize this is our second harvest here?" Nina asked. "It's a year ago today we arrived."

"No." Hazel sat back on her heels and stared at a ripe tomato in her hands.

Geoffrey scrunched his eyebrows together. "Me either. A year is a long time."

"You're not forgetting about home, are you?"

"Sometimes I forget what Mummy and Daddy look like." Hazel sounded as Canadian as any of the Wright kids, at least to Nina's ears.

Geoffrey found a tomato with its skin split and ants crawling around the fissure. He placed it in a separate pail for the chickens. "Me too. But then I look at their photograph and remember."

Nina nodded. Although she would know her parents instantly if they suddenly appeared before her, it wasn't always easy to envision their faces at will.

"When will we go home?" Geoffrey asked.

If only Nina had a real answer. "I don't know. Maybe by Christmas. Maybe not until next summer."

Hazel swatted a mosquito on her arm. "By next summer, I'll be nine!"

"I know." *And I'll be sixteen.*

"I'll be twelve. And Sully will be a big boy. He won't know us."

Nina sighed. "Not much point thinking about that now. You like it here, right?"

"It's okay." Hazel shrugged.

"It's better than home right now, even without Mum and Dad. Right? And we're having adventures." Geoffrey moved down the row, turning his back on his sisters.

"That's right. Fun, *safe* adventures," Nina said. "Not the kind where bombs are dropping around you and people are getting hurt or dying."

Hazel nodded. "Why do people have to drop bombs on each other? It isn't very nice."

"No, it's not. Say, guess what? Mrs. Wright is going to teach me to sew, and the first thing I'm going to make is a new dress for you to start school in."

"Can I pick out the color?"

"Um, well … she has two different fabrics, one for each of us. I'll let you choose first. How does that sound?"

"Good."

The girls carried the tomatoes inside, and Geoffrey jumped on Jim's bike. He'd been granted permission to visit Jessie Cain after the tomatoes were picked and obviously didn't want to waste a minute.

While Hazel kept Daniel occupied, Nina helped Mrs. Wright can the tomatoes. By mid-afternoon, the jars were lined up on the kitchen counter cooling. They turned to the sewing project. Mrs. Wright showed Nina how to take accurate measurements of Hazel and lay the pattern pieces on the fabric Hazel had chosen—red with small white polka dots. They cut out the cloth, allowing room for growth. With the pieces all cut out, the next lesson was learning to thread and operate the sewing machine. Nina practiced on some scraps of fabric until she could keep the rhythm of the treadle consistent with one foot while feeding cloth between the presser foot and throat plate.

"You're a natural seamstress, Nina." Mrs. Wright picked up two of the dress pieces she'd pinned together. "I think you're ready to start stitching this together."

"Nina. Supper." Hazel stood in the doorway.

Nina had stayed so focused on following directions and assembling her first garment, she hadn't heard Mrs. Wright call everyone to the supper table.

"Oh! All right." Rain pelted the window. How had she missed that? "After supper and chores, this is ready for you to try on before I go any further with it."

"Swell."

Nina rolled her eyes at Hazel's slang and followed her down the stairs. The entire family sat gathered around the table—a rare sight this time of year, but the rain must have brought the men in early. By the looks of Geoffrey's wet hair and change of clothes, he'd gotten caught in it while peddling home from the Cains. Nina took her usual seat beside Hazel.

"Before we say grace," Mrs. Wright took hold of Daniel's hands to keep them out of the food. "I just want to acknowledge that today marks one year since Nina, Geoffrey, and Hazel joined our family. It's a mixed blessing because we know your parents would love to have you home and you would love to be reunited with them."

Nina felt tears well up and stared hard at the flowery pattern on the plate in front of her.

Mrs. Wright cleared her throat before continuing. "We are also grateful that you are safe and healthy, and that we've been able to play a role in making that happen."

"Amen." Mr. Wright held out his hands and held Carol's on one side and Jim's on the other. "Let's pray. Lord, thank You for providing our needs this day, for this delicious meal, and for the ones who have prepared it. Thank You for what today represents for the Gabriel family. We ask for Your protection over them and over their parents and their little fella in England. Also, over David and our other boys who are serving. We pray for a swift end to this war. In Jesus's name, Amen."

Mrs. Wright had put together a cold meal for this hot summer evening, and they passed around plates of chicken, potato salad, sliced tomatoes, cucumbers, and bread.

"I think it would be nice to hear from each of you children about something you've learned in the past year with us here, or a favorite memory you have. Who wants to go first?"

"I will." Geoffrey said around a mouthful.

"Maybe after you swallow," Mrs. Wright coached.

Geoffrey finished chewing and swallowed, even while scooping up another forkful of potato salad. "I learned how to ice skate."

"Me too." Hazel nodded. "I'm not very good at it, though. Also, I learned how to speak Canadian."

The adults laughed. "You're *very* good at *that*!" Mr. Wright winked at Hazel and then turned to Nina. "How about you, Nina? Let me guess—learning to drive?"

Nina could feel the heat rising to her face. It had been hard enough to adapt to merely riding on the wrong side of the road, but when the Wrights had suggested Carol teach Nina to drive so she could take supper to the field, the lesson had not gone well. Carol's patience ran out the first time Nina stalled the truck.

Mrs. Wright jumped in. "Yes, well—thank goodness David stepped in and offered to teach you, eh?" She gave Carol a quick sideways glance. "And you've been doing just fine."

"I sure do miss that guy around here," Mr. Wright nodded. "Any word from him?" He looked at Carol.

Carol shook her head slightly. "Seems he's decided to write to the little kids first."

"Oh?" Her mother looked around the table, eyebrows raised.

Carol salted her food. "Yeah. A letter came for Nina today."

"From David?" Hazel spoke way too loudly and looked at Nina. "What did he say?"

Nina shook her head. "This is the first I've heard of it." David had actually written her? Did her heart just skip a beat?

"Where's the mail?" Mrs. Wright looked at Carol.

Carol shrugged. "I left it on the table by the front door."

Nina was dying to find it and rip it open, but she feigned calmness. "How lovely. I'll read it after supper."

Geoffrey let out a snort. "She'll run to her room and rip it open like Rosie tearing into a leftover pancake."

Both boys laughed. Carol only glared at Nina while her parents appeared to communicate something to each other without words.

Mrs. Wright cleared her throat. "Nina, we haven't let you answer the question yet about what you've learned or what your best memory is from the past year."

Nina's face grew warm, remembering the day she'd "rescued" her siblings and tried to run off. Thankfully, no one had been unkind enough to mention it, but she'd better start talking before Carol beat her to the punch and brought it up out of spite.

"Well … yes, learning to drive and to skate are not things I'd have learned in the last year at home. There's so much, I truly don't know where to start. I've learned to can tomatoes and make pickles and now I'm learning to sew. My mother can sew, of course. But she doesn't have a machine of her own." Suddenly overwhelmed with longing for her mother, Nina sucked in a rattled breath and stopped talking.

Carol pushed her plate away and rested her hands on the edge of the table. "Well, I've got news. Not that anyone's asking."

Nina let out a sigh of relief.

"What's your news, dear?" Mrs. Wright cut up some vegetables for Daniel to eat with his hands.

"As you know, the Canadian Women's Army Corps is

finally official." Carol had both her parents' full attention now. They turned serious faces toward her.

"Yes, and …?" Her mother coaxed.

"I've enlisted. They want me." Carol smiled at both parents and then flashed a sideways grin at Nina. "I leave in a week."

Mrs. Wright released a gasp. "You leave? So soon? You're not—"

"Ready? I am though, Mother. I've been ready for a long time. Well, since my last birthday. Prospective recruits need to be in excellent health, which I am. At least five feet tall and a hundred and five pounds. I'm five foot six and a hundred and ten." Carol began ticking off the requirements on her fingers. "No dependents. A minimum of a grade eight education. Aged eighteen to forty-five. A British subject. That's it. I'm all of those things and more. With my high school diploma, I'll probably be an officer in no time."

"Sweetheart, it takes a lot more than that to—"

"I know, Dad. They'll train me."

Mrs. Wright's face had grown pale. "I knew you were interested, Carol, but I thought it was just a … a lark."

"A lark?" Carol practically spat it out. "I'm not a little kid."

Mrs. Wright cleared her throat. "A passing interest, then. I thought we'd have you around here longer. What will they have you doing?"

"I don't know yet. Clerk or secretary, maybe. Glad I took typing and shorthand last year."

Mr. Wright shook his head. "Women in uniform. What's next?"

"You said that already, when we first heard the news on the radio." Carol scowled at her father. "I suppose what's next is, you're going to tell me a woman's place is in the home, not in a uniform."

"Well—"

"Quit being so old-fashioned, Daddy. Why can't you congratulate me for knowing what I want and going after it?"

"Carol." Her mother's voice was loaded with caution.

Her father let out a loud sigh. "No, she's right, Mother. I'm sorry. But … I'm sure you'll be staying here in Canada. They wouldn't ship girls overseas."

"Dad. Don't be too sure."

Mrs. Wright gave her head a shake as though to dismiss the thought. "Where do you go for training?"

"Either Kitchener, Ontario, or Vermilion, Alberta. I probably won't know for sure until I'm on the way."

"Oh my. So far. Either way." Mrs. Wright stood and began clearing dishes. "So soon." She moved to the sink and began filling the dishpan. "Girls, can you take care of these dishes, please? I need some fresh air." She removed her apron, hung it on its hook, and then pulled Daniel from his highchair. She carried him outside, letting the screen door slap shut behind her as she continued down the lane.

"Now look what you've done, Carol," Jim muttered. "Hope you're proud of yourself, upsetting Mum like that."

"Why can't anyone around here ever be happy about anything?" Carol stood and started removing serving dishes from the table, letting them land with a thud on the counter.

"Never mind, Jim. This isn't your concern." Mr. Wright rose and retrieved his cap from the hook by the back door. "Your mother just needs a little time, Carol. We all do. Come on, boys. Hazel. Let's get the critters looked after."

The tension in the room grew as Nina and Carol were the only two left. Nina gathered the remaining dishes and carried them to the sink. "I'm glad for you, Carol. That took courage." She didn't know what more to say. She'd seen plenty of women in uniform back home, serving in all sorts of ways.

"I don't need your two cents." Carol brushed a tear from one cheek with the back of her hand and started washing dishes.

"I only meant … you'll do well and learn a lot and—"

"You'll be glad to be rid of me. Well, you're not alone. I can't wait to get out of here." Carol paused her movements only briefly.

"Really?"

"Really. And I'd rather do these alone. Go read your precious letter."

Fine. Nina hung up the dish towel she'd picked up and moved straight to the little table by the front door. Sure enough, a letter addressed to her on military stationery lay among three or four other items. She carried it up the stairs and to her room, thankful for a moment of privacy.

David to Nina
August 1, 1941
Dear Nina,

Thanks for your letter. Please keep 'em coming and tell your siblings I'd enjoy hearing from them too. Any news from home is swell.

I'm still at the training base. They're instructing me on multi-engine aircraft, bomber command. I started on the link trainer this week, which teaches you the basics of flying skills. In classes, we learn a lot of math, plotting flight paths, that sort of thing. Aircraft recognition. Meteorology. Drills, of course. They get us up at six every morning—easy for me since I'm used to that, but some of the other fellas find it awfully early. Lights-out is at ten, and the training is pretty compressed, so we're busy, busy, busy. I've had a couple of weekends off so far. Visited the parliament buildings and walked across the big bridge over the river to Hull just to be able to say I've been to Quebec. Haven't done much else—they keep us hopping, and I need time to write letters. And sleep!

Thank you for confiding in me about your struggle regarding your baby brother. I don't think that makes you awful at all. Under the circumstances, I think it's perfectly understandable. I think you're a very brave and admirable girl, and if I ever do find myself homesick, you're the one I will tell. Not that I don't miss everyone, but so far, I have no desire to trade my new life and go back to the old. I'm not sure when or where I'll be next time I write, but I hope that won't stop you from writing to me. Wouldn't it be something if I am shipped to England and was able to look up your parents?

Keep studying hard. Try not to let Carol give you a hard time. I know she can be difficult, but … well, she has her reasons. I try to keep her in my prayers. And you too. Please pray for me when you think of it. I want to serve my country well, learn everything there is to learn, and make the Lord proud.

Your friend,
David

Chapter Seventeen

Ann Wright to the Gabriels

October 15, 1941
Dear Mr. & Mrs. Gabriel,

I apologize for not writing sooner. I realize you depend on my letters to provide a point of view besides that of your children. I'm certain you can understand the extreme busyness of the harvest season—not just the farm crops (wheat, oats, as well as hay to feed our livestock in winter), but our garden. We've been growing more vegetables than ever since the war began, and I'm pleased to report your children have been an enormous help with that. Especially Nina. I'm confident she could complete the entire tomato process from planting to shelving on her own if needed. But don't worry, she hasn't had to. We always work together.

We've also been sewing. Nina made a dress for herself and one for Hazel. They turned out quite well for a first attempt, and I know her next will turn out even better. I was able to make a shirt from brand new fabric for Geoffrey. Oh, I do wish I had a camera. All three of them have grown so much! Geoffrey and Hazel can now both wear the clothing that belonged to our Bart and Violet. We are happy to see their things put to good use.

Nina is a busy young lady you can be proud of. At times, I've had to remind her that she's still a schoolgirl and not responsible for her siblings every minute of every day.

Dr. Mitchell says Geoffrey's collarbone healed perfectly, so no worries there. He's never short of bumps and bruises from various exploits, but he's as happy and well-adjusted as can be expected. His best chum, Jessie Cain, comes from a family I'd trust with my own children. Geoffrey's school marks could be better, and I've tried to encourage him in that regard. He's certainly bright. There are simply too many things more interesting than schoolwork in his life!

Hazel is turning into quite the little Canadian. The other day I could hear her and Nina carrying on a conversation in the other room, and I could have sworn Hazel's friend Nellie Cain was over. Turns out it was Hazel. But not to worry, I'm sure she'll flip right back into her regular accent when she returns home. She's been a joy to have around and rarely needs to be reminded to do her chores.

Harold and Jim have the woodpile stacked nearly as high as the house. Well, the first floor of the house anyway. As we prepare for another winter, I'll be spending whatever spare moments I can find to ensure we have enough warm hats, socks, mittens, and scarves around here to keep everyone outfitted. With that, I'll close this letter and get back to my knitting needles.

Now that the Nazis appear to be focusing on Russia, I sincerely hope things have calmed down somewhat for you there. I hope your little one is thriving.

Sincerely,
Ann Wright

"You trying out for the Christmas play again this year, Nina?" Irene Jasper tied her shoe before opening her lunch box.

"Of course, she is. Right, Nina?" Emma nudged Nina with

her elbow. "Miss Simms wrote a part for an English storekeeper. Obviously, she had you in mind from the start."

Nina smiled. She'd read Miss Simms' script and had the same thought. "I probably will. It's a smaller role than I had last year—which is good. Grade ten is harder than nine. I can't afford to miss any study time. Are you trying out?" She addressed her question to Irene, knowing Emma preferred stage crew.

"Me?" Irene's eyebrows rose to meet her bangs. "I could never be on stage. I'd die of fright."

"Of course you wouldn't. I bet you'd be great." Nina remembered the encouragement she herself had needed as a much younger girl, back home, when she'd played a part in her first play. By the way Irene's eyes lit up at the idea, it wasn't hard to tell it was a secret dream.

"I don't know if my parents would let me." Irene bit her bottom lip. "And nobody wants to look at these hands…"

Had her parents convinced her of this? "They're not that bad, Irene."

"Well, they would be, because I'd be all nervous and when I'm nervous, it gets worse."

Irene hadn't participated in any extracurricular activities since Nina arrived, but Nina's words of encouragement must have gone further than she'd hoped. At the auditions held over the lunch hour the next day, Irene showed up. She stuck close to Nina. "I didn't tell Dad," she whispered. "But Mum said I could go ahead and try for a part."

"That's great, Irene!"

"Mum doesn't think I'll get one."

"Nonsense. Which part are you hoping for?"

"I don't even care. I'll even play one of the male parts if we don't have enough boys. That happens sometimes."

Miss Simms led them through a simple audition that consisted of sitting around in a circle, reading through the script as different characters. While the other kids traded parts frequently, Nina was assigned to read the English storekeeper's lines through the entire reading. No one was surprised when the parts were posted on the bulletin board at the end of the day. While the main roles went to two grade twelve students, Nina would play the storekeeper while Irene was cast as her Canadian-born daughter.

"Oh, what fun we'll have!" Nina put an arm around Irene, who came up to her shoulder. "You're already a storekeeper's daughter in real life. This will be easy."

Irene blinked rapidly. "I didn't think I'd get a part."

"Whyever not? It'll be great. Emma's going to be the wardrobe mistress." Nina put extra emphasis on the title, knowing Miss Simms was a stickler for professional theater terms and techniques. "We'll have gobs of time together backstage since we're not in every scene. We can help each other learn lines."

"I'll have to convince Dad first."

"Want me to go with you?" Nina had met Mr. Jasper a few times, and he always seemed like a friendly fellow.

"No."

Although Irene never divulged how the conversation with her father had gone, she apparently got permission to be in the play and showed up at the first rehearsal with lines nearly memorized. Miss Simms encouraged her and suggested she and Nina get together outside of rehearsal time to run lines together.

"I'll help you," Emma offered. "I can hold the script and prompt as needed. Besides, I've already collected a few costume possibilities for you both."

After their second rehearsal at the community hall, Emma pulled Nina and Irene into the girls' dressing room where a row of dresses hung, waiting to be tried on. "Since these are all borrowed, we can't really alter anything," she explained. "We need to find outfits that fit perfectly."

Nina stripped to her slip and took the first dress Emma

handed her. She pulled it over her head and then turned toward the mirror. She let out a gasp. Behind her, Irene stood clad in only her slip, her back visible in the mirror. One shoulder was completely purple and green.

"Irene! Whatever did you do?"

Emma looked up and saw what Nina was staring at. She gasped too.

"What?" Irene turned around.

"You're all bruised!" Emma took her by the arm and turned her around for a closer look.

"Oh, that." Irene let out an awkward laugh. "So embarrassing. I fell down the stairs."

"What? When?" Emma kept staring. "Why didn't you say anything?"

Irene stepped into the costume and pulled it up to thread her arms through the sleeves. "Would you, if it happened to you?"

"I guess not. I'm not sure. It's never happened to me."

"That's because you're not clumsy like me." Irene turned around again. "Help me button this up."

Nina took another glimpse at the bruises. "Doesn't that hurt?"

"Not much anymore. Just forget it." Irene turned to look in the mirror again. "What do you think? A couple of pigtails, and I could pass for a ten-year-old."

"That's the whole point. I think we've got a winner. That was easy." Emma turned to assess Nina's too-large outfit. "Looks like we'll need to try another option on you, though."

The incident was forgotten.

A couple of weeks later, at Miss Simms' suggestion, Nina went home with Irene after school to learn a little about the finer points of running a store, like wrapping meat in brown paper and string and operating a cash register. Irene was officially on duty until closing time, six o'clock. Nina observed everything she and her mother did. When the store was empty of customers, Nina practiced the different tasks so she could look natural doing them on stage while saying her lines. After closing time, the girls climbed the narrow stairs to the family's living quarters. Nina could see why the steep stairs would be easy to take a tumble down. In the little kitchen, she offered to set the table.

"Yes, thank you." Mrs. Jasper handed her three soup bowls.

"Where's Dad?" Irene sliced bread and placed it on a plate.

Her mother placed butter and jam on the table. "He telephoned to say not to wait for him. He got detained in Roseburg and would be late for the council meeting if he stopped at home for supper."

The girls spent a pleasant evening doing homework and practicing their lines for the play. At nine-thirty, they prepared for bed.

"Now I don't want to hear talking and giggling all night." Mrs. Jasper warned from the sitting room.

"We won't." Irene pulled a flannel nightgown over her head and pulled back the covers on her narrow bed. "It'll be squishy. You want to be against the wall or on the outside?"

Nina stared. Bruises on the undersides of Irene's arms and more on her shins had completely captured her attention.

"Nina? Which side do you want?"

Nina shook her head and pointed at the bruises. "Those aren't from your fall. They're too fresh. What happened?"

Irene looked down to see what Nina was pointing out. "I told you I was clumsy. I'm not even sure where I got those. I'm always stumbling into something."

"I've never seen you stumble at school."

"Plus, I bruise easily. Don't worry about it. You want the wall?"

Nina paused. "Sure." She climbed into the bed.

The girls did, indeed, talk and giggle longer than they should have for a school night but settled down when they heard Mr. Jasper climbing the stairs. Sometime later, Nina awoke to voices in the next room. She couldn't make out what they were saying, but Irene's parents were both clearly angry. Irene slept right through as the volume increased.

"Murdy, stop it!" Mrs. Jasper's voice was suddenly loud and clear. "We've got company!"

"Company? What are you talking about?"

"Irene's got a friend over. The English girl."

The conversation became subdued again. Then a loud smack punctuated the voices, followed by scuffling and silence.

Nina lay awake for a long time.

At breakfast, Mr. Jasper smiled broadly at both girls as they entered the kitchen. "Good morning, ladies. Good sleep? Hope I didn't wake you when I got home last night."

"You didn't." Irene helped herself to a bowl of oatmeal from the stove, indicating Nina should do the same.

Mr. Jasper returned to the newspaper he was holding. "Good. Glad to hear it."

Mrs. Gabriel to Nina
December 1941
My dearest Nina,

I'm delighted to learn you are once again acting in your school's Christmas play. Daddy and I wish more than anything we could see it as well as G & H's pageant. I know you will all do so well.

In my wildest dreams, I did not imagine a second Christmas coming around without our family intact. My heart is torn between the relief of knowing you, Geoffrey, and Hazel are safe and well cared for and the anxiety of missing you. Sully is approaching his first birthday and has no idea what peacetime life would be like or how different his life would be if his big sisters and brother were in it. I show him your pictures and say your names every day, but, of course, he doesn't understand you are real flesh and blood people who are as dear to me as he is. It breaks my heart.

Still, your father and I rarely regret sending you to Canada. I say rarely because on good days, when no explosions can be heard, no air raid siren … when we can gather around our table for a proper meal and can almost pretend all is well … it's easy to think we should have kept you home. But in our hearts, we are still convinced this is best. Most of your school chums are billeted on farms further inland. Do you hear from any? I visited Donna's parents after the disaster to tell them how sorry we were. Her mother mentioned that they'd received a kind letter from you. I've not seen or heard from her since. I fear she may be bitter, and who can blame her? It would be hard for her to even see us, knowing her daughter should be safe in Canada like ours is. It's all just too heartbreaking.

I'm sorry. I'm not normally so droll in my letters. Since Sully's arrival, I've not been active as a raid warden, but your father continues to serve. Mrs. Petrey from next door has offered to babysit Sully should I decide to return to work. I probably will, soon. It will be a mixed blessing. We need the income, and I know that by making wireless we are helping the war effort. But it will be hard to leave Sully every day. Oh, I do wish you could meet him. You would love him so dearly, and I can easily picture G & H having heaps of fun with him at this age. He laughs easily and brings so much joy into our home, even though his safety is constantly on our minds. When the prime minister declared war on Finland, Hungary, and Romania, we despaired that the entire world had, indeed, gone crazy, and this will simply never end. But now that the United States is involved, we're all hoping things will be reversed and come to an end soon.

Daddy sends his love. We miss you and pray for you every day. Work hard.

Lovingly,
Mother

Chapter Eighteen

Nina to David

05 April 1942
Dear David,

Mrs. Strong insists on us keeping up with current events, but there's been nothing but bad news lately. On our list of British ships that have sunk, we added *The Empire Arnold*, the *Cornwall*, the *Dorsetshire*, the *Hector*, *HMS Tenedos*, the *Gallant*, and the *Abingdon*—plus the American ship, *Byron D. Benson*—all in the past few days. It's incredibly disheartening. Sometimes I want to run outside when the news broadcasts come on and just scream. I don't, but I often go for a walk alone. Now that spring is well on its way, I love getting outside and filling my lungs with fresh air as though it could replace all the evil in the world. Then I think of you and realize you're in legitimate danger and with no escape. And my parents and little brother back in Middlesbrough. I realize I have so very much to be thankful for. When this all began, we couldn't imagine it carrying on for months, let alone years. Why are people so awful to one another? So stubborn and greedy for power?

I'm sorry. I know we're supposed to keep our letters light and encouraging, to give you something to smile about. But at the same time, you're someone I feel I can confide in—not someone who wants to play games of make-believe, pretending all is fine when it's not.

I do try to stay positive. I'm enjoying school. Maybe you

heard that Mr. Gordon joined up after Christmas. Old Mr. Jackson has come out of retirement to fill his shoes—did you ever have him for a teacher? Some of the kids poke fun behind his back (nicknaming him *Methuselah*), but I quite enjoy his stories and find him a good, patient teacher. Hard to believe another year will soon be behind us.

It's been different around the Wright household with Carol gone. Her parents found it really hard at Christmas, especially. Watching them gives me some insight into what my own parents must be going through even though it's different. I try to do all I can to ease the Wrights' lives … which includes trying to keep my brother out of trouble. Maybe your parents told you— Geoffrey and Jessie got the grand idea to start up your dad's tractor and took out a corner of a grain shed before it was all said and done. Jessie wouldn't admit it, but I'm certain Geoffrey was the instigator. (Doesn't Jessie already know how to drive that thing?) Anyway, both boys were assigned extra chores and given a stern talking-to. They won't be visiting each other's homes for a long time. I haven't mentioned the incident to my parents, but Mrs. Wright may have. I hope not. Mum and Dad don't need the extra worry. Your parents merely said, "At least no one was hurt." I suspect that may not have been your father's first thought, though. What do you think?

On another matter, what would you do if you suspected that a friend—and possibly her mother—was being mistreated by her father? Would you take your friend at their word when they say they are simply clumsy and bruise easily? Would you stay out of it, even if you doubted they were telling the whole truth?

I will close for now—homework calls. In your last letter, you asked whether I knew what I'd like to do after high school. If there were no limitations, I think I would dearly love to study theater and become an actress. But I'm practical enough to know that's next to impossible and highly unlikely. At best, perhaps I could become a drama teacher and maybe act in some community plays one day. Miss Simms says my accent is an advantage here even if it isn't at home. Who knows? Maybe I'll return to Canada one day and do all of that.

I trust you're well and enjoying your adventures. I am praying for you, David. Thanks for being my friend. Hazel says hello, and she'll write to you soon. Be warned. She is now smitten with a boy at school named Rodney and has changed her mind about marrying you. I'm sure she'll let you down easy.

Sincerely,
Nina

Nina, Emma, and Irene gathered around Nina's bed. They'd lain out three strips of fabric Irene's mother had given them.

"They're too small for a full dress, and they're taking up shelf space Mom needs for other fabric that *will* sell." Irene shrugged apologetically. "They're not exactly the latest, but—"

"Are you kidding?" Emma picked up a pink paisley. "Who around here wears the latest of anything? This is great. First thing is to decide which fabric suits which girl the best, then we'll figure out what to make from Mrs. Wright's patterns. You thanked her for us, right, Nina?"

"Yes. And I'll thank her again when we're done. She wants us to model whatever we make. That pink looks great on you."

Irene picked up a blue gingham and held it up to Nina. "This one accentuates your eyes."

"You think so? I was going to say it would look great on *you*." Nina picked up the third fabric, a heavier plaid. "Besides, I could use a new skirt more than anything."

Eventually, the girls matched fabric to patterns and spent an enjoyable Saturday cutting them out. Irene hadn't sewn before, and Nina proudly taught her how to use the machine to stitch her pieces together. Emma had excused herself to visit the outhouse when Irene's new garment was basted together and ready to try on. Once again, Irene's bare back was exposed to Nina. This time, Nina couldn't let it rest.

"It's nothing," her friend insisted. "I told you, I'm just clumsy. It's always something." She pulled on the blue gingham blouse she'd decided to make.

Nina shook her head. "You're not clumsy. I've never seen you be clumsy. At the very least, if you're bruising that easily, there must be something wrong in your blood. Maybe you need vitamins or something. Do your parents know?"

"Oh, sure." Irene shrugged and removed the basted blouse. "This is going to fit just fine. What do I do next?"

"Irene." Nina handed her friend's pullover to her. "Tell me the truth. Did your father do that to you?"

Irene took her time pulling the top over her head. "My father? Why would you think such a thing?"

"Wouldn't you think such a thing if you kept seeing bruises on me?"

"No. Well, I mean—I might. But … that's what parents do, isn't it? Discipline their kids? Don't worry about it, Nina."

"What's going on?" Emma bounced into the room.

Irene flashed a big smile Emma's way. "My blouse is ready to stitch together. Next lesson, buttonholes. Right, Nina?"

Nina couldn't help feeling Irene's smile carried a warning.

"How did the sewing day go?" Mrs. Wright handed Nina a clean dishrag and turned to finish clearing the supper table.

"Great! One more session, and we'll be all done. Thanks for keeping Hazel occupied."

"My pleasure." Mrs. Wright had taken Hazel to town for supplies and then given her a bread-baking lesson. "Sounded like the three of you were having a grand time. I'm so glad you're making close friends, Nina. I'm sure it helps your parents to know that too."

Nina nodded. "Can I ask you something?"

"Of course."

"You've known Mr. Jasper a long time, right?"

"Irene's dad? Sure, since we were teenagers. Why?" She picked up a dish towel and began to dry.

"Does he seem like the kind of man who would beat his daughter?"

Mrs. Wright froze. She slowly turned her head to look directly at Nina. "Never. Why would you ask such a thing?"

Nina took a deep breath and let it out slowly. "I've seen … bruises. On Irene. And not just one time."

"Did you ask her about it?"

Nina nodded. "Yes. She says she's just clumsy. But I've never seen her being clumsy."

Mrs. Wright paused before returning to her task. "Well. If that's what she says, then I would take her at her word. Why would anyone make that up?"

Nina put the last of the plates in the drain tray and plunged a potato pot into the water. "I don't know. I guess that would be an embarrassing thing to admit."

"The Jaspers have been upstanding people as long as I can remember. Her father's even a trustee on the school board. They're faithful at church—I think he served as a deacon for a while."

"Do you know what it means when people bruise easily? What's lacking?"

Mrs. Wright picked up the heavy pot and dried it. "I'm not sure, I'd need to consult my Family Medical Guide. Could be a shortage of some nutrient. Could be more serious, like a disease. Has she seen a doctor?"

"I don't think so. She doesn't seem sick in any way, except for eczema on her hands and arms." Nina gripped the edges of the dishpan to carry it outside.

"Leave that." Mrs. Wright hung up her towel. "I'll carry it out. I need to get outside for a bit. Try not to worry about Irene. If she says her father didn't hurt her, I see no reason not to believe her."

"All right." Nina dried her hands and headed for the stairs, hoping to get at least some school reading done before Hazel returned and started chatting up a storm. Mrs. Wright was most likely correct about Mr. Jasper. If only she could be sure.

Hazel to her parents

May 1942
Dear Mummy and Daddy,

Thank you for the photograph of both of you and Sully. He's getting so big. I love him. I wish I could put my arms around him and give him a big kiss on his little cheeks and feel his little hair. I bet it is so soft. Sometimes I want to come home and see you all. But mostly I wish you could come here with Sully. Where it's safe.

Guess what? Mrs. Wright showed me how to start little plants from seeds she saved from her garden last summer. We've got little baby tomato plants and beans and cucumbers, and I don't even remember what all. They are so cute! Next week we are going to plant them in the garden. We have to wait until it's warm enough and there's no danger of frost. If there is danger of frost, you have to cover all the little baby plants at night with old sheets and blankets which sounds like fun but it is not really. The blankets get dirty and you have to hang them on the line and it is a lot of work.

I also know how to make bread.

Nellie Cain is still my best friend. She is really pretty and nice. She's smart too, but I got better marks than she did on our last report card. We are getting ready for a field day at the end of June. We can do races and long jump and high jump and triple jump. I hope I get a ribbon this year. Last year I didn't.

I am not going to marry David Cain after all. He has gone to war. That isn't the reason why I changed my mind. I decided I'm going to marry Rodney instead. I don't know his last name. He's a new boy at school. He is shy so I haven't told him yet.

Please bring Sully for a visit as soon as you can. You can have our room. Carol went to the ladies' army so her old room is now Daniel's room. Mrs. Wright said Nina could have it, but Nina said no thank you. She said she wanted to stay with me, but I know it's really because Carol wouldn't like it if Nina had her room. I'm glad. I don't want to sleep alone. If you come in the summer, us kids can all sleep on the front porch. We did that last summer. It was fun except for the mosquitoes. Rosie loved it because she could sleep between us. She isn't allowed in the house. She has her own little doghouse, but she likes to be with people.

Mr. Wright is calling me. It's time to go take care of the chickens.

Love,
Hazel

Chapter Nineteen

Nina to her parents

July 1942
Dear Mum and Dad,

I finished grade ten (as they call it here) at the top of my class!
My lowest mark was in math (as they call it here) with a B+. I
confess I was shocked to learn I'd done that well in math as most
of it still leaves me feeling stumped. I don't think I will pursue a
career that requires working with numbers, not if I can help it.

So now we are on summer holidays again, though there is
little "holiday" to it when you live on a farm. We still rise early
and there is always work to do. After morning and evening
milking, the milk must be poured through a straining cloth into
the cream separator and stored in the ice box and cellar. (The
cream man comes around twice a week to collect it and pays Mrs.
Wright ten cents a pint.) Then the separator must be taken all
apart and carefully washed in hot soapy water and rinsed. The
straining cloth must be washed and hung to dry. (I've become an
even bigger stickler about this than Mrs. Wright, because the
smell of sour milk makes me gag. I can't bear it.)

We also do other jobs … washing clothes, ironing clothes,
baking bread, weeding the garden, picking potato bugs off the
potato plants (Hazel says it's disgusting. I don't disagree.),
cutting the grass, cleaning the house. We try to get tasks done in
the mornings before it gets too hot. In the afternoons, we may
sew or read. Mrs. Wright let me fill her big washtub with cool

water one hot afternoon. Hazie and Daniel had a swell time splashing around, but Mrs. Wright seemed very nervous. She stayed to watch them play even though she had work to do inside. The kids loved having her there, of course, but it left me feeling like she didn't trust me to watch them. Then she made us dump the water on the garden long before the kids wanted to get out.

The Cain family goes to a beach not far from here on Sunday afternoons. I got to go with them once, but Mr. and Mrs. Wright would not allow G & H to go. They've never taken us. It's on the shore of Lake Manitoba, which is so large you can't see across it. I could almost convince myself it was the Atlantic and I was at home at Redcar Beach.

David Cain is in England now. It seems so strange that he is there and I am here. In some ways, it makes the distance between us seem less. I would love it if he could manage to visit you, but I suppose we will wait and see. And I think I told you Carol has joined the CWACs (yes, they pronounce it "Quacks" which is terribly funny or unfortunate, depending on your point of view.) She does not write to me, but her parents have heard from her. She seems to be thriving in a secretarial type of position.

In Carol's absence, it has fallen on me to take meals to the men in the field, and Mrs. Wright has even entrusted me to take the truck to town by myself for groceries and mail. Hazel always comes along. I don't mind, but I do wonder if Mrs. Wright needs the break from Hazie's constant chatter as much as she needs the groceries. I haven't driven in winter yet. I'm told that's quite different.

The pastor here delivered an interesting message last Sunday. People are beginning to wonder, "what if this war never ends," and I have wondered that myself. I imagine that possibility seems even more likely for you there. He talked about how war never truly ends. It lies frozen for a time, or it hibernates. That it is peace that is elusive, not conflict. Conflict is always there, waiting to surface. That's scary to think about. But then he talked about spiritual warfare, how our real battle is not against nations or other people but against the devil and all his armies who are out to steal, kill, and destroy. The pastor said the only real peace comes from knowing God who made us and Jesus who gave His life to save us. That peace with Him is the highest prize, and that He promises one day all war will truly cease along with all death, heartache, pain, and tears. I'm not sure where that leaves us in the here and now, but I found it hopeful. I hope you do too.

Maybe we'll be home for Christmas this year?

Your loving daughter,
Nina

At last.

Nina climbed behind the steering wheel of Mr. Wright's truck and headed down their dirt lane. It was the first time she'd driven anywhere all alone. Hazel was at the Cains' place, so she was already out of Mrs. Wright's hair. The cucumbers were ready for pickling, and Mrs. Wright was out of vinegar, among other things. Nina headed down the road with a wonderful sense of freedom, a dollar in her purse to spend however she liked, and the anticipation of seeing Irene. While she'd seen Emma a few times this summer, she'd not seen Irene since their sewing day.

Mrs. Jasper was dusting shelves behind the counter when Nina entered the store.

"Morning, Mrs. Jasper."

"Oh, hello, Nina. How's everything in the Wright household?"

"Fine, thank you. Just need a few things." Nina dug through her purse to find Mrs. Wright's list. "Is Irene around? I was hoping for a quick visit."

Mrs. Jasper took the list and studied it at length before answering. "I'm afraid Irene is sick in bed—some kind of nasty virus. A cold. Maybe the flu. I'll tell her you came."

"Oh, I'm so sorry. Could I go up and say hello?"

"No, that's not a good idea. I'd hate for you to catch whatever she's got."

Something tingled at the back of Nina's neck. "I won't go close. I'll just stick my head in the door and say hello. Maybe I can cheer her up a bit. Besides, I'm healthy as a horse."

Mrs. Jasper shook her head without looking up from the list. "No, I'm sorry."

"Please?"

"Stop begging, Nina. It's for your own good. I'll be sure to tell her you said hello. I'll tell you what." She pulled a piece of paper and a pencil from a shelf below the counter and handed them to Nina. "Write her a little note, and I'll make sure she gets it. That will cheer her up. Maybe next week you girls can get together when she's better."

Reluctantly, Nina wrote the note while Mrs. Jasper gathered up the items on her list and totaled the bill. "Am I adding this to the Wrights' account?"

"Yes, please."

The bell over the door jingled and another woman walked in.

"Good morning, Rose."

"Hello, Eleanor." The new customer walked straight to the counter and held out a short strip of elastic. "Can you believe I'm in the middle of a sewing project for my girls, and I've run out of elastic? I really hoped to finish this today before we leave for the city tomorrow. Can you help me out?"

Mrs. Jasper took the strip. "Half-inch? I just got a new bolt in yesterday. It's in the back. I'll cut you a piece. How much do you want? Nina, when you're done with your note, just leave it here and feel free to take your groceries. I've got your total."

"All right."

Both women disappeared behind the curtain separating the back room from the storefront. How long did it take to cut a piece of elastic? Probably not long enough, but Nina was willing to take her chances to see Irene. She slipped up the staircase leading to the living quarters. At the top of the stairs, she knocked softly on Irene's bedroom door and then pushed it open, squeezed through, and stood with her back to the door.

Irene sat on a chair gazing out the window, her knees pulled up to her chest under her nightgown, her hands wrapped around her legs. She turned when she heard the door close. "Nina!"

Nina froze. Irene sported a black eye and a swollen, shiny red left cheek.

"What are you doing here?" Irene tried in vain to hide her face.

Nina hurried to her friend. "I came to see you. Oh, Irene." She raised a hand to Irene's face but stopped short of touching her. "You cannot tell me this is a result of you being clumsy."

Irene pressed her lips together, and her eyes welled up.

"We've got to get you out of here."

"No, Nina. I can't. It'll heal up, and I'll be fine."

"Until next time. Listen to me." Nina pulled a dress out of Irene's closet and tossed it to her. "Put this on." She began looking for shoes. "I told Mrs. Wright that I suspected your father was harming you, and she wouldn't believe me. She'll believe me if she sees this. You need to come with me."

"Nina, you're being ridiculous." Despite her protests, Irene pulled on the dress. "Nobody's going to let me go with you."

"We'll climb out that window." Nina moved to the window and raised it. The ground looked an awfully long way down. "We can tie one end of your sheet to the bed frame and let ourselves down like they tell us to do in a fire." Nina pulled the bedding from Irene's bed and began lacing one end of a sheet through the iron frame.

"This is never going to work. Even if I did go with you, what would happen? I can't just—"

"What's going on up here?" The door burst open, and Mrs.

Jasper stood glaring at Nina, hands on hips. "I told you not to come up."

"Mrs. Jasper, I know what's been going on." Nina stood to her full height and looked the woman in the eye. "How can you allow this to keep happening to your own daughter? I should think you above all people would want to keep her safe."

"Nina, don't—" Irene stepped between them.

Mrs. Jasper raised her arm and pointed her finger toward the door. "You need to leave. This is none of your business."

"She's my friend, and she's hurt, so it *is* my business. She won't fight for herself. Somebody has to."

"Well, that somebody is not you. Now take your groceries and get out of here."

"Nina, you better just go," Irene pleaded.

But Nina stepped between her friend and her mother again. "What kind of mother allows this? My parents sent me all the way to Canada to keep me safe, and you let this happen to your daughter right under your own—"

Smack!

Nina felt the sharp slap against her cheek before she saw the hand coming at her face. Before she could react, Mrs. Jasper gripped Nina's right arm in a snake bite and began dragging her toward the door.

"You! It's been *you* doing this all along." Nina looked at Irene for confirmation, but the girl only stood there sobbing.

"You will leave these premises now. Do you understand me?" Mrs. Jasper stopped short of pushing Nina down the stairs. "You established yourself as a troublemaker when you first arrived, English girl, so no one is going to believe a word you say. We've been upstanding citizens of this community since long before you were born."

Nina caught one last glimpse of Irene's tear-stained and shame-filled face before she descended the stairs. No one was in the store. Nina grabbed the box of groceries waiting on the counter and headed out the door. Who could she tell? Mrs. Jasper was probably right. No one would believe her. Mrs. Wright had already made that clear, and if she didn't believe Irene's father capable of mistreating his daughter, she'd never believe it about Mrs. Jasper.

Her mind still on Irene, Nina placed the groceries on the seat of the truck and crossed the street to the post office. Disappointed that there were no letters for her or her siblings in the mailbox, she pulled out the Wrights' mail, including a letter from Carol. As she turned to leave, Miss Simms entered the post office.

"Oh, hello Nina." Miss Simms stuck a key into one of the mailboxes. "Looks like you're getting some sun on your face. Are you having a good summer?"

"Um. Yes, thank you." Nina stepped away from the boxes to give her teacher space. Was Miss Simms someone she could tell about the Jasper family?

"Glad to hear it." Miss Simms pulled one envelope from her box, examined it, and closed the box. "Any news from home?"

"Not today. Um. Miss Simms? Do you have time to chat a bit?"

Miss Simms raised her eyebrows. "Certainly, Nina. Would you like to go for a little walk?"

Nina nodded, raising a quick prayer that she was telling the right person. Miss Simms led the way to her own cottage where she offered Nina a glass of lemonade. Nina poured out the story from the beginning.

"So that's not sunburn on your face. I wondered why it was only on one side."

"No, ma'am. She did this too." Nina held out her arm where more red marks had formed from the twisting motion. "Irene isn't safe, but she won't speak up for herself, and I don't think anyone will believe me."

Miss Simms studied Nina's face. "I'm not sure what you want me to do."

"Believe me, for a start. I don't know. Isn't there something we can do?"

Miss Simms took a deep breath and let it out. "It's not that I don't believe you, Nina. I just—" She looked around her little home and glanced out the window. "Mr. Jasper is on the school board. I could get in deep trouble. Maybe lose my job."

Nina stared at the teacher she had enjoyed and admired. "I see. So you won't help her?"

"It's not that. I simply need time to think. If Irene won't admit to anything, I don't see how—"

"Never mind." Nina set her glass on the table and turned to leave. So that's how it was. No point saying more as she'd likely only say something she'd regret later. She left without a goodbye and nearly ran back to the truck still parked in front of Jaspers' General Store. She peered up at Irene's bedroom window. The blind had been pulled all the way down.

David to Emma

June 1942
Hey Emma,

Sorry I don't have time to write you a long letter, but I'll tuck this in with my letter to Mum and Dad so you've got something of your own. Hey, can you do me a favor? If Mum's peonies are still blooming when you get this, could you pick a big bouquet and take them to Nina? I don't know how much she tells you, but I can tell from her last letter she's been pretty discouraged and maybe homesick. And who can blame her? I'm glad she's got you for a friend, Sis.

Got to go. Will write more when I can. Be good, kiddo.

Love,
David

Chapter Twenty

Nina to Alice

Christmas, 1942
Dear Alice,

I'm sorry I haven't written in so long, but a lot has been going on, and I've been terribly busy with school and preoccupied with feelings for David. But I'll get to that later. First of all, I wanted to bring you up to date on Irene. I think I told you about my suspicions. I couldn't just do nothing, could I? Yet it seems the adults refuse to help. Mrs. Wright didn't believe me. I went to our English teacher, Miss Simms, but she was more worried about losing her job than helping Irene. I went to the pastor, but he didn't believe me because Irene's parents have been part of the church forever, and Mr. Jasper was a deacon or elder or something.

But guess what? When I returned to school in September, neither Irene nor Miss Simms were there! I won't go into the long, awful story, but it turns out it was Irene's mother who was harming her—can you believe it? Apparently, Miss Simms spoke up after all, although no one tells me anything, and I was right to go to her. According to some of the other students, Miss Simms took a job in another school division. I've had no word from Irene, but rumor has it she's gone to Winnipeg to live with an aunt. I've seen no trace of Mrs. Jasper. Every time I've been in the store only Mr. Jasper is working. Either his wife has left town too, or she sees me coming and disappears, or she's locked up somewhere. Neither of them have been in church. I don't know for sure what's going on. I miss my friend, but I pray she's safer now.

I miss Miss Simms too, although the new teacher, Mr. Rubins, is all right. (The kids call him "Rooster" behind his back. The hair at his crown tends to stick straight up, and he walks with a pronounced limp which is probably why he's here and not been drafted. Anyway, I like him.) All that to say—I'd love to know the whole story. On one hand, I am learning I need others' help and can't rescue people on my own no matter how much I'd like to. On the other hand, I'm learning that not all adults can be counted on to care. No wonder our world is at war.

Speaking of war …

David's letters, while infrequent, have done nothing to lessen my feelings for him. His sister Emma is my closest friend here. She had her mother take a photograph of us girls posing under a tree in their yard, and she sent it to David. In his next letter to me, he said (and I quote), "You are turning into a beautiful young woman that any man would be proud to have on his arm." It was all I could do to stop from squealing when I read it! I realize that it's possible he told his sister the same thing, but still. I've read it over and over. Did I tell you he recruited her to bring me flowers last summer? "To cheer up Nina," he said. Big, gorgeous peonies, half of them pink and half of them purple. (Unfortunately, they were crawling with ants which Hazel and I discovered soon after I set them in our bedroom. She was not impressed. I think she was just jealous.)

How I'd love a whiff of those fragrant flowers now. Winter's back with a vengeance, and you can be SO grateful you're in a milder part of the country, weather-wise. Christmas will be quiet again. Carol Wright is stationed in Ontario and didn't make it home for the holidays. Whenever her parents read aloud one of her letters, she mentions David less and an

American fellow named Roger more.

Mum and Dad tell me that Britain is now loaded with American and Canadian soldiers. Some are billeted with nearby neighbors, so Mum and Dad see them coming and going and are starting to recognize them. With the victory over the Germans at El Alamein, spirits are up, and everyone is hopeful it will be over soon. It's hard to imagine going home, isn't it? I've seen photos of the bombed-out buildings in London, heard about the shortages of everything, even worse than when we left, and I wonder what we'll be going home to. Why is abundance so easy to grow accustomed to while hardship is not? I suppose that's why it's called hardship. Mum says it all serves to build character. If that is true, this world should be filled with people of the highest character after it's all over.

I trust your family is well. I need to close—the family is setting up the Christmas tree tonight, and it sounds like they're ready to begin. The wireless is cranked up and Bing is crooning "White Christmas."

In friendship,
Nina

Nina tried to feign enthusiasm, but her heart wasn't in it. Compared to their first Christmas, this one felt empty and sad. The Wright family missed Carol, and Nina missed David. Though she looked forward to another afternoon with the Cain family, David's absence left a gaping hole. For the sake of her siblings and the Wright family, she smiled brightly as she helped make pancakes for breakfast, served with canned strawberries from last summer. When they were done eating, Mr. Wright read the Christmas story from the second chapter of Luke and prayed a special prayer for the soldiers, particularly for David and Carol.

They moved into the living room to unwrap gifts. Nina, Geoffrey, and Hazel opened their presents from their parents first—sweaters for each of them. From their unique colors, Nina knew immediately where the yarn had come from. In a labor of love, Mum had unraveled two jumpers of Dad's and one of her own, reworking them to fit her children.

Next, the Wrights opened gifts from the Gabriel children—artwork from Hazel, embroidered handkerchiefs from Nina, and a pinecone collection from Geoffrey. He'd painted the tips white to look like snow, and Mrs. Wright proudly placed them in a basket on the dining table. Nina opened a box of stationery and a piece of skirt fabric from the Wrights. Hazel received a nightgown and a set of toy dishes. Geoffrey got pajamas and a model plane.

The entire family spent the afternoon at the Cain home, enjoying a turkey dinner. With David away, no one had kept the pond free of snow for skating. Instead, they stayed indoors and worked on jigsaw puzzles. Nina and Emma managed to sneak away into Emma's bedroom for their own conversation. Most of it surrounded the contents of a new issue of *Chatelaine* Emma had received from her siblings for Christmas.

Late in the afternoon, the girls were called downstairs to gather with the family around the radio to hear the King's Christmas speech. Mrs. Cain managed to settle everyone down— the youngest children seated on the floor, each with a peppermint stick. Though her parents would have listened to the live speech hours before, Nina closed her eyes and pretended Mr. and Mrs. Wright were Mum and Dad and Daniel was little Sully. She pushed everyone else, except her siblings, from her imagination and pictured her own living room at home. King George spoke with an occasional stammer, but his words were clear.

"It is at Christmas more than at any other time that we are conscious of the dark shadow of war. Our Christmas festival today must lack many of the happy, familiar features that it has had from our childhood. We miss the actual presence of some of those nearest and dearest, without whom our family gatherings cannot be complete."

A murmur of agreement went up from both mothers in the room.

"But though its outward observances may be limited, the message of Christmas remains eternal and unchanged. It is a message of thankfulness and of hope—of thankfulness to the Almighty for His great mercies, of hope for the return to this earth of peace and goodwill. In this spirit, I wish all of you a happy Christmas. This year it adds to our happiness that we are sharing it with so many of our comrades-in-arms from the United States of America. We welcome them in our homes, and their sojourn here will not only be a happy memory for us but, I hope, a basis of enduring understanding between our two peoples. The recent victories won by the United Nations enable me this Christmas to speak with firm confidence about the future."

He went on to describe fleets and forces advancing toward each other in various theaters of the war. Nina's mind wandered, imagining David on the battlefield of the air. He wasn't allowed to share in his letters any information about where his duty took him. Had he been involved in any of the exploits the King now spoke of? Would she get to hear about it all one day?

"We still have tasks ahead of us, perhaps harder even than those which we have already accomplished. We face these with confidence, for today we stand together, no longer alone, no longer ill-armed, but just as resolute as in the darkest hours to do our duty whatever comes. Many of you to whom I am speaking are far away overseas."

"Hey, that's us!" Geoffrey said.

"We realize at first hand the importance and meaning of those outposts of the Empire which the wisdom of our forefathers selected, and which your faithfulness will defend. For there was a danger that we should lose much, and this has opened our eyes to the value of what we might have lost. You may be serving for the first time in Gibraltar, in Malta, in Cyprus, in the Middle East, in Ceylon, or in India. Perhaps you are listening to me from Aden or Syria, or Persia, or Madagascar or the West Indies, or you may be in the land of your birth, in Canada, Australia, New Zealand, or South Africa.”

At the mention of Canada, Nina felt tears roll down her cheeks, but she kept her eyes closed.

“Wherever you are serving in our wide, free Commonwealth of Nations you will always feel at home. Though severed by the long sea miles of distance you are still in the family circle, whose ties, precious in peaceful years, have been knit even closer by danger.

“The Queen and I feel most deeply for all of you who have lost or been parted from your dear ones, and our hearts go out to you with sorrow, with comfort, but also with pride. We send a special message of remembrance to the wounded and the sick in the hospitals wherever they may be, and to the prisoners of war, who are enduring their long exile with dignity and fortitude. Suffering and hardship shared together have given us a new understanding of each other’s problems. The lessons learned during the past forty tremendous months have taught us how to work together after the war to build a worthier future.”

“Oh Lord, I hope he’s right about that.” Mr. Cain broke in.

“On visits to war industries in every part of the country, the Queen and I have watched with admiration the steady growth of that vital war production, the fruits of which are now being used by every branch of our forces. We are thankful for the splendid addition to our food supplies made by those who work on the land, and who have made it fertile as it has never been before. Those of you who are carrying out this variety of duties so willingly undertaken in the service of your country will, I am sure, find new associations, new friendships, and new memories long to be cherished in times of peace.”

Nina’s new friends and the memories she was now making came to mind. She could hardly imagine life before Emma or David. The Wright family. Irene.

“On the sea, on land, and in the air, and in civil life at home, a pattern of effort and mutual service is being traced which may guide those who design the picture of our future society.”

Would the society of the future look anything the same?

The King continued, "A former president of the United States of America used to tell the story of a boy who was carrying an even smaller child up a hill. Asked whether the heavy burden was not too much for him, the boy answered, 'It's not a burden. It's my brother!'

"So let us welcome the future in a spirit of brotherhood and, thus, make a world in which, please God, all may dwell together in justice and peace."

Nina slowly opened her eyes as an orchestra played "God Save the King." The little kids, proud to know the words, sang along. Grownups wiped their eyes. Teenagers looked somber, thoughtful. When the anthem ended, Mrs. Cain turned off the radio, and Mr. Wright stood.

"Well, gang, we need to head home. The cows don't care about Christmas or the King's speech."

That evening, after a light supper, Nina washed the dishes and Jim dried.

"Hazel's been awful quiet. Did you notice?" Jim stacked the plates on a cupboard shelf.

"Mmm." Nina felt chagrined to realize she hadn't noticed. "Now that you mention it … yes. She might be feeling a little homesick. Wonder where she's off to now?"

"I saw her head upstairs after supper."

"Probably playing with her new toys."

But when Nina went up to their bedroom a few minutes later, the new tea set rested in its box, and Hazel wasn't there. Across the hall, the door to Carol's room—now used by Daniel—stood closed. Nina saw shadowy movements from the crack under the door. *Uh-oh.* What was Hazel getting into? Without warning, she opened the door. Hazel sat in the middle of the floor, surrounded by letters and notebooks and a flowered box from which they had clearly been removed.

"Hazel!" Nina shut the door behind her before anyone else saw. "What are you doing?"

Hazel made no move to hide her activity. Instead, she

focused on the notebook in her hand. "I think you need to read this."

"What is it?"

"Carol's diary."

"Diary? Hazel! Put that away right now!" Nina began gathering letters and stuffing them into the box. "You know better than to snoop. You'll get us both in trouble."

"I don't care. You need to read this."

"No. I'll not." Nina held out her hand to take it, but Hazel pulled it away. "Put it in the box."

Hazel stared back. "Fine." She laid the book in the box. "But I'm telling you what I found out."

Nina's curiosity immediately rose to the surface, but she wouldn't let it get the best of her. "If it was any of our business, we'd already know." She shoved the remaining items into the box and closed the lid. "Where did you find this?"

Hazel took the box and carried it over to the closet. "We sort of already *do* know. We just don't know *this* part."

"I don't know what you're talking about." Nina waited for Hazel to shut the closet door and then opened the door to the hallway. "Come on. Let's get out of here." Nina crossed to their own room.

Hazel followed and closed the door behind her. Standing with her back to the door, she looked solemnly at Nina. "I know how the Wrights' other children died. It was Carol's fault."

"What?" Nina wasn't sure she wanted to hear this. "Hazel, you shouldn't say such things. Don't you ever go snooping in Carol's stuff again. Or anyone else's."

Hazel sat at the table and chair set that had belonged to the Wright children and began removing her little dishes from their box. "Well, maybe it isn't Carol's fault. But *she* thinks it is."

Without a word, Nina sat on the little chair opposite Hazel and waited for her to continue.

"She wrote about it in her diary. It's from 1938."

"Two years before we came."

Hazel nodded. "Did you ever wonder why the Wrights don't swim in their pond like the Cains do?"

"Yes …"

"They used to." Hazel arranged the dainty cups and saucers on the table. "A long time before we came."

Images rose to Nina's mind. Mrs. Wright hovering over Daniel and Hazel while they played in the tub. The Wrights' refusal to take their children to the lake on a hot summer day. The two small graves at the cemetery with matching dates. *Bartholomew and Violet.*

"Did Bart and Violet drown?"

Hazel nodded solemnly.

"What makes you say Carol thinks it's her fault?"

"She was in charge of them. Her mum and dad weren't home."

Nina let the information sink in. *Poor Carol.* Oh, how well Nina understood the burden. She moved to the frosted window and breathed on it until she'd cleared a circle big enough to gaze out across the winter wonderland under the moonlight. Beyond the barn, she could make out the dugout pond from which Mr. Wright watered his animals, the gentle mounds around it now covered in white. By July, the pond would be muddy with cow hoofprints on one end, but the other end would indeed look like an inviting swimming hole. Nina had asked about it once, only to be told in no uncertain terms that it was "unsanitary and unsafe."

"Nineteen thirty-eight," Nina murmured. "Carol would have been only … fourteen. Same age I was when we came." Those days on the ship and the train flooded Nina's heart now, recalling the angst of trying to watch over her siblings. The urgency of needing to keep them together after they arrived.

Hazel nodded. "Carol was very sad about it. I think she still is. That's why she's mean to us."

From the mouths of babes.

"She wrote some really nasty things about us."

Nina spun around to face her. "About *us*? How many diaries did you *read*?"

"All of them. The last one in the box is from last year."

Nina let out a massive sigh. "We mustn't let on that we know about this, Hazie. Not unless someone tells us."

"Should I tell Geoffrey?"

Nina kept her back to the window waiting until she'd made eye contact with Hazel. "No. It's possible he already knows if he asked Jim. But in any case, it's best to leave it be."

Mrs. Gabriel to her children.

Christmas 1942
Dearest Nina, Geoffrey, and Hazel.

Oh, how I wish we could be together but since it's not possible, I hope you are having a lovely Christmas there in Canada—although I suppose it may be late January by the time you receive this. We feel a special connection to you this year, as the Canadian soldiers hosted a Christmas party for local children at their camp, and Sully was invited. Since he's so young, I volunteered to be one of the adult chaperones. The children were loaded into army lorries and on arriving at the camp, each child was assigned a Canadian soldier as an honorary uncle for the day. Each received a bag of sweets, chocolate, and chewing gum. They were also served "Coke." Most of them had never had the strange drink before. A massive tea was laid out. It looked like a feast to us!

A Santa Claus with a Canadian accent handed out gifts. Sully's was a picture book. Older boys received toy tanks and the models used to teach aircraft recognition. We saw tears in the eyes of the soldiers as they loaded the children back into lorries to send them home. I'm sure they were remembering their own loved ones in Canada. Each child was given yet another bag of sweets as they left the lorries. I made Sully put his away and am allowing him one each day.

Despite the blackout, we went carol singing through nearby streets. I don't know how people managed it, but at various homes the children were given fruit and sweets, even half-crowns. In one flat lives an elderly couple who fled Germany right before the war—maybe you remember the Heimbergers? I had seen them around town but had not really spoken to them. They seem shy and polite, with only enough English to get by. Someone suggested we sing "Silent Night" at their home. I didn't think they would appreciate it, being Jewish, but they came to the door and listened and then asked us to sing the first verse again. We gladly obliged, and they were mouthing the words along with us—in German, I am certain. We wished them a Merry Christmas and left them smiling at us as we continued on our way. It was a special moment, to be sure.

Our train station has been repaired after the bomb last August—I think I mentioned it? One train (no passengers aboard) was badly damaged as well as the station roof. But the station was out of action only two weeks.

Everyone feels that this Christmas is the beginning of better days—certainly more peaceful than the previous three years. Surely, before long we will see the end of the war and bring you all home for keeps. It's hard to believe Sully is nearly two years old and has not met his siblings yet. Oh, how my heart longs for us to be united at last. I love you all. Dad and I miss you very much. Please keep writing as often as you can.

Lovingly,
Mother

P.S. I did ask a couple of the Canadian soldiers if they'd heard of David Cain, but they had not. There was one boy from Manitoba, though, and after they pointed him out to me, we had a good chat. His name is Henry Forsythe, and I'm sorry, I've forgotten the name of his town. He knew of Cedar Bluff, but not of David. He did promise to mention us to David should they ever cross paths.

Chapter Twenty-One

Nina to Carol

February 1943
Dear Carol,

I know I've never written you before, so I hope you're not shocked. I just thought you might enjoy hearing from someone else for a change. Your parents read your latest letter aloud at supper. Sounds like you're having lots of new experiences and making friends. I'm glad for you.

We are doing well. You'll see a huge change in your brothers when you come home, especially Daniel. He's tall for a three-year old and his favorite activity is following Hazel around, asking "Why?" nonstop. She's not always patient, I'm afraid, but he adores her anyway.

I wasn't on stage for the Christmas play this year but worked as a stagehand. It was a nice break to not have to memorize lines and kind of fun to wear all black.

I think your mum has mentioned to you that she's taught me to sew. I quite enjoy it, although I'm sure I'll never be as good as she is—or you. Emma and I hatched a plan to get jobs in a garment factory in Winnipeg for the summer, but I don't expect it will come to anything. Where would we stay? I doubt her parents would agree to it, even if mine (and yours) did. I can't say I enjoy having four parents who need to confer on things, but Geoffrey in his infinite wisdom reminded me that we should be grateful to have so many adults who care about us.

I also wanted to apologize for my attitude when we first came here. At the time, all I could think of was myself and my siblings and how I could keep us together. Since then, I've tried to imagine my own family and home being "invaded" by strangers—strangers looking to my parents to provide for them, to treat them as their own children—and I know I would not handle such a thing graciously. (You remember how upset I was when I learned about Sully? If I had trouble accepting my own flesh-and-blood brother, how much harder would it be to accept strangers?) So please forgive me for not being more understanding. I wish we could have gotten off to a better start and been friends. I was so focused on thinking I alone was responsible for my siblings and terrified that I couldn't do it. I am (slowly) learning that if bad things do happen to them, it's not my burden to carry.

When I was eight years old, my mother had a stillborn baby boy. Geoffrey and Hazel were four and one at the time and to this day, they are unaware. My grandmother, whom I'd never met before and never saw again after, came to visit. I can still hear Mum's sobs if I let myself think about it. I was too young to understand everything that was going on, but I overheard my grandmother say to my parents, "it would be easier to lose your oldest than one of these precious wee ones." I still don't understand why Grandmama would say such a thing, but I've never forgotten her words. I think perhaps I have spent the years since then trying to prove that I deserve to live and to make sure my parents never lose another child.

I've never told anyone this before. I hope you understand.

In friendship,
Nina

On Friday, March fifth, Nina woke to the aroma of cinnamon and the sound of Hazel's voice singing "Happy Birthday." She opened her eyes just enough to take in the ridiculous image of Hazel in her nightgown, her hair a halo of tangles around her head, standing on the bed at Nina's feet, crooning at the top of her lungs. She dragged out the final "you" and dropped to all fours. "Get up, Nina! You're seventeen!"

Seventeen. The age Mum was when she married Dad. And I've never even had a real date. Nina groaned and rolled over, pulling the covers over her head.

"C'mon!" Hazel tugged the blankets off Nina. "Mama Wright is making a special breakfast and everything." No trace of Hazel's English accent remained, and she'd taken to calling their foster parents "Mama and Papa Wright."

Fifteen minutes later, the family was gathered around the kitchen table enjoying French toast made from Mrs. Wright's home-baked bread dipped in a mixture of eggs from her own chickens and milk from her own cows. Even the butter and syrup were their own, the latter made from wild chokecherries the children had helped pick the previous August.

Mrs. Wright poured a little syrup over the piece of French toast on her fork and tasted it. "This should be sweeter and thicker. Dang sugar rationing."

"It's fine." Mr. Wright reached for another slice. "Did you ever think you'd be in Canada long enough to celebrate three birthdays with us, Nina?"

Nina shook her head. "I had no reason to think I'd have even one birthday here. Six months, they told us."

Mrs. Wright reached out a hand and gave Nina's forearm a little squeeze. "I'm sorry you can't be home with your family. I hope you know we count it a privilege to have you here with us."

"Thank you." Nina thought back to their first day and their rocky start. Now she better understood Mrs. Wright's reluctance to host all three of them.

After breakfast, the three Gabriels piled into the truck with Jim at the wheel. After they dropped off Geoffrey and Hazel at their school, Jim spoke up. "How's it feel to be seventeen?"

"Same as sixteen."

"Oh yeah? It won't for me." Jim would turn seventeen in another month.

"How do you know?"

"Well, for one thing, I can enlist."

"Enlist?" A sudden, sisterly urge to protect came over Nina. "But you're just a—" She stopped herself before *kid* came out. "Why enlist?"

"I don't want to be a zombie."

"A what?"

"That's what they're calling the fellas who get drafted before they volunteer."

"Well, I don't think that's quite accurate." Nina had heard the news. While the government initially promised there'd be no conscription, they now promised not to force anyone into active duty. Draftees would be allowed to refuse overseas duty and be put to work on the home front—and apparently, nicknamed *zombies*. "Why not wait until you see if you get drafted? Then you could volunteer for active duty if you're so sure that's a good idea."

"Why wait? If I enlist, I'll be called up that much sooner, trained sooner, and have more options. Maybe become an officer eventually."

Nina sighed. "You've obviously thought about this. Do your parents know what you're thinking?"

"Not yet."

"Well, if I were you … better sooner than later. Your dad needs you on the farm, and they've already lost so much. Give them some time to prepare."

"I suppose." Jim pulled over to pick up his classmate, George, who stood waiting at the end of his lane for a ride to school.

Nina felt flushed as her classmates sang "Happy Birthday" to her. When Mr. Rubins asked what she would wish for, her first impulse was to give the same answer most of the other students had given—for the war to end. The only ones who gave different answers were the boys eager to join up. At the last second, she changed her answer. "I wish everyone could experience just enough of the war—without being harmed—to realize it's not a game."

The room grew quiet. Some of the boys glanced at one another with half grins. One or two cleared their throats.

"Well said, Nina." Mr. Rubins picked up a piece of paper from the top of a stack on his desk. "On that note … it's time for our English lesson. I planned to have you read aloud the poems you wrote for your last assignment. I think we should begin with Nina's. C'mon up, Nina."

Already self-conscious from the attention, Nina felt sweaty and hot. In front of her, Emma turned around with an encouraging smile and a thumbs-up. "Just pretend you're in a play," she whispered.

While acting came easy, sharing your own heartfelt words with your peers was another story. Nina pushed herself to her feet and counted ten steps from her desk to Mr. Rubin's. She accepted the paper from his hand. A bright red A+ had been scrawled in the top corner. She could have recited it from memory but was grateful for something to hold and look at. She took a deep breath, determined to play the role of a woman with five times her confidence.

"'The Bomb Shelter,' by Nina Gabriel." Nina took a quick glance at her classmates before continuing.

"That delicious moment between waking and sleeping
When all's right with the world, when shadows are deepening.
Then suddenly—*WHAM!*—the siren's shrill blare
Pulls me back to a world full of care.
The rudest of intrusions, the darkest of night
As I and my family must now take to flight.

Will we reach the shelter before the bombs drop?
Will we manage to dodge every blast, crack, and pop?
Will we return to our home before the night ends?
Will our city survive what the enemy sends?
We'll emerge without knowing—do we still have a home?
Do we still have a country? Will we be all alone?
Stay if you must. Leave if you dare.
The bomb shelter and I have a love/hate affair."

The room was so quiet, Nina was certain the students in the back row could hear her swallow. She held the poem out to Mr. Rubins, who gently shook his head. "Keep it. Thank you, Nina. That's a powerful piece and straight from your heart. You can return to your seat."

Mr. Rubins distributed the remaining poems to their authors and asked two or three more students to share their work aloud, but Nina barely heard anything they read. She had succeeded in transporting herself back three years and thousands of miles to that neighborhood bomb shelter where she'd huddled with Geoffrey and Hazel while Mum and Dad performed their duties as wardens, organizing people and keeping them calm.

"That poem was amazing," Emma told her as the girls walked to the post office at lunch time. "Sometimes I forget what you've been through. I hope reliving it like that hasn't spoiled your birthday."

"No." Nina pulled a mailbox key from her pocket. "If anything, it makes me more grateful to be here."

"You must miss your parents, though."

Nina nodded.

"Do you worry about them?"

"Every day."

Nina pulled three items from the Wrights' mailbox—a letter from Carol to her parents, something that looked like a bill, and a letter for Nina. "Hey, look, it's from Irene!"

Unable to wait, Nina tore the envelope open while Emma brushed snow off a bench outside the post office. They sat while Nina read Irene's words aloud.

March 1943
Winnipeg, Manitoba

Dearest Nina,

First of all, I'm sorry for not writing sooner. I confess I was terribly angry with you at first. I truly believed you had no right to interfere with my family and I was petrified of what might happen. I had no reason to think life could improve for me. In fact, I felt convinced it would only get worse. I guess things did get a bit worse, for a while. I don't know who you spoke with or what all transpired, but within days after you came to my room and confronted Mum, she left. Then Dad sent me to live with my Aunt Sadie (his sister) in Winnipeg for a while until they could sort things out. I adore my aunt, so that part was all right. But I was terrified at the thought of attending a city school.

Anyway, this terribly long-overdue letter is to say thank you, Nina. You were a true friend when I didn't know how desperately I needed one. After a month here, my eczema cleared up completely. The doctor says it was caused by stress. Now that I feel safe, I suppose I'm not under stress anymore. I didn't even know it was possible to live like this! Aunt Sadie is helping me see that the way we lived was not normal. She's the best. She is engaged, but her fiancé is in service overseas. She and I have long talks about what it means to be in love and all that. Plus, she works for Eaton's and has the nicest clothes!

Yes, it was scary to go to school at first (there are four hundred students in four grades!) but I love the opportunities to take courses not offered back home—like chemistry with a real lab. I've made friends and even gotten involved in drama and the yearbook. I just started a Saturday job at a corner store two blocks from home. Of course, it came easy for me. Dad tells me that Mum is "getting help" and will soon be able to come home. Between us, though, we've agreed that I will stay on here through graduation.

So Nina, once again—thank you from the bottom of my heart. I love my life! I didn't know it was possible to go to bed at night looking forward to the next day, or to wake up in the morning without an instant sense of dread. I miss you (and Emma, of course—please tell her I say hello), but I am so happy to be here, and I owe it to you. My father even apologized for allowing things to go on so long. For the record, Dad never laid a hand on me or Mum though they argued plenty.

You are a good friend, and I hope we can see each other before too long. Maybe this summer? Maybe you and Emma could come for the whole summer and work in the city. We'd have a grand time!

Lovingly,
Irene

Chapter Twenty-Two

David to Nina

London, England
June 1943
Dear Nina,

I'm across the pond. The voyage was an adventure. Let's just say this prairie boy may not have been created to spend his life on water, and I was really glad to find solid ground under my feet once more. If I can't get up the courage to do it again, I'll have no choice but to stay here until such time as flying home would be an option.

Now I'm in your country, and you're in mine. Wish I could visit in happier times—there's so much beauty and history. So many places I've read about but never dreamed I might have the chance to see—Tower Bridge, Buckingham Palace, Hyde Park. I remember how you said you've never been to London. It seems kind of unfair that I am getting to see some of these places before you. I've seen a lot I'd rather not see too—the damage from the shelling is, sadly, all too evident. I'm not supposed to go into detail about where we're based or the missions we're assigned, but I wanted to let you know I received several of your letters at once, along with some from my family, when we arrived. For a while, I kept the photo of you and Emma tacked up over my bunk. But the other fellas were so nosy, I tucked it into my Bible instead. They'll never look there. I told them you are both my sisters so they wouldn't be rude. Not sure if they believed me, but the teasing stopped. They're not wrong, though—you've both turned into beautiful young women who would turn any fella's head. My one regret about not being home is that I can't fend off the creeps who are no doubt pestering you both for dates.

I am looking into the possibility of catching a train to Middlesbrough to look up your family, but I would need more than a day's leave and that isn't likely to happen any time soon. If I can make it work, I sure hope we can have a photo taken together—your parents, Sully, and me. Wouldn't that be something?

By the time you receive this, you'll be on summer holidays with only one year of high school left! Don't work too hard. You're only young once, so have some fun. Keep writing. Your letters always give me a lift.

Affectionately,
David

Carol was coming home for a week-long vacation. Nina vowed to treat her with kindness and compassion. Even though she had not received a reply to her heartfelt letter, she'd felt encouraged when Mrs. Wright shared part of her own letter from Carol. "Please thank Nina for her letter and tell her I'll write when I get a chance." Hopefully, their relationship could improve, now that Carol knew they shared a similar heartache.

Mrs. Wright put everyone to work as though the Queen herself were coming. While Mr. Wright tackled the scraping and painting of the picket fence his wife had been nagging him about for two years, Jim repainted the railing on the front porch. Geoffrey was on grass-cutting duty. Nina and Hazel spent two days washing windows and scrubbing floors. Even little Daniel was assigned to assist his mother in the kitchen, preparing as many of Carol's favorite dishes as rationing would allow.

When the day of Carol's arrival came, Nina volunteered to stay home with Geoffrey and Hazel while Carol's parents and brothers picked her up at the train station in Cedar Bluff. As soon as they left, Nina recruited her siblings to help her fill the house with bouquets of flowers from Mrs. Wright's expansive perennial beds. By the time the family arrived home, the house was filled with the fragrance of roses and lilies. The three Gabriel children waited on the front porch and watched Rosie run to the truck, tail wagging.

Nina wasn't sure she'd have recognized the woman who stepped down from the truck. Carol had always appeared classy and well put together, but in her CWAC uniform, she exuded an air of confidence and authority. Even after a half day of warm summer traveling, she looked fresh as a daisy—every hair in place beneath her cap, her khaki suit with its brass buttons and notched lapel neatly pressed. Brown shoes shiny, black tie knotted tightly. Over one shoulder, she carried a canvas bag with a leather strap. Jim hopped out next and retrieved his sister's duffel bag from the back of the truck while Carol paused to greet Rosie.

Nina, Geoffrey, and Hazel rose. "Welcome home, Carol. We made lemonade."

Mrs. Wright responded. "Thank you, Nina."

"Yes. Thank you, Nina." Carol's smile did not extend to her eyes, but Nina chalked it up to fatigue. Everyone followed Carol inside and gathered in the living room where Carol fielded questions from Jim and her father and plenty from Geoffrey too.

At supper, Mrs. Wright made an announcement. "I've arranged a little party so you can see all your friends at once, Carol. Tomorrow night, here. A bonfire starting at eight. We began spreading the word as soon as we knew you were coming. How does that sound?"

"Fine." Carol shrugged one shoulder.

Mr. Wright raised an eyebrow. "Just fine? Try to contain your enthusiasm."

"Oh, it's not that. I appreciate it, Mum. As long as I can be free the rest of the week to see whomever I wish."

"Well, of course." Mrs. Wright pushed the food around on her plate.

"I think she's on to you, sweetheart." Mr. Wright chuckled.

Mrs. Wright raised her head. "I have no idea what you're talking about."

"I do." Jim volunteered. "You said it yourself, Mum. 'If Carol can see all her friends at once, we might stand a chance of seeing her ourselves for more than a few minutes.'"

"Oh, I did not." Mrs. Wright's protest sounded weak, even to Nina.

"Perfectly understandable, dear. I don't blame you a bit." Mr. Wright turned to his daughter. "Carol, please be sure to carve out a little mother-daughter time while you're here. She's too proud to come right out and ask."

"Harold!"

"Now that wasn't so hard, was it?" He grinned and dug into his potatoes.

"Sure, Mum. I won't be going far. Besides, it's not the same without David around."

At the mention of David, Nina felt the heat rising on her face. What would Carol think if she could see David's recent letters? Though he claimed to think of Nina as a sister, he wrote to her four times more often than he wrote to his real sister. His letters typically ended with "your friend," but his words were increasingly intimate as he shared his heart and expressed his pride in Nina's accomplishments.

"He's definitely got it bad for you," Emma had proclaimed. "He just doesn't know it yet. His letters to *me* are mostly questions about *you*!"

Emma's words were enough to raise Nina's hopes. Enough to make her refuse any other boys who showed interest beyond friendship. Enough for her to fall asleep at night with David foremost on her mind, prayers for his well-being on her lips. Now Carol's statement made her wonder if it was all a childish illusion. Thankfully, Mr. Wright asked the question Nina was dying to ask but never would.

"Are you and David still an item? I would think you've met plenty of other fellas by now."

Jim let out a snort. "Carol and David were never an item. Except in Carol's head."

"Jim. Don't be mean," his mother scolded.

Carol tossed her head. "I haven't heard from David in months. I only meant that the old gang won't seem the same without him. He was always the life of the party."

"Well, there are lots of other fellas away now too." Mr. Wright reached out and ruffled Jim's hair. "This one will be next."

"What? Really?" Carol turned to study her brother as though seeing him for the first time. As the conversation shifted to Jim's plans, David Cain was forgotten for the rest of the evening—except by Nina.

They spent the following day preparing for the party in Carol's honor. Emma, Julia, and Jessie Cain arrived first and were put to work, although Julia would be relegated to the house with Hazel once the party was underway. After the boys created a table with an old door and two sawhorses, Nina and Emma decorated it with one of Mrs. Wright's tablecloths and more fresh flowers. Mason jars of black-eyed Susans and white daisies added color to the faded cloth. Nina put extra effort into arranging them just so.

"I don't understand why you're being so nice to Carol," Emma muttered. "She's never been nice to you."

Nina straightened the tablecloth before answering. "I think she's really hurting. She needs some true friendship."

"What do you mean? She's got a whole trio of girls who hang on her every word. And that's just the ones she left behind."

Nina studied her friend a moment. "How much do you know

about … the drowning?"

Emma paused. "You mean Bart and Violet?"

Nina nodded.

"I remember it, of course. It was awfully sad." Emma pinched the tablecloth together in one corner with a clothespin to hold it in place. "Can you pull on that side?"

Nina pulled the cloth taut and held it in place with another clothespin. "What else do you remember?"

"The funeral. The church was packed, with more people standing outside. Lots of sad faces. The Wright kids were never allowed to go swimming with us after that. Mom and Dad told us to be understanding and to not talk about it."

"What about Carol? Did she seem … different after that?"

Emma twisted her lips while she thought about it. "I think they were *all* a little different. Sadder, for sure. I mean, who wouldn't be? But Carol always had a bit of a mean streak if you ask me. Even before."

The girls were interrupted by the arrival of a carload of young people from town, quickly followed by several more. Some came on bikes, some on foot. One boy showed up on horseback. Carol emerged from the house in a gorgeous pale peach summer frock that had been hanging in her closet, tempting Nina to try it on. Some of the girls greeted Carol with shrieks, others just seemed glad for an excuse to get together. While the adults congregated in the house, the boys built up a nice bonfire. The youth gathered around it on benches and stumps, devouring cookies, fresh strawberries, and watermelon. Carol enjoyed the limelight, telling stories of her army life, her clerical duties, and the social aspect of being part of it all.

Jim's friend Billy pulled out his guitar and the campfire choruses began—some silly, some serious. Between songs, the night air was filled with laughter and stories. When Emma smiled warmly at her, Nina couldn't help thinking about how far she'd come from her first few weeks in Cedar Bluff. She truly felt she belonged and couldn't think of anywhere she'd rather be. Only David's presence was needed to make it perfect.

"I've applied to be stationed overseas," Carol announced. The group grew quiet. "Italy, maybe. More likely England."

"Hey, maybe you'll come back sounding like Nina here!" Jim gave his best imitation of Nina's accent.

"Well, I don't even know if I'll get to go." Carol's words sounded modest, but her grin betrayed her. "The competition is fierce."

"Wouldn't you get desperately homesick?" one girl asked.

Another piped up. "You could get some pointers from Nina. She knows all about being far from home."

Carol turned and looked in Nina's direction. "Oh, I don't think Nina had any trouble leaving *her* home. Her parents can't get rid of their kids fast enough. Isn't that right, Nina?"

Nina stared at her, speechless.

"That's not true!" Geoffrey scowled at Carol.

Carol's friends giggled awkwardly. The fire popped and crackled.

Emma gave her head a shake. "Why would you say such a thing?"

"Nina knows why." Carol grinned in Nina's direction. "She told me herself. Didn't you, Nina?"

"I … I don't think that's what I said. I miss my parents a lot. We all do. And I know they miss—"

"Her mother had a dead baby and said it would be better if Nina had died instead. Then, guess what? A few years later, they shipped all their kids off to Canada at the first opportunity. I mean, how much do you have to hate your kids to send them to the other side of the world with Nazi U-boats infesting the ocean? I should think anybody would be glad to get away from a home situation like that. Right, Nina?"

Nina's heart pounded. She had trusted Carol, felt sorry for her. Offered her compassion by sharing her own pain. Now Carol was using it against her.

Jim came to her rescue. "Carol, that's mean. And it's not true."

"You don't know anything about it, little brother." Carol

stood. "Oh, who cares? Who wants to go for a walk? Bring your guitar, Billy."

As the rest of the kids followed Carol's lead and were soon walking down the road singing and laughing, Nina, Emma, Geoffrey, and Jim stayed behind. Nina stared into the fire.

"I'm sorry, Nina." Jim began spreading apart the burning pieces with a long stick. "I don't know why my sister's so mean to you."

"Why did she say that? Did Mum really have a dead baby?" At thirteen, Geoffrey's voice rose and dropped in pitch—especially when he was upset, like now.

Nina sighed. "You were little. Mum had a baby boy, but he died before he was born."

Geoffrey took in the news, wide-eyed, trying to remember. "Did she really say she wished you had died instead?"

Nina swallowed. "No. She never said that."

"Why would Carol say such an awful thing? How does she even know?"

Emma looked at Nina. "Yeah, how does she know?"

"I … shared it with her. In a letter."

"Why?"

Nina was beginning to wonder the same thing. She'd convinced herself she was being vulnerable to help Carol. Deep down, was she really seeking understanding for herself? "I … don't know. Let's forget it. Geoff, please don't say anything to Hazel about this."

"If you say so."

The four of them doused the fire pit with water and cleaned up the party mess. For the remainder of Carol's week at home, she spent most of her time visiting friends. When she was home, Nina kept her distance as much as possible. When it was time for her parents to take Carol back to the train station, nobody was happier than Nina.

Mrs. Gabriel to Ann Wright

Middlesbrough, England
July 1943
Dear Ann,

Thank for your recent update on the children. It's impossible to imagine our Nina as a grown-up young lady attending youth events as you mentioned, but we are so grateful for your guidance in her life and your ongoing care and concern. I've no doubt you and Harold are both a blessing for which she will be grateful all her days. You've been supremely patient with our Geoffrey. When we read your words, "we felt as proud as if he were our own" about his school's awards day, it warmed our hearts beyond what I can describe. I suspect Hazel is the bigger handful now. Nina tells me she has become quite the little Canadian, and one of my biggest fears is that she will have no desire to return home when the time comes. As always, we owe you a debt of gratitude such that we can never repay.

My mother-in-law is staying with us as her flat was bombed. I dearly hope it's temporary. Between you and me, I find her presence more trying than the war at times. Things have calmed down for us somewhat here in Middlesbrough and we're hopeful the fighting will soon end altogether.

My bigger concern these days is Sully. Please don't tell the children yet as there may be nothing to worry about, but it seems there may be something wrong with his hearing. Our doctor has written a specialist. If his referral is accepted, we will be taking Sully to London for further testing and possible surgery to correct the problem. It's all very frightening, but of course, we want to do the best for him. Everything is just so much more difficult due to travel restrictions, bombed-out hospitals, beds taken up by wounded soldiers, nursing shortages … well, shortages of every kind, really. If you could remember this concern in your prayers, I would be very grateful. And if you have any advice at all or know someone with a deaf child, I would dearly love to correspond with someone who has walked this road.

Please know that you are in my prayers every day, along with our children and yours. May God grant you wisdom, patience, and love. May he fill your home with peace.

Sincerely,
Margaret Gabriel

Chapter Twenty-Three

Middlesbrough, England
October 1943
My darling children,

By now I'm sure you have heard that the new government of Italy has confirmed its allegiance with the Allies and declared war on Germany. Surely, it won't be much longer now. Oh, my heart longs to see you all, to wrap my arms around you, my precious children. Wouldn't it be wonderful if you could be home for Christmas this year? I'll not let myself hope for that, but possibly next summer. Let's plan a picnic at Redcar Beach.

Your father and I took the train to London last week with Sully. I haven't wanted to say anything, but now I'm asking for special prayer for him. The bad news is, Sully has limited hearing, which we think he was born with. The good news is, the specialist who examined him has performed a surgery numerous times that he believes will correct the problem … he explained it to us, but frankly, I was too distraught at the idea of surgery to really grasp what he was saying. Anyway, a date has been set. We'll be returning to London where Sully is scheduled for surgery on 21 January at the Hospital for Sick Children on Great Ormond Street. Mrs. Dowden from church has a friend who lives near the hospital. We hope to be able to stay with her. Sorting out the details. Please pray that the surgery will be a success, that Sully's hearing will be completely restored, and that he will quickly be able to catch up wherever he's fallen behind because of it.

Grandmama Gabriel's flat was bombed so she is staying with us here in Middlesbrough until she can make other arrangements. It will be good to have someone in the house while we're in London.

I have so enjoyed reading each of your letters about the start of a new school year—Nina, I cannot believe this will be your last! Please apply yourself as you always have done, even if it's tempting to coast along as you near the end. And sweet Geoffrey, this will be your final year at the country school. Mrs. Wright explained that a lot of boys your age don't go on to high school, but your father and I—as well as Mr. and Mrs. Wright—are in full agreement that you must keep going. Trust me when I say you will be glad you did. And, dear Hazel, I know your education has not come easily for you, but to be starting "grade five" as you call it, is a terrific accomplishment. You are at such a wonderful age—old enough to think for yourself and to carry on real conversations, young enough to still be a little girl when you want to. We love you all so much and hope you have a perfectly lovely school year … and that next year, you'll be enrolled right here in Middlesbrough once again!

Lovingly,
Mother

January 1944

Nina was focused on her science textbook when Mr. Rubins tapped her on the arm. She blinked in confusion and looked up to see concern in his eyes.

"Nina," he whispered. "Sorry to interrupt your studying. You need to come with me. Bring your books."

What was going on? Nina looked around. The attention of

all her classmates was pinned on her. She focused on Emma, who shrugged with one shoulder. When she followed Mr. Rubins into the hallway, Mr. and Mrs. Wright both stood waiting, their faces grim.

Oh no. "What's happened?" Nina's heart pounded, and her hands began to shake. Something had happened to Geoffrey or Hazel, maybe both. What else would bring them both to town to pull her out of class in the middle of the day?

Mr. Rubins mumbled something that sounded like, "I'm so sorry," and returned to the classroom.

Nina searched the faces of her foster parents.

"We've received a telegram," Mrs. Wright said.

A telegram? Nina noticed the folded paper in Mrs. Wright's hand. Her mouth went dry, and she couldn't form any words. Not her siblings, then. Could something have happened to David? No. The Wrights knew David and Nina were growing closer through their letter-writing, but if something had happened to him, it would be Emma being pulled from class, not Nina.

Mr. Wright placed a hand gently on Nina's elbow and guided her toward the door. "Let's go to the truck."

Numbness fell over Nina as she paused at the coat hooks to put on her parka and boots. Once she was seated in the truck between Mr. and Mrs. Wright, she finally found her voice, weak though it was. "Please tell me."

"It's terrible news, Nina. I'm so sorry." Mrs. Wright looked at the telegram in her hands. "It's from CORB. Do you remember the news from the other day—the bombing in London?"

Nina nodded. They'd heard it on the radio first. The next day, the front page of the newspaper Mr. Wright brought home from town was filled with horrid photographs showing the destruction. Nina had shuddered, thankful the Germans were staying away from Middlesbrough.

"It seems your parents were in London," Mr. Wright said. "For Sully's surgery, we presume."

Sully's surgery. Nina had not connected the date.

Mrs. Wright blinked several times. "Your parents were

caught in the bombing."

Nina held her breath while she let this sink in. "Are they … going to be all right?"

Mr. Wright cleared his throat. "I'm so sorry, Nina. They didn't make it."

No. It was the only thought that would register. It couldn't be true. "It must be a mistake."

Mrs. Wright handed Nina the telegram and wrapped an arm around her shoulders.

Nina stared at the telegram. Plain as oatmeal and cold as ice. It was sent from Mr. Cress at CORB to Mr. Wright.

REGRET TO INFORM YOU EUGENE GABRIEL AND MARGARET GABRIEL OF MIDDLESBROUGH ENGLAND KILLED IN LONDON SHELLING 22 JANUARY 1944. PLEASE CONTACT US BY TELEPHONE ASAP TO DISCUSS NEEDS OF GABRIEL CHILDREN.

At the bottom was a telephone number for Mr. Cress in Winnipeg.

"Have … you called him?" Nina managed to ask.

Mr. Wright shook his head. "No. We wanted to tell you first. We can pick up Geoffrey and Hazel on the way home … take the evening to think of all the questions we need to ask. Then we can try to call tomorrow. Does that sound all right to you?"

Nina nodded, still numb from the news. She needed more details—where had Mum and Dad been? The newspaper report said the attack came at night. Was the house they slept in shelled? Did they suffer long or die instantly? When she tried to picture their faces, all she could drum up was the photo they'd sent of themselves with Sully when he was about six months old. She let out a gasp. "Sully! It doesn't mention anything about him. Is he all right? How do we find out?"

Mrs. Wright patted Nina's knee. "We must assume he's all right—he would have been in the hospital, recovering. We'll try to find out as much as possible when we call tomorrow. Maybe they'll have more information by then. For now, let's get you home. This is a horrible shock."

No one said a word until they pulled into the yard of the one-room school.

"Class will be let out for recess in a few minutes," Mr. Wright said. "No point disrupting everything. We can wait here."

As soon as the first student emerged from the building, Mr. Wright went inside to speak with the teacher.

When she spotted Hazel, with Geoffrey not far behind, Mrs. Wright stepped out and called them over. "You'll be going home a little early today."

With puzzlement on their faces, Geoffrey and Hazel piled in. Hazel sat on Nina's lap, clearly dying to ask questions but receiving the message from Nina's face that now was not the time. Mr. Wright emerged from the school building carrying the children's lunch boxes. Not until he started up the truck and headed down the road did Hazel speak.

"Has something awful happened?"

Nina pushed a stray hair from Hazel's face and tucked it under her knitted hat. "Yes. I'll tell you when we get home."

At the farmyard, Mr. Wright dropped them off and carried on to the Cains' where they'd left Daniel. Hazel and Geoffrey hurried into the house.

Mrs. Wright placed a hand on Nina's arm. "Are you sure you want to be the one to tell them, Nina?"

Nina nodded. "Yes. May I have the telegram, please?"

Inside, Mrs. Wright asked the children to gather in the living room while she put the kettle on for tea.

Geoffrey sat stiffly on the couch. "This is about Mummy and Daddy, isn't it?"

Nina sank down beside him and pulled Hazel toward her, holding to her hand. "Yes. It is. You're very astute, little brother."

"Just tell us."

Nina did her best to relay the same news she'd heard only thirty minutes earlier as gently as she knew how. She showed them the telegram, and Geoffrey read it aloud.

"What's going to happen to us?" Hazel's voice was barely above a whisper.

Nina held her close. "I don't know for sure, Hazie, but try not to worry. You'll be looked after."

"We need to get home." Geoffrey sucked in a deep breath. "Don't we need to get home?"

Nina shook her head. "We can't go home. Even if we could, there's nothing we could do."

"We could find Sully."

Nina had no idea how to answer him. What was going to happen to the little brother she'd never met? Who would bury her parents, and where? Would there be a funeral?

Mrs. Wright served them tea. Nina sensed that she too was laden with questions but kept them inside for now. Jim came home from school with his regular ride, and Nina could hear his mother quietly explaining things to him in the kitchen. At supper, no one felt much like eating.

"Jim and I can take care of all the chores tonight." Mr. Wright patted Geoffrey's shoulder.

"Please don't." Geoffrey stood. "I'd rather keep busy if that's all right."

Mr. Wright nodded. "Very well. What about you, Hazel?"

"You can do my chores."

Mr. Wright allowed himself a grin as he rose and moved to the back door to grab his chore jacket. "You've got it."

"You can help me with dishes, Hazie," Nina started gathering soup bowls.

"I can do that." Mrs. Wright brushed breadcrumbs from Daniel's lap and helped him down from his chair. "Why don't you girls go rest a bit?"

"I think we should keep busy too," Nina said over her shoulder.

That night, Nina and Hazel lay awake long after they'd gone to bed.

"Is it bad that I'm not really, really sad?" Hazel asked.

"No. But it's all right if you *are* too. It's okay to cry."

"It's just — I don't really remember them. I'm sad for Sully, but I don't even know him either. I think I would be sadder if Mum or Dad Wright died."

Nina swallowed back the lump in her throat. Her eyes remained dry. An old lullaby came to mind that Mum had sung to all her children, and she began to hum it now in hopes that it would trigger a pleasant memory for Hazel. "Hush-a-bye, don't you cry … go to sleep, little baby …" Gradually, the lyrics came back and she sang softly, stroking Hazel's hair until her breathing became slow and even.

Slowly, she slipped out of the bed and tiptoed to the doorway of the boys' room to check on Geoffrey. Satisfied that he was asleep, she crept down to the kitchen for a drink of water. Instead of returning to bed, she went to the living room and sat on the couch with her knees drawn up to her chin beneath her nightgown and her arms wrapped around her legs. Her eyes adjusted to the darkness, and she focused on the nearly full moon visible through the window. She might never sleep again, not until there was a plan in place for Sully.

The creaking of footsteps on the stairs turned her attention to the bottom of the staircase where Mrs. Wright emerged in her flannel nightgown, a blanket around her shoulders. She rounded the corner. "I heard you come down but not go back up. Can't sleep?"

Nina shook her head.

Mrs. Wright tucked the blanket around Nina. "I'll warm some milk for us both."

Soon, the two of them sat side by side with their warmed milk. Neither spoke, but Nina felt comforted by the presence of another mother figure.

"I want to tell you something," Mrs. Wright said. "Before I lose my nerve."

Nina turned her head but remained quiet.

"You know that I was born in England, right?"

"Yes." Nina had known that, but whenever Nina had asked for more details, Mrs. Wright had been evasive.

"Did you ever wonder why I don't have any family members around here?"

Nina nodded. "It's crossed my mind."

Mrs. Wright took a deep breath and let it out through her lips. "Have you heard of the Home Children?"

"Home Children?" Nina narrowed her eyes, trying to think where she'd heard the term. "I … think so. Isn't that kind of what we are?"

Mrs. Wright shook her head. "Big difference, really. The Guest Children, like you, were all sent here for your safety, by your parents' arrangements and with the intention of returning."

Nina nodded.

"The Home Children … well, that's another story. They are boys and girls from the United Kingdom sent to British dominions for a better life. Some were orphans, but most had at least one parent. One parent with financial troubles. No work. Often these parents couldn't afford to feed them and believed they had no choice but to put their children into the care of an orphanage. Some kids were sent away without their parents' knowledge. Many of them came from the streets."

Nina stared. Had Mrs. Wright been one of these children?

"The plan was to have younger children adopted by Canadian families and to have older children provided with shelter and food in exchange for farm help until they were eighteen years old. Some were treated as part of the family, but some … well, they became indentured servants. Slaves, really." She paused, pressing her lips together. "Remember how welcomed you felt as you traveled across Canada, like celebrities?"

"Like royalty, almost."

She nodded. "It wasn't that way for these kids. They were considered gutter snipes. Dirty and diseased, not fit to share your table. Thieves, and worse." Now Mrs. Wright stared beyond the ceiling as though Nina was no longer present. "Being a Home Child was not something to be proud of. Just the opposite. You tried to hide the fact if you possibly could."

Why was Mrs. Wright telling her this? She was making it sound so impersonal. Nina wondered if she was even going to continue, and when she finally did, it was as though she was starting over.

"I was born in Liverpool in 1898. I had one big brother and two younger ones. When I was four years old, our father died. I don't really remember him. I barely remember my mother—lying on a couch, sick … or… possibly drunk, I don't know. It seems we all lived in one room. One day a woman came and took my older brother, Edward, and me to an orphanage. When I was six, we boarded a ship to Canada. I was seasick the entire trip. That's all I remember of it."

"You were only six?" Nina swallowed. "What happened next?"

"My brother and I were separated. They took me to a farm twenty miles north of here. I was one of the lucky ones—anyone who wanted a six-year-old girl wasn't looking for a strong laborer. My people hadn't been able to have children of their own and truly wanted me. At first, anyway. School was another matter. There were other home kids, and we were all treated as gutter rats—even the ones who excelled in school."

"Did you?" Nina asked softly. "Excel?"

Mrs. Wright shrugged. "I held my own."

"Was your family kind?"

"At first. Then God blessed them with four children of their own, in four years. I became the babysitter. When the mum took sick, I … well, I pretty much did it all."

She stopped abruptly, and Nina got the feeling there was more she wasn't saying.

"After she died, I … well, I was fifteen by then. Things got worse for me and I left."

"You ran away?"

Mrs. Wright nodded. "I got a job with a family down the road from here. That's how I met Harold. I was still sixteen when I married him."

"Did you ever see the other family again?"

"No. Never wanted to."

"Did you ever find your brother?"

Mrs. Wright pressed her lips together tightly. "He found me. Eventually. He'd been less lucky than I was—at least I was able to sleep in a real bed, go to school, and have enough to eat. His master made him sleep in the barn and work from morning until night, every day—or be beaten. We were all supposed to be sent to school, but Edward was not. Nobody ever came to check on him. When he turned eighteen and was finally free to leave, he tried to collect the money that was supposed to have been held in trust for him, but there wasn't any. After he tracked me down, he rode the rails until the Great War broke out. Then he joined up." She took another deep breath and let it out. "He's buried in France."

Nina felt compassion rise inside. "I'm so sorry. What about your other brothers, did you ever contact them?"

She shook her head. "I don't even remember their names." She took a deep breath. "Almost no one knows all this about me, Nina. I've not even told Harold all of it. It was such a shameful thing. No one talks about it, even though it's still going on. England decided it was a great way to rid their overcrowded cities of unwanted children and populate their colonies—two birds with one stone, I suppose. Maybe it wasn't a bad plan, I don't know. I can't possibly know what my life would be like if I'd stayed in Britain. I'm telling you this because … well … I want you to understand that I am completely sincere when I tell you that I will do everything in my power to help you find Sully and make sure he's safe. All right?"

Nina nodded, her head still spinning with questions.

"We can talk more tomorrow. You really need to get some rest. I just want you to know you're not alone. Do you understand?"

"Thank you," Nina whispered. For the first time since she received the tragic news, a tear released itself from one eye and found its way down her cheek.

Nina to David

January 1944
Dear David,

Reports of accelerated fighting fill our hearts with dread for your safety, but also with hope that things are finally coming to a conclusion. You are in my prayers constantly.

I don't suppose there is any way you could know this, but we've received word that both my parents were killed in the shelling in London last week. We are still in shock, I think. Geoffrey is being stoical. Hazel is clinging to Mrs. Wright more than usual. She claims she hardly remembers Mum and Dad, even though she was seven when we left. That's not so young, is it? I worry she's deliberately forgetting them to lessen the pain.

I am sick with worry for our little brother. All I know is that he was scheduled for ear surgery at the Hospital for Sick Children on Great Ormond Street in London on January 21. Mum and Dad died on January 22. CORB was able to obtain confirmation that the operation did take place and that Sully was still registered as a patient on the twenty-fourth. Through them, I was able to relay contact information for my grandmother in Middlesbrough. But David—here's the thing. My grandmother is not a good person. The thought of her caring for Sully sickens me, but we really have no other family left. Mum's only brother has been missing in action for three years. Dad has a sister somewhere, but they were estranged, and I've never even met her.

I know I shouldn't be placing this worry on you on top of everything else, but please—if you have an opportunity to find out what's happened, could you please? I can't get the image out of my head of a poor little tot left in a strange hospital and not having his mummy and daddy come back for him as they promised. I have no idea if the operation was a success. If he can suddenly hear well, it might all be more disorienting for him than if he can't. I'm beside myself wishing there was something I could do.

I realize there must be an untold number of war orphans there by now, and I should be grateful we are safe and provided for here. If I could, I would go find Sully myself and bring him here to be with us. If it's of any help, his full name is Sullivan George Gabriel, born on January 18, 1941. My grandmother is Elizabeth Gabriel. Our house is at 47 Abbey Court in Middlesbrough. I don't know what else to tell you.

Nina

Chapter Twenty-Four

David to Nina

April 1944
Dear Nina,

I received your letter last week and finally have a moment to write. By the time I got it, I'd received one from Mum and another from Emma, so I already knew about your parents. Nina, I can't tell you how sorry I am. I want you to know I've been praying for you, Geoffrey, Hazel, and little Sully. I trust by now you've received more information about his welfare. I may be in a position to do some investigating in a few weeks—that's all I can say right now. Please know that I will do everything I possibly can to help.

Emma tells me things are gearing up for your graduation, and I hope you've been able to focus on school and maybe even have some fun despite everything. My sister confided that she's grown to love you so dearly that part of her dreads graduation. Do you have any plans for afterward? Can you stay with the Wrights until the war is over? I bet you never dreamed you'd be finishing high school in Canada, eh? I'm thankful you're safe, and I'm thankful my sister has found such a dear friend in you. You have my deepest sympathy in your loss but glad you are in a good home. I've seen so many wounded people everywhere— and I don't just mean physically—it's easy after a while to think that what I see is normal. To forget that back home in Canada, people can still sleep in relative peace. Let's pray we can keep it that way.

I'll take this opportunity to wish you a Happy Graduation in case I can't get another letter to you in time. I know your parents would be beaming with pride. Perhaps they can see from Heaven.

With sympathy,
David

With the assistance of CORB, Nina learned that Sully had been discharged from the London hospital into the care of a Red Cross volunteer who would deliver him to his grandmother in Middlesbrough. Nina wrote repeatedly to Grandmama Gabriel for confirmation, asking a thousand questions. Was Sully's surgery a success? Did the community hold a funeral? What had become of Mum and Dad's belongings? Was Grandmama able to stay on in the house?

She received nothing in return.

The weeks wore on. Mr. and Mrs. Wright encouraged Nina with "no news is good news," and advised her to throw herself into school as much as she could, both her studies and other activities.

"I'm sure they're right," she told Emma. "All I can do is keep writing letters and wait. I may as well get the best marks I can."

"Well, don't study too hard," Emma quipped. "You'll make me look bad."

Emma had written faithfully to Larry Nickels. A spark had begun before Larry ever enlisted, and now their letters back and forth were laced with promise. As a result, Emma spent more time daydreaming than studying. She even brought home a *Chatelaine* magazine with a bride and groom on the cover—she in white silk, he in military uniform—and pored over every page. While she sympathized with Nina's loss, joy bubbled over in everything Emma said and did.

"It feels wrong that our lives haven't changed," Nina confided to Mrs. Wright over dishes one evening. "Other than no longer receiving letters from our parents, everything is the same. Yet it's not."

Mrs. Wright nodded thoughtfully. "That's not necessarily a bad thing. Your lives were so disrupted when you first came. Better to keep things as consistent as possible, especially for Geoffrey and Hazel. It will go easier for them."

"I suppose." Nina sorted forks and knives into the drawer as she dried them. "I'm just not sure what I should be doing. Everything feels up in the air."

"I know. Just keep doing your best with whatever is right in front of you each moment. Right now, that's school."

A week before graduation, Nina sat at the kitchen table studying for her final history exam after all the other kids had gone to bed.

"Why don't you take a little break?" Mr. Wright pulled his wife's sweater from a hook and held it out to Nina. "Join us on the porch?"

Surprised, Nina pushed her book forward but didn't close it. "Sure." She pulled the sweater on, squeezing her eyes closed a few times. "My eyes could use a rest."

Mrs. Wright waited on the porch swing and patted the seat beside her. "Join me, Nina."

Nervous there might be more bad news, Nina slid wordlessly onto the swing. Mr. Wright flipped an old wooden chair around and sat on it backward. "We thought it might be time to have a little chat about your future," he began. "Have you given much thought to what you want to do after graduation?"

Nina looked at them both. Where to begin? "I have."

"Tell us what you're thinking," Mrs. Wright coaxed.

"Well … I guess … ultimately, I need to go home. Find Sully. But … since we have to wait out the war, I just—I …" For the first time since learning of her parents' deaths, tears began to fall in earnest. "Will our return fare even be covered if Mum and Dad aren't there anymore?"

"Oh, honey. That's what's worrying you?" Mrs. Wright stroked Nina's back.

"Not only that. It's everything. Even if I could sail home the day after grad, I couldn't leave Geoffrey and Hazel behind. I can't leave them behind, but I've got a brother over there who needs me … who doesn't even know me! I … it's all too much." She shrugged and brushed the tears away on the sleeve of Mrs. Wright's sweater before realizing what she'd done. "Sorry."

"You have every right to cry." Mrs. Wright looked at her husband and raised her eyebrows.

He picked up the conversation. "Nina, we've been talking. We have an idea we'd like to run past you." He cleared his throat. "You and your siblings have become like our own children to us. You're old enough to be on your own, graduating soon. We spoke with Mr. Cress, and he said this is an unprecedented situation, but he thinks you would or could eventually be named your siblings' legal guardian—if you wanted that. But we were wondering if … well, what would you think if we were to pursue the possibility of adopting Geoffrey and Hazel? I mean, if you have no family members or anything …." His voice trailed off.

Nina stared, not certain she'd understood. "Adopt them?"

"Only if they—and *you*—agree." Mrs. Wright added. "We haven't talked to anyone else about this yet. We wanted to hear your thoughts before we even looked into it."

Mr. Wright folded his fingers together on the back of the chair. "They could keep their own last name if they want. They could still be Gabriels."

Nina's thoughts spun. "You would want to do that?"

"Shucks, we'd adopt you too, Nina, if you were younger."

Mrs. Wright leaned in. "He's right. With you finishing school soon, you'll want to make your own plans. We think it would be the least disruptive thing for Geoffrey and Hazel if they stayed and became officially ours. They already feel like ours. You too."

Nina looked from one to the other. "What about your own kids?"

Mr. Wright shook his head. "Jim loves you three. And Daniel has no memory of you ever *not* being in our family. He'd be devastated if you all suddenly left."

Nina knew both those things were true, but it wasn't quite what she'd meant.

"What about … Carol?"

Mrs. Wright stared at her hands. Her husband waited a moment. Then he cleared his throat again. "Carol is responsible for Carol. You're not. Neither are we now that she's grown."

"I think she'll come around." Mrs. Wright said the words, but the tone was less than convincing.

"You don't have to say anything now, Nina." Mr. Wright leaned forward. "Think about it. If you can find a way to raise the idea with Geoffrey and Hazel … you know, feel them out … do that. As we said, we don't even know if it would be possible. If you think we should go ahead and pursue it, we'd love to do that. Take your time."

"Whatever you decide … and however this goes," Mrs. Wright added, "we will always consider you and Hazel and Geoffrey part of our family. You have a home here as long as you want."

Nina looked out toward the garden she'd help plant a month earlier. The moonlight revealed silhouettes of tiny lettuce leaves and beet tops swaying in the gentle evening breeze. This home had become a haven, a place of provision and support—except for Carol. Mr. and Mrs. Wright could not possibly understand how much their daughter despised Nina and her siblings. Carol's words from months before played like a skipping record in Nina's brain. *How much do you have to hate your kids to send them to the other side of the world with Nazi U-boats infesting the ocean?*

The ocean. Even if Nina could find a way to cross it now, two thousand miles of land separated her from its nearest shore. The Wrights had said nothing about adopting Sully, and how could Nina dare ask them to when they were already being so generous and kind? If only Grandmama Gabriel would respond!

"I'll think about it," she murmured. She returned to her books at the kitchen table but with every word her eyes skimmed, her heart and mind were on other things. Though their intent was only for good, her foster parents had just complicated the situation even more in Nina's mind.

The history exam behind them, Nina and Emma left the classroom and headed outdoors to find a shady spot to eat their lunch.

"That wasn't so bad. How do you think you did?" Emma plopped down beneath the only tree in the schoolyard.

"I don't know." Nina sighed as she sank to the ground. "I think I passed, but it won't be an A. I've been too distracted to study. You?"

Emma shrugged. "I did okay, I think." Her smile lit up her face.

"What?" Nina dug a sandwich out of her bag. "You look like the cat that stole the canary."

"I was going to wait until we'd finished our last final, but I can't. It's too exciting." She pulled a letter from her skirt pocket.

"Okay. I'll bite. Is that from Larry?"

"No. It's from Irene."

"Oh, good. Let's hear it." Nina took a big bite out of her sandwich.

"Guess what? She submitted our applications to her company, and we can start in two weeks."

Nina almost spit the food out of her mouth. "What? What applications? What company? I don't remember filling out any applications!"

"You didn't. But we talked about it, remember?"

"About going to work in Winnipeg? Sure, but that was ... I

don't know … pie in the sky."

"I applied for us both."

Nina squinted at her friend. Was she serious? "You can't do that—can you?"

"Well, you had so much going on, what with your parents and everything. And grad was approaching. I decided to go ahead. I knew how to answer all the questions they asked—your name and age and sewing experience and all that. They even know you're a Guest Child."

Once again, Nina had the sinking feeling her life was being planned for her. Still, the enthusiasm in her friend's eyes, and the notion of living in the city did raise her heart rate a little. "But—"

"Irene says we can live with her and her aunt. It'll be squishy but splitting the rent four ways will make it easy. We'll have a ball, Nina! Just think. We'll get real paychecks! On our days off we can shop, go see movies. We can even—"

"Let me see that." Nina snatched the letter out of Emma's hand and skimmed it. Sure enough, Irene's words confirmed everything. "Two weeks!"

"Why would we need more than that? Graduation is on Friday. All we have to do is pack our bags and buy a train ticket."

Nina shook her head. "I have a lot more to do than that. I don't know if the Wrights will be okay with this. How can I leave Geoffrey and Hazel? Especially now?"

"Don't you see, silly?" Emma took the letter back and tucked it into her pocket. "This is perfect. You told me yourself the Wrights have already offered to adopt those two. I mean, sooner or later, the idea is that you won't be around, right? You'll be off living your own life. This way, you can consider it a trial run. No long-term commitment. See how it goes."

Nina considered her friend's words. "That does sort of make sense."

"Of course, it does. Maybe by fall, the war will be over."

Nina bit her lip. What would the end of the war even mean for her now?

"Plus, it might be easier to look for Sully if you're in

Winnipeg, with the CORB office and government officials there."

Nina stared at Emma. "Well, how can I say no now?"

"Why would you want to? Please say yes. I don't want to do this without you, Nina."

That night, Nina pulled both her siblings onto the bed she and Hazel shared. "I need to talk to you two about something. A couple of things, really."

Hazel's big eyes threatened to melt her heart. "It's not more bad news, is it?"

"No." Nina took Hazel's hand into her own. "You know that I'm graduating soon, right?"

They both nodded.

"Well, I have an opportunity to go to Winnipeg with Emma and work in a garment factory."

"Sewing?" Geoffrey raised his eyebrows.

"Yes. We can stay with Irene and her Aunt Sadie. Emma really wants me to come, but I won't if you two don't like the idea."

Hazel's bottom lip began to quiver. "Forever?"

"No, certainly not! For the summer. Or until the war ends, whichever happens first."

"Then what would happen in the fall?" Geoffrey asked.

"Well, then we evaluate. If it's working out for everyone, I could probably stay on. But if not—I could come back."

Geoffrey shrugged. "I don't see why not. You need to do something after grad, right?"

Nina almost felt hurt. "You wouldn't miss me? Even a little?"

"One less person bossing me around."

Nina shoved him off the bed with a laugh.

He landed on the floor on his rump. "See? Like that."

"How about you, Hazie?"

Hazel frowned. "Would you come home for visits?"

"Oh, sure. We'd come home for a weekend now and then. Who knows, maybe you could even come visit me."

At this, Hazel's face lit up. "Really?"

"Well, not by yourself. But maybe with a grownup."

Geoffrey picked himself off the floor and wandered to the girls' dresser. He fingered the items on top of it thoughtfully. "If fall comes and the war's still on and you decide to stay in the city … you know I start high school next year, right?"

"Right."

"You wouldn't be around. I don't know if I like that so much."

"Jesse will be going with you."

Geoffrey nodded. "Yes. I mean … eventually … what's going to happen, Nina? Would we come live with you? Get jobs too?"

"That's a long, long way off, little brother. But I'm glad you asked because it leads to the other thing I wanted to talk to you about." She took a deep breath and let it out. "Mr. and Mrs. Wright love you two very much. You know that, right?"

Hazel nodded. "They love you too."

"Yes. But I'm old enough to be on my own soon. What would you think of the idea of them adopting you?"

Nina to the Red Cross

June 1944

To Whom It May Concern.

My name is Nina Gabriel. I am eighteen years old, and I'm from Middlesbrough, North Yorkshire. My two younger siblings and I came to Canada in 1940 under the CORB program. Our parents were killed in the London bombing last January, and I am trying to locate our little brother, Sullivan George Gabriel, age three. I know only that he was accompanied back to Middlesbrough by one of your Red Cross volunteers from the Hospital for Sick Children on Great Ormond Street in London. He was left in the care of my grandmother, Elizabeth Gabriel, who moved in with my parents after we left—at 47 Abbey Court. I have written repeatedly to my grandmother but have heard no reply. I have reason to believe she is not stable, and I am deeply concerned about the welfare of my brother. Can you please help me or direct me to someone who can? I would be deeply grateful.

Most sincerely,

Nina Gabriel
PO Box 26
Cedar Bluff, Manitoba
Canada

Chapter Twenty-Five

Nina to David

July 1944
Winnipeg
Dearest David,

I hope this letter finds you well and safe. I have so much to tell you, I don't know where to begin!

Graduation was great, but you've probably heard all about it by now from Emma. I confess my emotions were up and down all day. I had to keep reminding myself that Mum and Dad wouldn't have been able to attend even if they hadn't died. *Died.* I can still hardly believe it's true. Anyway, Mr. and Mrs. Wright beamed as though I were their own, which warmed my heart immensely. They gave me a two-piece set of luggage which is fantastic because the old case I came with was pretty much falling apart by the time we arrived. Plus, they knew I was going to need it, because…

As you probably also know from Emma, we're now residents of Winnipeg! We came by train just a week after grad. I hadn't seen Union Station since my arrival four years ago. The place hadn't changed (although at the time I was too exhausted to notice much of anything, so I can't be certain). I feel like a completely different person from the fourteen-year-old I was then. Irene and her Aunt Sadie met us at the station, and we're all living together in their apartment. They are gobs of fun. Sadie works for Eaton's and we three girls work at the Keinbaum

Garment Company, but we don't really see one another during the workday. So far, they've got me stitching the same basic seams on the same basic shirts over and over, in assembly-line fashion. As I earn trust and get more skilled, I'll have a little more variety. I don't mind. I'm luckier than Emma—she's sewing on buttons all day long.

Our apartment has two small bedrooms. Emma and I share the one Irene used to occupy, and Irene moved in with Sadie. Our kitchen has a hotplate, icebox, sink, and four cabinets. The little dining table (with two chairs) nearly fills the remaining space. (It will truly be full once we find two more chairs.) Sadie is the organized one and has us on a bathroom schedule for both mornings and evenings, as well as a rotating cooking schedule for dinner. Breakfasts and lunches are "every girl for herself." We take turns shopping and all pitch in the same amount for groceries. The building's basement has a shared laundry room with hot and cold running water, large wash tubs and boards, a wringer, long clotheslines, two ironing boards, and electric irons. Quite handy, really, as long as you don't miss your scheduled time. If that happens, you'll find everything in use by others.

We don't spend much time in our apartment. Work keeps us gone from eight until six, Monday through Friday. In this lovely summer weather, we spend evenings exploring our neighborhood parks. Saturdays, we venture farther and do a little window shopping or take in a matinee. The newsreels before the movie always make me pray for your well-being. My memories of the nightly bombings are still vivid, but I no longer startle as easily as I used to. The other girls don't understand any of that, which can make me feel lonely sometimes, but I know you understand.

On Sundays, we attend Irene's church with her. It's the biggest church I've ever attended. Sermons are less interesting than our own pastor's at Cedar Bluff, but the music is magnificent. Sadie is Catholic and goes to her own church. (She is also exotically beautiful and engaged to a soldier.) Sunday afternoon, I usually write a letter to Mr. and Mrs. Wright, whom I am now addressing as "Mom and Dad Wright." Funny how it took moving away to make that leap. Or perhaps it's simply easier to write than to say.

Emma and I are learning the trolley routes and have only gotten mixed up once, resulting in a far longer walk than we wanted. We talk about buying bicycles, but we're told they can't simply be left outside or they "disappear," so we'd need to find space inside—not likely! We are having a lovely time playing "grownup" while your parents (and you too, I suspect) are grateful to know we're under Sadie's watchful eye rather than being completely on our own.

Now here's a piece of news I made Emma promise not to tell. The Wrights want to adopt Geoffrey and Hazel! Can you believe it? After thinking about it for all of ten minutes, G and H were fairly smitten with the idea. Since we are officially British war orphans, CORB is working together with the government on the Wrights' behalf. If there is no one to contest it (and I can't imagine who would), they could be adopted as early as next January—after a year has passed since our parents died. I don't mind telling you there is part of this that is an enormous relief to me. It frees me up to search for Sully. We have still not had confirmation of his whereabouts—or my grandmother's whereabouts, for that matter. I considered joining the Canadian Red Cross Corps with hopes that doing so would get me passage to England. But the training involved would delay everything, and I'd be left with no certainty because I'd have to go where they tell me to go. I think I'm better off working to save for my own passage. I intend to squirrel away as much money as I can (a bit tricky with Emma constantly putting forth ideas for how we could spend our earnings). If I can buy my own passage home, I don't have to wait for CORB and possibly not even for the war to end.

At the same time, the idea of Geoffrey and Hazel being adopted is difficult in ways I'm still trying to sort out. I suppose because it seems so final. It means Mum and Dad are really gone and not waiting for us to come home. As well—and this is embarrassing to admit—I have just a smidgen of jealousy over being excluded even though I realize how silly that would be. Oh, I'm not explaining it very well. Thanks for "listening" anyway.

I must close, as it's nearly dinnertime and my turn to cook. Potato pancakes are on the menu—something I learned from your mother one weekend in your home. She said you love them. I wish you were here to share them with us. You'd love the laughter around our little kitchen—even though you'd have to stand through the meal or fight someone for a seat.

Love,
Nina

"I need a plan." Nina brushed her hair vigorously as she sat on the edge of the bed she shared with Emma. "If I don't make a plan, nothing will ever happen."

Emma crawled into bed on her side. "For finding Sully?"

"For getting back to England."

"So you can find Sully."

"Yes." Nina lay down the brush, turned off the light, and got into bed. "I'm going to Union Station tomorrow after work to ask some questions."

"Want me to come along?"

Nina felt touched by the offer. Unless… "You're not going to try to talk me out of it, are you?"

"Wouldn't dream of it."

"In that case, I'd love for you to come along. Thank you."

Emma rolled onto her side, facing Nina. "Let me ask you something, though. Suppose you can get there, and suppose you find him. Then what? Wouldn't there be a whole lot of red tape to bring him back here? How would you ever have enough money for that?"

"I thought you weren't going to try to talk me out of it."

Emma sighed. "I'm not. I just think you need to think the whole thing through a bit."

"If I do that, I'll never get anywhere. It's too overwhelming. I have to take one step at a time and cross bridges as I come to them. That means a trip to the train station, to start. I appreciate your support." Nina let the sarcasm drip as she flipped over with her back to Emma, and Emma said no more.

After work the next day, the girls caught a different bus than usual and got off at the corner of Main Street and Broadway, right in front of Union Station. Nina scanned the ticket windows and chose the one operated by a woman in a railroad uniform and curly grey hair.

"Can I help you?" Her smile featured a gap between her two front teeth.

"I hope so." Nina pressed herself as close to the ticket window as she could while Emma hovered behind her. "I need to know how much it would cost to get from here to England."

"England?"

Nina nodded. "Yes. Well—from here to Halifax first, of course."

"Oh, I can get you to Halifax—provided you're willing to be bumped in case our troops need the seats. They get first priority."

"Yes, I understand. How much would that cost?"

The woman flipped through a thick book to check the numbers and named the fare.

Emma let out a whistle behind her. Nina did some calculations in her head. She'd have to work and save until Christmas just to get to Halifax.

Not to be deterred, she asked the next question. "And how about from there to England?"

The woman looked at her over the top of wire-rimmed glasses. "How well do you swim?"

"Uh—" Nina stammered.

"Got a rowboat? Because you're not going to be a passenger on a ship to England unless you're military or a Red Cross volunteer. Not 'til this war ends."

Nina never felt so stupid. She should have realized. In school, they'd done a project on how the *Queen Mary* had been retrofitted from a luxury passenger liner to serve as a troop ship dubbed "The Grey Ghost."

"You sound like you came from there. England." The ticket woman said.

Nina nodded. "Yes. Four years ago." She glanced at Emma and saw both relief and compassion in her eyes.

"Well, honey, I'm afraid you're stuck on this side of the pond for a while. I'd be grateful for that if I were you. Still want that ticket to Halifax?"

"Um … no. No, thank you. Not today. Thanks for your time." Nina turned away.

Emma linked arms with her as they left the building. "We could have accomplished that over the telephone."

"Yes, I suppose."

"Are you terribly disappointed?" Emma led the way to a bus stop bench and sat.

"I feel more foolish than anything."

"Well, at least now we know."

Nina loved how Emma used terms like *we*, as though this were her mission as well. "Thanks for coming with me."

The remaining weeks of summer flew by. Nina doubled her letter-writing efforts to her grandmother and made an appointment to visit Mr. Cress at the CORB headquarters.

"Nina! I'm not sure I'd have recognized you if you hadn't called ahead." Mr. Cress indicated a chair for Nina to sit on. "How are you? I was so sorry to hear about your parents. You have my deepest condolence."

"Thank you." Nina sat. Mr. Cress may not have changed as much as Nina, but stress and fatigue showed around his eyes. Since he already knew all about the Wrights' hopes for adoption and the ongoing search for Sully, she got right to the point. "I'm told I can't return to England to find my brother until the war is over."

Mr. Cress sighed and reached for a file folder lying on top of his desk labeled *Gabriel.* "Even if you could, it wouldn't be advisable, Nina." He opened the folder and began sifting through the papers inside. "This says he was delivered safely to your grandmother."

"Who, as I told you, is not stable. It's been seven months, and she hasn't written me even once. Is she dead or alive? She was never a safe person to begin with, Mr. Cress. Now Sully's a war orphan who—"

"One of thousands, Nina. Your government, the Red Cross, churches … many experienced, capable people are doing everything in their power to help these kids and other displaced people. I'm not sure you understand the magnitude of it."

"I'm sure I don't. Does that mean I shouldn't do anything? How can I do nothing?"

Mr. Cress pressed his lips together and let the air slowly out through his nose as his shoulders dropped. "You've done plenty with the letters you've written. I've done all I can, for now, as well. I'm sorry this is so hard, but like thousands of others who are waiting for news of loved ones, we must wait and trust that your brother is in good hands."

"Trust?" Nina shook her head. "My parents trusted me to look out for my siblings when they sent us over here, and now—"

"And you've done an admirable job. You should be proud. Look how the Wrights have come to love you all—"

"—my parents are dead. They had another child, and then they died. I don't know who to trust. They wouldn't want me just doing nothing—" A sob escaped Nina's throat, and she stifled it, embarrassed. Maybe she should have brought Emma along.

Mr. Cress tented his fingers in front of his face, elbows on his desk. "Nina, you've had a lot to process, a lot of responsibility on your young shoulders. It would be only natural for you to feel a certain amount of anger at your parents. Even though it's not their fault that they died, being angry is part of the grieving process. The whole situation with your little brother makes it more complicated. More grievous."

Nina sniffed and dug a handkerchief out of her handbag to wipe her eyes and nose.

"I know your parents would not want you to put yourself in harm's way."

"Not even to find Sully?"

He shook his head. "That would be inconsistent with the difficult decision they made when they sent you and Geoffrey and Hazel here, *out* of harm's way."

Carol's words played yet again in Nina's mind. *How much do you have to hate your kids to send them…?*

"They loved you very much, Nina." He made a note on the inside of the folder. "I'll tell you what. I'll write again to the Red Cross and make a note to keep writing until something develops. May I suggest you write one more letter to someone else?"

"Who?" Nina felt fresh hope rise.

"It might be helpful to write a letter to your parents, even though you can't send it. Express everything you're feeling, and don't worry about holding back. No one needs to see it."

Nina thought of the letter she'd written but never sent after learning of Sully's birth. It had felt like a useless waste of paper.

She rose to leave and tried not to sound sarcastic as she muttered, "Thanks for your help."

A week later, Nina made her way alone to a section of railroad track separated from any streets by a rambling cemetery. She found a flat rock to sit on and waited for a train. When one came thundering along at full speed, she pulled from her pocket the letter she'd written the evening before. With no one to hear a word over the rumble of the train, she read the letter, starting out at normal volume. "Dear Mum and Dad: How dare you? How dare you do this to us? To *me*? How dare you put me in charge of Geoffrey and Hazel? How dare you send us to the other side of the world? How dare you have another child? How dare you die! How dare you leave us with no instructions for what to do next?" She was yelling now.

"How am I supposed to find Sully?

"What am I supposed to do?" Nina hollered out every word at the top of her lungs.

"I'm so angry at you! So angry. Why did you even have us?

"I hate this so much. I hate this, I hate this, I hate this!"

Chapter Twenty-Six

David to Emma

September 2, 1944
Dear Emma,

How's my little sis? Thanks for your latest letter. It doesn't surprise me a bit that you and Larry are "practically engaged," as you say. He had a crush on you when you were only thirteen, and I told him to keep his distance if he knew what was good for him. (That's true, by the way. I did say that. I guess he didn't know what was good for him.) I'll be nicer to him next time we meet— I promise. He's a decent fellow, and I think you two are a good match. However, I also believe it's irresponsible for any of us to be making—or even suggesting—commitments before the war is over.

That's why I have tried to keep my letters to Nina on a "friendship" level, but gosh, it's hard. I don't know how she feels about me, but I find myself thinking of her far more than I ought. Don't tell her any of this—I just need to say it to someone. My pal Brodsky caught me staring at her photograph. He told me I was only fooling myself if I figured Nina was merely a friend. Well … he's not wrong. Except I don't think I'm even fooling myself anymore. As much as I appreciate letters from you and the rest of the family, I can't even describe what happens in my heart when I see one from her. I suppose I need to tell somebody, and confessing my true feelings to her seems unkind right now.

It also feels unkind—downright cruel, even—to tell her

what I discovered today. I decided to tell you so that you can tell her in your gentle way, and Nina doesn't have to read it in a letter. I managed to take the train to Middlesbrough and find the address Nina gave me for her parents' house. Two children were playing in front of it, so I said hello and asked if this was the Gabriel residence. Naturally, I wondered if the boy might be Sully although he looked too old. They stood there with their mouths hanging open, gawking up at me as though they'd never seen a soldier before. Hat in hand, I knocked on the door. A woman answered, and I told her my name and that I was searching for Elizabeth Gabriel and her grandson, Sullivan.

"Oh, maybe they lived here before us," she said. "You'd have to ask the landlord."

The woman told me she'd been there two months, and that her husband was off fighting. She gave me the landlord's name and address. Before I left the neighborhood, I knocked on the doors of the two nearest neighbors. No one was home at the first place. At the second, a couple confirmed that Nina's parents and grandmother had lived there, how sorry they'd been to hear they'd been killed, but they had no idea what became of the grandmother or the little boy. Their accents sounded so much like Nina did when she first came.

I then found my way across town to the landlord's house, although I was running out of time. If I didn't catch the only train back, I'd be in hot water for being late and might never get another pass. The landlord, Mr. Godfrey, was not home but his wife answered the door and was happy to invite me in as soon as she saw the Canadian uniform. When I explained my mission, she shook her head sadly.

"Oh, 'twas an awful thing."

My heart sank. She explained that after Nina's parents died

in January, no one came by with the rent money. Mr. Godfrey wrote a letter the first month and then visited the grandmother the second month. She said the state of the house was deplorable. The little boy appeared neglected while the grandmother had been taking in stray cats. (Don't tell Nina all this!) Mr. Godfrey contacted a child welfare agency—she didn't know the name—and evicted Mrs. Gabriel. She thought the grandmother might have ended up in what she called an "old folks' home" but didn't know about the boy. "There are dozens of orphanages," she said. "He could be at any of 'em or none of 'em." She knew nothing about his deafness or surgery.

To her credit, she did apologize for not being more helpful and promised to gather more information when her husband got home. I raced back to the train station and quite literally jumped aboard as it began moving. (I'm on the train now, on my way back to our base.) I was fortunate enough to find myself next to a man from Middlesbrough and when I asked, he gave me the names of three orphan homes in the area. I will do my best to contact them by telephone first and by letter if I need to.

None of this is the news Nina wanted to hear, but it certainly confirms her assessment about her grandmother. Her fears were not unfounded. Please find a way to tell her I'm making progress in the search—for as frustrating as it was, I realize it is still progress. I just don't know when I'll have another minute to work on this.

In other news, we're dropping bombs on the jerries, and it won't be long now, Sis. Hitler is getting very nervous. I hope you get to see this beautiful part of the world someday when it's not so bleak. It really is something … everything seems so old compared to home.

Your loving brother,
David

As tempting as it was, Nina knew better than to ask Emma if she could read David's letter for herself. Clearly, if her friend wanted her to see it all, she'd offer instead of simply telling her his news. It would be unfair to ask. On the one hand, she loved David even more for the effort he was making on her behalf. On Sully's behalf. But her heart sank at the information Emma shared. While she felt little compassion for her grandmother, tears surfaced if she allowed herself to think about Sully in an institution with strangers. The poor little boy must be so confused. Whether he was still hard of hearing or whether the surgery had been a success and he'd been suddenly thrust into a world with sound but without anything familiar, she didn't know. Either way, she couldn't bear to imagine it.

"A weekend at home will do us a world of good," Emma announced. "We said we'd visit. Now summer is over, and we haven't been home even once."

Nina didn't argue. With no end in sight for the war and their work going well, the girls had made the decision to stay on for another six months. Though she was diligently saving as much money as she could, being able to hug her siblings and enjoy Mrs. Wright's cooking would be well worth the train fare. Hazel's letters had indicated she loved having a bedroom to herself and she'd been allowed to have Nellie Cain sleep over at least twice, but Nina read more between the lines. Hazel missed her.

Sure enough, Hazel bounced on the platform when the train pulled in—despite the rain. Nina and Emma gathered their belongings and stepped down from their car just in time for Hazel to launch herself into Nina's arms and hang on like a monkey—at eleven years of age, far too tall for Nina to carry as she once had.

"Couldn't convince her to stay home and dry." Mr. Wright chuckled as he handed Nina an umbrella and picked up the girls' bags.

"Didn't expect to see you here in the middle of harvest time." Nina hurried toward the truck. "I suppose that's because of the rain?"

"That's exactly right." Mr. Wright placed the bags in the back and threw a piece of canvas over them. "Welcome home, both of you. Your parents would have come themselves, Emma, but I suggested they save their gas and promised to bring you straight home."

"Thanks, Mr. Wright."

As the girls climbed into the truck's cab, its familiar smells of fuel and burlap, once distasteful to Nina, now filled her with a warm sense of home. She kept an arm wrapped around Hazel and listened to all the news about school, new kittens, and Junior Red Cross projects. Images surfaced of her first ride down the gravel road between Cedar Bluff and the Wrights' farmyard in Mr. Cress's car. How strange it had all been. Now, she knew every field, every tree, every dip in the road. She knew who lived in each house they passed, which ones had dogs that would run out to chase their truck, and which had lost boys to the war.

Mr. Wright interrupted her thoughts. "You just missed Carol. She was home for a few days. Did you know she requested a discharge?"

Nina was surprised. "No. Why?"

"She's determined to go overseas and has given up on CWAC getting her there. She's joining the Red Cross Corps instead."

Nina glanced at Emma. "I thought about doing the same."

True to his word, Mr. Wright drove right past his own place to drop off Emma, who disappeared into the waiting arms of her family on the Cains' front porch.

When they pulled into their own yard, Mrs. Wright, Jim, Geoffrey, and four-year-old Daniel waited with big smiles. Even Rosie wagged her tail, although Nina suspected that was more about Hazel's return than her own.

"Hi, Sis!" Geoffrey hugged her first and then quickly pulled away. "Guess what? You were right. High school's great so far.

I didn't need you at all."

"What did I tell you?" Nina swallowed the chagrin she felt at her brother's declaration of independence and turned to accept hugs from the others. For the next hour, she felt like a celebrity as she sat at the kitchen table answering questions while the others bustled around. She presented them with a treasured box of chocolates, which Mrs. Wright declared must be saved for later. An apple pie waited on the sideboard and a full-course meal of roast chicken, garden produce, homemade bread, and jam soon filled the table. Everyone took a seat.

"Let's pray." Mr. Wright reached out to grab the hands of those nearest him and the others followed suit.

Nina swallowed a lump at the familiar gesture and prayer.

"Come, Lord Jesus, be our guest. Let this food to us be blessed. By Your hand, we all are fed. Thank You, Lord, for daily bread." This time, Mr. Wright tacked on some extra expressions of gratitude before he closed. "Thank You for bringing our Nina home to us for a visit. Please bless our time together. Amen."

"Amen." Mrs. Wright echoed. When she smiled at Nina, her eyes glistened.

Nina returned the smile and then looked at her lap. Did Mr. Wright realize he'd called her *"our* Nina?"

Nina and Hazel spent Saturday helping Mom Wright in the kitchen, taking lunch to the men in the field, and canning the last of the tomatoes. Visiting all the while, Nina described what she was learning at the garment factory. "We're making military uniforms now, so at least I feel I'm contributing to the war effort. That, plus saving our tin cans and bones and whatnot."

"What's it like to share a small apartment with three other women?" Mom Wright raised an eyebrow and grinned.

Nina's chin rose a bit at being referred to as a woman. "Oh, we've had some minor disputes, but we have tons of laughs. I do miss the open spaces out here," she admitted. "Which is pretty funny, because when we first came here, I thought I wouldn't be able to bear it. I wanted to go back to the city."

Mom Wright smiled. "You weren't used to it."

Hazel wanted to know what movies were in theaters and what the mannequins in the store windows were modeling. Eventually, Mom Wright sent Hazel out to the pigpen with a bucket of tomato skins.

"Any word about Sully?" Mom Wright asked as soon as Hazel was out the door.

Nina told her what David had discovered.

"Oh, dear."

"I know. He didn't even write me about it—he told Emma first."

The older woman nodded. "That was thoughtful."

"I can't help wondering if he's washed his hands of it."

"Oh, I'm sure that's not true. He no doubt thought it would be easier for you to hear it from Emma. In person." Mom Wright wiped out her big wash tub and hung it on its nail. "Don't you think?"

"I suppose. But I wouldn't blame him if he's weary of it. It's not really his responsibility."

"No. But we all want to help. I've been writing letters myself and will continue to do so. I hope you know that. You're not in this alone, Nina. I know it's awfully hard."

"What's awfully hard?" Hazel came back inside with the empty slop pail, letting the screen door slap behind her.

"Not seeing this silly face every day." Nina cupped her hands on Hazel's cheeks and kissed her forehead. "Come up to the bedroom. Irene gave me a skirt I think we can resize for you."

No more was said about Sully.

On Sunday, when Nina would have normally sat with Emma in church, both girls were content to sit with their own families. Familiar faces welcomed them. They gathered news from other girls about who was dating whom, who had been drafted, and who had shipped out. Afterward, the Wright family went straight to the Cain home for a backyard picnic of sandwiches, raw carrots, pickles, and watermelon. Nina grinned at the activity around her—fathers swatting flies, kids running around, mothers fussing over food. Mr. Cain opened the windows wide and turned up the radio loud so they could have some music. A game of kick-the-can carried on for hours.

"Hush, everyone!" Mr. Cain called out at five o'clock. "The news is on."

When the announcer said that Canadian troops had liberated Abbeville, France, French troops had liberated Lyon, and the British and the Americans had liberated parts of Belgium, everyone cheered.

"Won't be long now!" Dad Wright smiled at Mr. and Mrs. Cain. "Your boy will be home."

"And your girl," Mrs. Cain added.

"You suppose David was part of those liberations?" Emma asked. Nina had wondered the same. Of course, no one knew. *Oh Lord, let him be safe.*

After the news broadcast, Mr. Cain drove Nina and Emma to the train station. This time, Emma's sister Julia rode along. Nina's heart warmed as she watched the sisters hug and say good-bye on the platform. Prior to her move to Winnipeg, she'd witnessed nothing but spats between those two girls. She turned to their father.

"Thank you, Mr. Cain."

"You're welcome, Nina. Hope you'll be home again soon. Christmas, for sure."

"Yes. Good-bye. 'Bye, Julia." Nina stepped onto the train and sank into the nearest seat. She watched as Emma hugged her father and then hustled onto the train herself.

With a sigh, Emma took the seat next to Nina. "What did I tell you? It was good to be home, wasn't it?"

Nina nodded. "It was. You were right. As usual."

"As always." Emma smirked as she laid her head against the seat and closed her eyes.

Nina focused out the window as the train chugged away, leaving Cedar Bluff behind. It had been good to be home.

David to Nina

November 1944
Dear Nina,

Thank you for your last letter and for understanding why I didn't write you in person about what I discovered at your old home. Please don't think for another moment that I've tired of trying to locate Sully. I've not yet been able to return to Middlesbrough, but I've got news good and bad. The landlord's wife, Mrs. Godfrey, wrote to say her husband sold the contents of the house to cover the back rent. I checked into that, and apparently, it's allowed, although if he made more than was due, the balance should have gone to your grandmother or someone. I'm guessing he got whatever he could for it and would argue it still wasn't enough. I'm so sorry. I know there must have been belongings of yours—keepsakes from your childhood and mementos of your parents that you would have liked to keep. It's all horribly unfair.

Mrs. Godfrey didn't provide any suggestions as to where your grandmother might be.

The positive news is, she gave me a list of five orphanages with telephone numbers and addresses. I've already been in contact with two of them. The first is a convent where the nuns take in children until their families can be found. They have no record of Sully or any boy resembling his description, but they did take my name and address (as well as yours) in case anything develops. The second place turned out to be a residential school with no children under six. I will keep trying as time allows.

I also contacted the London hospital where Sully had his

surgery and, with great persuasion, was able to get a telephone number for the house where your parents were staying the night of the bombing. Eventually, this led to an address and the discovery that a doodlebug landed on the house that night. No one survived. I tried to visit the street, but the area was blocked off and impossible to access. From what I have seen, Nina, your parents did not suffer. Given the time of day, it's highly likely they went straight from their sleep to be with Jesus. I'm sorry I haven't taken the time to try to track down where they might have been buried. I'm assuming that Sully is our first priority.

Hopefully, I'll have more for you soon, but I'm off on another mission in the morning and wanted to at least bring you up to date with what I've learned, even if it is merely a process of elimination. Please try not to worry. This country seems to do everything in its power to care for its children. People are, for the most part, good and kind and willing to help one another out in these trying times. Keep praying. I believe God hears. He knows where Sully is, and He's watching over him the same as He's watched over you and Hazel and Geoffrey.

You asked about what I'm doing. Some of it's tough to write about, but it feels good to tell you. The worst was the time we got lost over Germany with our compass stuck due to violent evasive action. Thinking we were coming home, we instead found ourselves dodging flak over Berlin at eighteen thousand feet. There must have been a hundred searchlights aimed at us. I dropped her to two hundred feet and told my gunner to open up. We took out seven searchlights in about thirty seconds. I thought I was going to cut grass before I was able to pull back up and head for the nearest aerodrome in England—our hydraulic system shot to blazes, fifteen minutes of fuel left, and the aircraft looking like a sieve. It was hard to settle down that night, I'll tell you. I kept reliving it every time I closed my eyes. Maybe don't share all that with Emma.

I think it's swell that you're making uniforms, and I love

what you said about how you pray for the soldier that will wear each one as you push the fabric through your machine. I'm hoping for a replacement uniform soon, as mine is wearing out and no longer fits properly—too snug around the shoulders, too loose around the middle, ha ha! When I do get one, I will wonder whether it might have passed through your pretty hands—although I suppose we'll never know. Please take care, work hard, have fun when you can, and try not to worry.

Yours,
David

Chapter Twenty-Seven

Carol to her parents

December 1944
Mum and Dad,

I'm writing to tell you I won't be home for Christmas as I'm heading overseas. We ship out in just two days, and I can't tell you how glad I am to have made this decision. I don't yet know where I'll be or what I'll be doing—could be anything from cooking to driving an ambulance. But at least something exciting is finally happening.

I need to tell you that even if I were not leaving, I would not come home for the holidays because I'm far too angry at you both. Angry and shocked. I'll return after you've come to your senses—once you see how preposterous the idea of adopting those English kids is. I can't believe you made this decision without consulting your real children, but I'm confident you'll realize your error before you sign any papers and it's too late. Until then, I just can't be at home pretending to go along with this idiotic plan—not even for Christmas.

Give my love to Jim and Daniel.

Carol

Nina tossed and turned until Emma's patience wore thin. "Would you settle down? Tomorrow won't get here any faster if you stay awake."

"Sorry," Nina mumbled. She rolled over, determined to lie still even if she couldn't sleep. Tomorrow was January thirty-first. The entire Wright family—minus Carol—was catching the train from Cedar Bluff to Winnipeg. The official signing of final adoption papers for Geoffrey and Hazel would take place at a provincial courthouse.

"I wouldn't miss this occasion for the world," Nina had replied to Mom Wright's letter telling her the date of the ceremony. She'd even managed to book the afternoon off work.

What she hadn't managed was to sort out her feelings about it all. She'd observed from a distance as Mom and Dad Wright had filled out multiple forms, written countless letters, and subjected themselves to interviews and home visits. They'd worked together with CORB, with the National Child Adoption Association in Britain, and both the Children's Aid Society and the Child Welfare Board in Manitoba. Nina herself had been interviewed via telephone. Of course, she'd given a glowing report of the Wrights' home and family life, saying nothing about the coldness of their daughter or the little she knew about the children they'd lost. She was convinced this was the best possible outcome for Geoffrey and Hazel. With their adoption would come Canadian citizenship. If there was still an England to return to after the war, and they chose to do so, it would be their own decision.

So why couldn't she sleep?

What was that trick David had written about? *It works better if I tell myself I don't have to sleep. I simply need to lie here with my eyes closed. My body will rest. My eyes will rest. I don't have to sleep.* He'd written about how he repeated these words to himself on a night before a bombing mission and found it far more conducive to sleep than telling himself "I gotta get to sleep."

Nina tried it now. It must have worked, because the next time she opened her eyes, daylight peered over the snow-covered rooftops of the city outside her window. She and her roommates hurried off to the factory. Work helped the morning speed by, and when the whistle blew for the lunch break at noon, Nina realized she'd succeeded in not dwelling on the adoption. She skipped lunch and took some time to clean up and comb her hair in the washroom before catching the right bus. The law courts on Broadway Avenue stood across from the Manitoba Legislative Building with its statue of the Golden Boy on top. Nina hopped off the bus, nervous that she wouldn't be able to find the right courtroom.

She needn't have worried. Before the front door closed behind her, she heard her name in a high-pitched squeal.

"Nina!" Hazel flew toward her, and the two sisters exchanged a quick hug. "You made it!" Hazel wore a new navy blue dress with a white collar and buttons, no doubt made for the occasion by Mom Wright.

"Wouldn't miss it." Nina looked up to see Geoffrey, Jim, Daniel, and Mom and Dad Wright waiting with smiling faces. "C'mon, little brother. Getting too old for a hug?"

Geoffrey obliged. He looked very grown-up in a white shirt and navy tie.

"Good to see you, Nina." Mom Wright gave Nina a quick hug as well. "It's time for us to go in."

Nina followed the group into a mid-sized room where everyone was invited to sit. Two social workers were already in the room. A judge soon joined them. He looked over the forms and asked a few questions.

"I'm sorry for your loss, children." The judge looked at them with kind eyes. "But how fortunate you are to have a loving family ready to step in. How do you feel about this adoption? Geoffrey?"

"Fine, sir. We've already lived with them for four years, so I don't expect much will change really." Geoffrey sounded so business-like that Nina had to stifle a grin.

The judge glanced down at the forms. "And you, Hazel? Do you agree this adoption is a good idea?"

"Yes, sir." At first, Hazel's response was timid. Then, like an afterthought, her face lit up. "I don't even want to go back to England. I'm glad we get to stay forever and be Canadians."

At this, the judge chuckled. "Well, that's just fine." With no further fanfare, he signed the papers and gave one copy to Mrs. Wright. "I wish you all the best."

The whole thing was over in five minutes.

The little group stepped out into the hallway, where Mom and Dad Wright shook hands with the social workers, thanked them, and said goodbye. Hugs were exchanged all around.

"You're still our sister, though. Right, Nina?" Hazel gripped Nina's hand.

"Of course. I'll always be your sister." A lump formed in her throat, and she tried to swallow it back. Now was not the time for tears, but she avoided eye contact with Mom Wright, knowing there'd most likely be tears in her eyes too.

"Where shall we go for our celebratory lunch?" Dad Wright asked. "We can walk to the Fort Garry from here."

"Oh, Harold, that will be much too expensive!"

"Hey. This is a once-in-a-lifetime event." He gave his wife a fake scowl. "We can afford it."

Fifteen minutes later, the family was seated at a round table in the famous hotel's dining room. While the rest of the family ordered chicken or roast beef, Hazel and Daniel asked for spaghetti. When the food came, Dad Wright got everyone to hold hands and led in prayer just like he always did at home. "Lord, thank You for this special day. Thank You for this wonderful gift to our family and thank You that it's now official. Please watch over Carol. We know she's going to come around and gladly join this circle in due time. Thank You for this food we're about to enjoy. Amen. Dig in, everyone."

"Thank you for adopting us." Hazel pushed her fork into a meatball and popped the entire thing in her mouth.

Mom Wright smiled and ran a hand over Hazel's hair. "You're welcome." She turned to Nina. "And you, my dear, are just as much a part of the family. You know that, right?"

Nina felt the tears well up again, but this time she let them come. She pressed her lips together and nodded, unable to speak.

Nina to David

February 1945
Dear David,

It's official. Geoffrey and Hazel are legally the children of Harold and Ann Wright. Even though I witnessed the event and even though I know it's best for them … part of me feels torn in half. The kids were given their own choice about their names. Initially, both of them thought they wanted to change their names to Wright. Then Geoffrey changed his mind. "I'm the only boy to carry on the Gabriel name," he announced, as though he's forgotten entirely about Sully. And why shouldn't he, I suppose. He's never met him. For all we know, he could be in another home with another last name of his own by now.

Then Hazel decided she should stay a Gabriel too. "I'll change my name when I get married anyway," she told the family around the dinner table. Probably to Cain." (I honestly don't know if she's once again carrying a torch for you, or if she's moved on to one of your brothers.) "No point changing it twice."

Mom and Dad Wright laughed and commended her practicality. I think they're fine with it, and deep down, I felt relieved. They need to hang onto something from their roots, don't you think?

So, I suppose if it weren't for the issue of Sully, I could feel I've fulfilled my responsibility as promised to my parents. It is good to know I don't have to worry about G and H, that I'm free to pursue finding and rescuing Sully. I'm so grateful to have your support in this, David. I hope you know that. I feel so helpless here but knowing you're doing all you can brings me great comfort and hope. You are under no obligation to even care, let alone devote your free time to this. I do appreciate it so very much.

Work is going well. I have only one "station" left to learn—zippers—before I can be placed in the regular two-week rotation. This keeps the work from becoming completely humdrum and keeps us sharper, they say. It also means we can serve as "floaters," filling in anywhere that's needed if workers are sick or away. I can't say I enjoy any one task above the others, but there are certainly gals who are more fun to work near. Of course, we're not supposed to socialize while we work—and the noise level makes that nearly impossible anyway—but still. I'm sure you know what I mean. Some people you're simply drawn to more than others. I hope you're making some good friends.

I've been thinking a lot about something you wrote—about how God is the best counselor in the world, giving us the Holy Ghost for just such. I looked it up in John fifteen like you suggested. I like how you said telling God our concerns and troubles—no matter how big or small—can be exactly like sitting with a wise and loving counselor. How we can tell Him anything we're thinking and feeling, and how we can listen for His wisdom. I'm trying to learn how to do that—especially as it concerns Sully and what I'm supposed to be doing about him. You're right—it's enormously helpful! Though I still have a long way to go in the listening department, the Bible is filled with wonderful words of wisdom, and I'm learning to "lay this at His feet" as you say. It's given me a lot more peace in my heart and strength to keep going.

I'm praying for you too. Every day. You are never really out of my thoughts, David. My one big fear now is that, as much as

I want this war to end soon, CORB might ship me back to England before you're sent home, and I'll never see you again. I have no idea what will happen, but until I turn twenty-one or can arrange private passage, I fear I'm at their mercy. Even in that, however, God is teaching me to trust Him for His best.

Please take care.
Lovingly,
Nina

Hazel to Buckingham Palace

February 1945
Dear Your Majesties,

I'm writing to ask you to kindly disregard my previous letter in which I asked whether you might consider adopting my brother Geoffrey and me. I hope you and the princesses will not be too disappointed, but guess what? We have already been adopted! Mum and Dad Wright are now our real, forever parents, and we will stay here in Canada with them. We even signed some papers with a judge and everything, and then we had spaghetti in a fancy restaurant! Perhaps you can visit us one day after the war is over. I'm sure Princess Elizabeth and Princess Margaret would like to meet the brother and sister they almost had. I can show them around our farm. We have cows, chickens, pigs, cats, a dog, and sometimes turkeys and geese.

Now that we are no longer available, maybe you can adopt some other orphans, as there are a very great many. Which is really sad, but I am one of the lucky ones. I am not an orphan anymore.

Yours sincerely,
Hazel Gabriel

Chapter Twenty-Eight

Carol to her parents

April 1945
Dear Mum and Dad,

I'm sorry it's been so long since I've written and will try to catch you up on my life here.

I spend my days driving and have become so used to driving on the left side of the road that it will be harder to adjust when I return home than it was when I started here, I think. Although I've hauled people around more than once (a carload of pregnant war brides one day!), most of what I deliver is supplies to hospitals. It's quite safe. Troops are everywhere, and motorcycle dispatch riders ride alongside every convoy and lead us past long lines of vehicles when they see the Red Cross insignia. We've all been granted the rank of "lieutenant," and I was issued a laissez-passer which reads, "This is to certify that Lieutenant Wright is a driver for the Canadian Red Cross Society. Her work involves the conveyance of supplies and personnel to Canadian Military Hospitals, some of which are in the restricted area. She always returns the same day. It is requested that she be allowed to carry out these services."

I've also been privileged to see some lovely scenery when we venture into the countryside—although getting around can be tricky. Earlier on, they removed all the road signs and name places to confuse the enemy in case of invasion. But since the names of the pubs haven't changed, receiving directions sounds like one big pub crawl. "Take a left at the Rose and Crown. Then go straight on until you see the White Hart." I also got to drive through the gates at Buckingham Palace once, although I don't know whether the King and Queen were there. The flag was not up, but I don't imagine they announce the King's presence during wartime. I also delivered a package to Number Ten Downing.

Your weekly letters have been arriving like clockwork, which is pretty amazing when you see what life is like here. I truly had no idea. I think I mentioned in an earlier letter how my first impressions shocked me—bombed-out buildings with ragged flaps of blackout curtains still fluttering from what used to be windows. Barrage balloons adding spooky shadows to an already grey landscape. There was something else I couldn't quite put my finger on, but now I realize it's the people. They all look so worn out. I don't know how else to describe it. Tired and downtrodden. Shabby clothes and shoes. Undernourished. I am beginning to understand what five years of war does to people, with the nightly blackouts and air raid sirens. Sleeping in the bunkers with strangers, never knowing what you'll see when you come out. The stress of having to constantly be on guard, wondering whether the next bomb might drop on your car, your home, your head.

Just last week a little house was destroyed that belonged to some friends who had hosted us for a happy gathering only days before. I walked past today to see, and it was as though a massive knife had sliced right through it like you might cut the corner off a cake. Like a giant dollhouse, but with dust still rising from the rubble.

All that to say, my perspective has changed. I've had a change of heart and want to apologize for my attitude. What you're doing by adopting the Gabriel kids is a beautiful thing to be proud of. Please forgive me for being so childish and selfish. For causing so much grief. I only wish it hadn't taken all this for me to have my eyes opened. I am working on a way to make it up to them, but please don't mention anything. I would hate to get their hopes up, but I am using my connections here to see if I can find their little brother.

All in all, I'm doing well. Don't worry about me, but don't stop praying either. I'll write again when I can.

Love,
Carol

Nina and her roommates huddled around their little kitchen table eating canned vegetable soup and arguing about whether to turn on the radio.

"It's time for the news." Emma reached for a piece of bread. "I'm sick of the news."

Irene agreed. "We should wait five or ten minutes. Then they'll go back to music."

"Well, I, for one, like to stay informed." Sadie rose to turn on the Zenith. "If you want dinner music, we either need to eat earlier or later. Besides, it's *my* radio." She turned the dial, and the radio slowly crackled to life. Johnny Mercer was crooning the last few bars of "Ac-Cent-Tchu-Ate the Positive."

"I don't see how we're supposed to accentuate the positive and eliminate the negative when all the news is so bleak," Emma grumbled.

"Sh-h!" Sadie scrunched her eyebrows at the familiar beeping of breaking news.

"We interrupt this program to bring you a special news bulletin from CBS World News. A press association has just announced that U.S. President Roosevelt is dead. The president died of a cerebral hemorrhage. All we know so far is that the president died at Warm Springs, in Georgia."

Around the little table, the girls stopped eating and stared at one another. Had they heard correctly? The news continued, explaining that Vice-President Truman would now be sworn in as president and how FDR was the first president to die in office while the country was at war.

"What's going to happen now?" Emma's eyes were as big as a Kewpie doll's. "They loved him, didn't they? The Americans?"

Irene nodded. "I wonder what kind of president Mr. Truman will be? He's got big shoes to fill."

"Poor Eleanor." Sadie shook her head. "And they've got four boys in active duty too."

Poor Eleanor, indeed. Nina bit her lip to keep from mentioning the rumors she'd heard about FDR having an extramarital affair. No point speaking ill of the dead, especially one who'd led his country through the greatest economic crisis and a world war, all without the use of his legs. Somehow, people in leadership seemed to be excused—at least the men.

"Why couldn't it have been Hitler?" Emma rose, gathered her dishes, and carried them to the sink.

Two and a half weeks later brought the first day of May. Nina decided she'd step out for some glorious sunshine as soon as lunch break arrived. With only a minute or two before the whistle would sound, Mr. Keinbaum himself stood on the walkway outside his upper-floor office. The room grew eerily quiet as the machines stopped. Nina wondered what could be important enough to stop working even a few minutes early.

"I wanted to be the first to tell you." He cleared his throat. "CBC radio just confirmed that Adolf Hitler and his wife, Eva Braun, are dead. They're reporting it as suicide."

Nina half expected the room to burst into cheers and applause, but the somber news was met with silence instead. Out of shock, relief, or reverence, she wasn't sure. Perhaps all three.

It didn't last long. The room quickly began to buzz as chairs were pushed into place and workers filed out of the room and toward the cafeteria. The news had lifted the mood as the chatter around the tables included phrases like "Surely, it'll all be over soon," and "Good riddance to bad rubbish!"

It took a week, but the May seventh issue of the *Winnipeg Free Press* proclaimed in huge letters, "Defeated Germany Surrenders. V-E Day to be Celebrated Tuesday. War in Europe Is Ended at Schoolhouse in France."

Canada's Finance Minister announced that the next day, May eighth, would be a national holiday. The girls heard the ruckus outside their apartment windows and ran to look out. People banged pots and pans and honked horns. Nina, Emma, Irene, and Sadie grabbed pots and lids to join in the revelry. Streets flooded with people celebrating. Church bells rang. Nina breathed in the fresh spring air, alive with relief and hope.

Where had David been when he heard the news? What was he doing now and how long would it take for him to come home? Perhaps most importantly, how much had the war changed him?

That evening, the girls were eager to huddle around the radio to hear what Prime Minister Mackenzie King had to say to Canadians.

"In the name of our country, I ask the people of Canada at this hour to join with me in expressing our gratitude as a nation for the deliverance from the evil forces of Nazi Germany. We unite in humble reverence and thanksgiving to God for His mercy."

He went on to acknowledge the great price and the many losses, the grieving families, and to all who'd served at home and abroad. "You have helped to rid the world of a great scourge."

Nina listened patiently but was far more interested in

hearing what the British might be saying. When the other girls decided to go out, Nina stayed home and found a station that was rerunning King George's speech.

"Today we give thanks to Almighty God for the great deliverance. Speaking from our empire's oldest capital city, a war-battered but never for one moment daunted or dismayed, speaking from London, I ask you to join with me in the act of thanksgiving."

A shudder went through Nina. If Mum and Dad had only stayed home in Middlesbrough, they would still be alive now, anticipating a reunion with their children. She shook away the image of dropping bombs and tried to listen as the King continued.

"And let us remember those who will not come back. Their constancy and courage in battle, their sacrifice and endurance in the face of a merciless enemy. Let us remember the men and women in all the services who have laid down their lives. We have come to the end of our tribulation, and they are not with us at the moment of our rejoicing."

Nina's latest letter from David had arrived just yesterday, written three weeks prior. He was fine then, but that could have changed in a moment. What if he were one of the ones who wouldn't return and they simply hadn't received word yet?

"And then, let us salute in gratitude the great host of the living who have brought us to victory. Armed or unarmed, men and women, you have fought, striven, and endured to your utmost. No one knows that better than I do, and as your king, I thank with a full heart those who bore arms so valiantly on land and sea or in the air, and all civilians who, shouldering their many burdens, have carried them unflinchingly and without complaint. With those memories in our minds, let us think what it was that has upheld us through nearly six years of suffering and terror."

Tears began to escape Nina's eyes. She barely remembered an England that was not at war. Now she would be returning—to what? She'd have to go alone, leaving Geoffrey and Hazel behind with their new family. Once she found Sully, then what? The

Wrights had advised her to bring him back to Canada, but they weren't offering to adopt him. Nor could Nina expect that. What if she didn't find him?

"So let us resolve to bring to the tasks which lie ahead the same confidence in our mission. Much hard work awaits us, both in the restoration of our own country after the ravages of war and in helping to restore peace and sanity to a shattered world. This comes upon us at a time when we have all given of our best for five long years and more, hearts and brain, nerves and muscles have been directed upon the overthrow of Nazi tyranny..."

Nina wiped her tears. The King was right. She had a mission. Rescuing Sully would be her part in this restoration he talked about. But even as she declared it to herself, thoughts of earlier "rescue" attempts came to mind. That night she tried to get her siblings out of their host homes would have been a disaster if Mr. Wright had not found them, or if the Wrights had washed their hands of all three of them. Her "rescue" of Irene would have gone nowhere without the intervention of others. How could she hope to rescue Sully on her own?

"There is great comfort in the thought that the years of darkness and danger in which the children of our country have grown up are over. And please God—forever. We shall have failed and the blood of our dearest will have flowed in vain if the victory which they died to win does not lead to a lasting peace founded on justice and goodwill. To that then, let us turn our thoughts on this day of justice and triumph and … and then take up our work again, resolved as a people to do nothing unworthy of those who died for us and to make the world such a world as they would have desired for their children and for ours. This is a task to which now honor binds us. In the hour of danger, we humbly commit our cause to the hand of God as He has been our strength and shield. Let us thank Him for His mercies and in this hour of victory, commit ourselves and our new task to the guidance of that same strong hand."

King George's reference to God caused Nina to slowly turn the knob to the "off" position and slide to her knees. Resting her elbows on the chair, she folded her hands and tried to pray.

Words wouldn't come.

Nina to David

June 1, 1945
Dear David,

I can't tell you how relieved and pleased I was—we all were—to learn you have survived the war "in one piece," as they say. I admire your bravery in fighting for Canada and the Commonwealth, and I pray daily that any "inside" wounds will heal completely and leave you an even stronger man. We are all praying that victory will occur in Japan any day as well. You must be so excited about coming home. Emma is beside herself to see you, and … well, to be completely honest, I am as well. I hope it's soon because I have exciting news.

I've booked my passage to England. After trying numerous times to get on one of the previous return trips with CORB (at first I was told I needed my parents' signature, if you can imagine that, which caused delays), now that the war is over and I've reached eighteen, I'm booked to leave Halifax July 14 on the *SS Pasteur*. I'm told this ship is so fast, it doesn't travel with convoys, and we could make the crossing in four days or less. Can you picture it? Three days on the train to get only halfway across Canada, and then almost that quickly across the Atlantic?

I'll be leaving Winnipeg on the seventh in case there are any delays along the way. The weekend before that, I'm returning to Cedar Bluff to say my good-byes. I don't even want to think about that. The only way I can bear the idea of saying good-bye to Geoffrey and Hazel—or the Wrights—is to assume I'll be coming back. *With* Sully. I don't know how I can make that all happen, but since I can't bear the other option either, I have no choice but to go. The idea of sitting here in Canada while Sully's whereabouts and situation are still unknown would be torture. I must try, even if it takes me the rest of my life.

I don't know whether to pray you get home before I leave or pray you're still in England when I arrive. Not seeing you again is simply one more thing I cannot bear to think about. Pray for me, David. My parents told me to "be a brave girl" when I left home to come here. I thought I was, but this return trip seems to be taking more courage than I can muster. If somehow the worst should happen and this is the last you hear from me, I don't want to let this opportunity pass without telling you the truth. I've loved you since the day we met. I will never forget that day you rescued Hazie and me from that silly old goose, Adolf. I had no idea then how prophetic that would one day seem, or what a true hero you would turn out to be. Thank you for your service. Thank you for all the ways you've shown care for me. Thank you for your efforts to find Sully. I love you, David.

Yours,
Nina

Chapter Twenty-Nine

David to Nina

04 JULY 1945

LIVERPOOL, ENGLAND

CABLEGRAM TO NINA GABRIEL, WINNIPEG, MANITOBA, CANADA

LETTER RECEIVED. BOARDING SS ILE DE FRANCE TODAY. DUE HALIFAX 13 JULY. PIER 21. MEET ME RAILROAD STATION CLOCKS. URGENT.

DAVID CAIN

Nina stood beside Dad Wright's old truck, surrounded by loved ones and the farmyard that had become home. She pulled Geoffrey into a tight hug, all too aware that the fifteen-year-old was a solid five inches taller than she. "I love you, little brother. Be good and take care of Hazie."

"I will." Geoffrey blinked hard several times as he backed away.

Hazel squeezed in for an embrace. At twelve, she'd caught up to Nina in height as well. "I'm going to miss you so-oo-oo much!"

"Oh, you'll hardly notice I'm gone. We've already spent months apart, haven't we?" Nina held her close.

"Yes, but I always knew you were only a two-hour train ride away. This is different."

Nina pulled back but kept her hands on Hazel's shoulders. "I know. You understand why I have to do this, though, don't you?"

Hazel nodded. "Yes. Please just come back soon."

"I promise I will. As soon as I can."

Jim and Daniel both moved in for quick hugs, followed by their mother. Mom Wright wrapped her arms tightly around Nina and held her for a long moment.

"Thank you for everything," Nina whispered. When she pulled away, the woman's eyes glistened with unshed tears.

She cleared her throat. "Be careful, dear girl."

"I will."

"We're not going to make that train, Nina," Dad Wright called from the driver's seat.

The passenger door hung open. Nina gave Hazel one last kiss on the cheek before climbing into the truck and pulling the door closed. She rolled down the window and waved all the way down the lane, trying to swallow the lump in her throat.

"They'll be fine." Dad Wright swiped away a tear of his own, warming Nina's heart. "Best roll that window up before this cab fills with dust."

Nina obeyed and turned forward to watch the gravel road and the familiar sights along the way—a green field of wheat on one side, a pasture on the other with a dozen Herefords grazing contentedly. It was hard to shake the nagging feeling that she might not make it back. CORB would cover the cost of her trip one way, which meant she could use her savings for the return trip and to live on until she found Sully. But what if that took too long? What if she'd need to find work and housing back in England—or worse, use up her savings just to live?

"How're you holding up, girlie?" Dad Wright kept his eyes on the road, but his voice held the same affection it did for his own children. "Excited to be going home?"

Nina swallowed. "This has really become my home."

He nodded. "I'm glad to hear it. You nervous?"

"Scared silly." They both laughed, and Nina began to relax.

At the station, Nina checked in while Dad Wright waited in a quiet corner. Ticket in hand, she walked toward him with a triumphant grin. "Three minutes to spare."

"Would it be all right if I prayed for you right here, Nina? I mean, I know Mother prayed for you last night, but I just thought—"

"Of course it's all right. I'd love it." With her free hand, Nina reached for the cuff of his sleeve and held onto it while she bowed her head.

Dad Wright placed his other hand on her shoulder and leaned in. "Lord, thank You for bringing Nina into our home and thank You for the strong young woman she has become. Please grant her journey mercies and courage. Provide for her needs in ways she would never have anticipated. Help her to locate her brother and return to us swiftly. Keep them both safe, I pray. In Jesus's name, Amen."

Nina couldn't even echo his *amen* for fear her voice would crack. She stood on tiptoes and kissed his cheek gently. "Thank you. For everything."

Dad Wright pulled his handkerchief from his pocket and swiped at his eyes. "Now let's get you on that train, or we'll have to do this all over again."

Back at their apartment, an excited Emma in her pink chenille bathrobe met her at the door. With curlers in her hair and bright red nail polish on only one hand, she waved a telegram back and forth in her unmanicured hand. "He's on his way. David's coming home!"

"He is?" Nina grabbed the telegram and dropped her suitcase. "Hey, this is for me."

"I know. I signed for it. He got your letter. He's going to be in Halifax when you get there."

"I see that." Nina read it over carefully. "The arrival times of those ships are pretty unpredictable, though. If his ship is late, I can't just wait around—"

"Oh, isn't it just so romantic?"

"Romantic? In all likelihood, we'll miss each other." Nina was ready to burst into tears. "Honestly, I was hoping he'd stay in England until I got there…and for some time after that."

"He probably didn't have much choice in the matter." Emma sat at the kitchen table where her nail polish waited.

"No, I suppose not. Why do you think he said *urgent*?"

Emma shrugged. "Probably just doesn't want to miss you. Once he's back, he can finally declare his love for you. Oh, isn't it so romantic?"

"Emma." Nina moved to the sink to fill the tea kettle.

"What? It *is* romantic." She let out a sudden gasp. "Oh! Maybe he's going to propose. Right there at the train station. Maybe he already has a ring and everything!"

Irene wandered in from her bedroom. "Who has a ring?"

"No one." Nina lit the stove, placed the kettle over the burner, and then turned to pull the teapot down from its shelf. "Emma's just excited her brother's coming home."

"Just Emma?" Irene and Emma exchanged knowing smiles. "I heard about one fella that came home with a wedding band for his girl, fashioned out of shrapnel they took out of his leg. What do you think of that?"

"Eww. No, thanks." Emma held her freshly painted fingers up and examined them for flaws. "That poor bride."

"Well, thankfully, David hasn't taken any shrapnel. Besides, we're nowhere near that point in our relationship."

"Oh, c'mon. You love my brother, and you know it."

Nina grinned as she poured hot water over the tea leaves. "I don't mind admitting it. I'm just saying—we're not at the place yet where there'll be any talk about rings or weddings. I've got a mission to accomplish, remember?"

"What's the latest word on that?" Irene took the chair

opposite Emma.

Nina sighed. "Nothing new, really. I received a letter from the last orphanage on the list. They never heard of Sully. They wished me well in my search but reminded me there are thousands of missing and displaced people trying to reunite with loved ones."

"That poor little kid." Emma tightened the lid on her nail polish. "Does he even know he has sisters and a brother?"

Nina could only shrug and shake her head. "I'm grateful for the work David already did on this. Even if he didn't get far, he saved me some steps." She took down three cups and poured tea into them through a strainer. "I assume you both want some?" Nina carried two cups to the table for the others and then leaned against the counter to drink her own.

"Thanks." Irene turned her cup. "Sure won't be the same around here without you."

"Don't say that." Emma blew on her fingernails. "She'll be back before we know it."

"We don't know that, Em." Nina set the hot tea down. "I'm too fidgety to even drink this right now. I need to go repack and wash out a few things."

Abandoning the tea, she grabbed the bag she'd dropped at the door and carried it into the bedroom she and Emma shared. Closing the door behind her, she leaned against it and tried to keep the tears in check. David was coming home. She should be thrilled about that, for his sake and for the whole family, if nothing else. But even if she did manage to meet him in Halifax, they'd only have to say good-bye again and she wasn't sure which was worse.

"God, if You're there and You hear me," she whispered, swiping a tear from her cheek. "I need Your help. It felt easier to leave home at fourteen and go far away into the unknown than it feels now."

The door thumped against her back.

"Nina?" Emma called from the other side. "You all right?"

Nina turned and let her friend in.

"I thought I heard you talking to someone."

Nina couldn't hold back the tears. "Just to God. But I don't think He's listening."

"Oh, honey." Emma pulled her tight. "Of course He is. He loves you very much, and He already knows what's on your heart. Maybe you could tell me, if that's easier."

Nina gave her nose a good blow as Emma led her to the bed. They sat on the edge.

"I used to think I was so brave, so independent." Nina sniffed.

"You are."

"Maybe I was. Before I knew better. Now I'm just afraid. Part of me wants to forget the whole thing. Just settle in here and wait for David to come home."

Emma nodded. "That's … a possibility."

"But how can I, Em? I will never be able to forget I have a brother over there, somewhere. The longer I wait, the harder it will be to find him. I have to do this, but I'm so afraid I won't succeed."

"Then we'll just have to believe that you will. God will help you. He'll help you in ways you never dreamed. You'll see."

Nina gazed into Em's pretty blue eyes, wanting more than anything to believe her words.

Mrs. Garrison, the CORB escort on the train to Halifax, concentrated her attention on the younger kids. Nina recognized none of the other CORB evacuees and made little effort to figure out whether she should. They'd all aged five years. They'd all had different experiences. While she might ordinarily be curious to hear their stories, her mind was far too preoccupied. She spent the trip reviewing all the notes she'd made and letters she'd received in the search for Sully, trying to figure out where she'd start once she reached England. She also memorized David's telegram, trying to determine if she'd missed anything between the lines. Was Emma right about David's love for her? Even if she was, how long could she expect David to wait? Where was he now? Would they miss each other, possibly by mere hours, or would he be waiting in Halifax? The closer she got to the East Coast, the more she found herself hoping for the latter.

The salty Atlantic air greeted Nina as she stepped off the train onto the platform in Halifax. She paused long enough to close her eyes and listen to the cry of the gulls circling above. For a moment, she was transported back to childhood in Middlesbrough. The jostling around her didn't allow her to linger long, and she followed the flow of passengers. Her gaze rose to the overhead walkway connecting the station to the Hotel Nova Scotian and to the nearby Pier 21 terminal where David's ship would dock.

The railroad station had not changed and was, if anything, even busier than it had been five years before. Troops in Canadian uniform filled every bench, surrounded by khaki duffel bags. The biggest difference was the attention that came Nina's way. While the soldiers of 1940 had ignored the skinny fourteen-year-old, many of these fellows smiled and gave Nina appreciative nods, making her more uncomfortable. She scanned every face even though it was doubtful David's ship had arrived yet. Breaking away from her group, she made her way to the clocks that displayed the time in at least ten different zones. Not a familiar face in sight. She approached a ticket counter.

"Excuse me? Can you please tell me whether the *Ile de France* has arrived?"

The short, balding man across from her pointed one hand at the schedule on the wall without saying a word or bothering to look up from whatever he was doing. The sign said the *Ile de France* was due to arrive July 13, just like David said.

"Nina! Come on." Mrs. Garrison called out. "Please stay with the group. Our rooms are waiting and tomorrow's a big day."

At the Hotel Nova Scotian, Nina shared a room with three other girls. While the others chattered eagerly about returning home and what they might expect, Nina's heart grew heavier. Torn between her hopes of seeing David before she boarded her ship and dreading the task ahead once she disembarked, she slept little. She was the first to rise and dress the next morning. Slipping out of the hotel room, she ventured outside. A ship waited at the dock, a French flag flying high. That could be either David's ship or hers. She ran to the terminal and learned it was, indeed, the *Pasteur*. They were to board that afternoon and leave the next day.

With a heavy heart, she walked back to the train station. She was supposed to be joining the others for breakfast at the hotel, but she had to know how far out the *Ile de France* might be. Once more, she made her way past the row of clocks to the ticket counter.

"Nina!"

Convinced Mrs. Garrison was chasing her down, Nina ignored the voice and continued in the direction of the counter.

"Nina! Stop!"

Wait a minute. She knew that voice, and it wasn't Mrs. Garrison's.

Nina stopped and swung around. Racing toward her through the crowd in her Red Cross uniform, was Carol Wright.

"Carol?" Nina froze. "What are you doing here? I thought you—"

"We arrived in the middle of the night." Carol set down a suitcase and reached for Nina's hand. "Oh, I'm so glad we found you. We thought we were going to miss you." To Nina's surprise, Carol pulled her into an embrace. "Oh, thank God."

"I'm … so confused. I thought—" Nina's head spun.

"I know. I'm so sorry I couldn't let you know sooner. Everything happened so fast. By the time I was able to wire Mum and Dad, you'd left. I hoped and prayed we'd catch you before you left Canada."

"We?"

"Well, I had no idea David Cain was on the same ship, and he had no idea I was either. We spotted each other our second day at sea."

"David? You've seen David?"

Carol took Nina's elbow and pulled her toward a bench. "C'mon. You look like you need to sit down. I have so much to explain."

Nina sank to the wooden bench. David and Carol had journeyed back together. Were they an item after all? Had she completely misunderstood? "So…" she looked around the station. "Where is he?"

"He'll be right back. They went to the men's room and were going to circle around that way in hopes of spotting you."

"They?" Nina was convinced she was dreaming the entire encounter.

"Yes." Carol sat next to her and took her hand. "I need to tell you something, Nina. Like I said, things happened so quickly that I couldn't—"

But Nina didn't hear any more. Walking toward her was David, more handsome than ever and three years more mature. She could tell the moment he spotted her because his whole face lit up into a gorgeous smile. "Nina!"

Nina rose so she'd be able to greet him with a warm hug. Then she noticed his companion. Clinging tightly to David's hand, a boy of three or four trotted to keep up.

Nina stared at David, and then Carol, and then back at the boy. His short pants, little jacket, and hat made him look so much like Geoffrey had when they left England, it made Nina's head spin.

Carol rose. "Nina, I have someone I want you to meet." She smiled down at the boy. "This … is Sullivan George Gabriel. Your brother."

Nina continued to stare while David squatted and spoke to

the boy. "Sully, I'd like you to meet your big sister, Nina. Can you say hello?"

The boy looked up at Nina shyly but managed to say, "Hello, Nina." Then Nina saw it. He had the same eyes as Geoffrey and the same dimple in his left cheek as Hazel.

She dropped to her knees and gazed into his face, uncertain whether she could even speak but not wanting to frighten him. "Hello, Sully. I'm … pleased to meet you." She shook her head and turned back to David. "I don't understand. How—?"

"It was all Carol's doing." Still smiling and clinging to Sully's hand, David moved to the bench and sank into it. "You want to explain, Carol?" He patted the seat beside him, and Sully scrambled up and leaned into David, clearly tired.

Carol took the bench facing them, and Nina sat beside her.

"Well, it's a long story. But as I said, in the end, things happened so fast. David had already done much of the legwork. With my connections through the Red Cross, I was able to find Sully. Turns out he was taken in by an elderly German couple, the Heimbergers. Loveliest people I ever met. They said they wanted to repay England for taking them in before the war."

"Oh, thank God." Nina rested one hand across her chest. "And … my grandmother …?"

David ran his hand through Sully's fine hair and cast compassionate eyes on Nina. "I found her, Nina. She's extremely unwell. Doesn't seem to remember any of you, not even your father. The staff at the nursing home told me she has cancer and could be gone within the month."

Sully slipped off the bench and moved closer to Nina. Resting one hand on her knee, he looked up into her face. "Are you really mein schwester?"

Nina glanced at Carol, who nodded quickly.

"Yes, I really am." She wrapped his little hands in hers.

"And do I really have another schwester named Hazel and a bruder named Geoffrey?"

Nina loved his jumble of English and German. "Yes, you do. They will be so happy to meet you, Sully." She wanted to pinch the boy's skin to convince herself he was real. Instead, she patted the bench beside her. "Would you like to sit here by me?"

Sully shook his head. "I sitzen by David." He turned around, and David pulled him onto his lap. "I'm hungrig."

"Me too, pal." David stood, hoisting Sully onto one hip. "Let's go find something to eat, shall we? I'll introduce you to something Canadian. Ladies, watch my duffel, will you?"

Nina watched them walk away. "He speaks clearly, apart from the blended languages. His hearing must be good."

Carol nodded. "The surgery was successful. Your parents made the right choice for him. I mean … even though it cost them everything…"

"What a beautiful boy."

"Isn't he?" Carol swiped at a tear. "I've grown fond of him very quickly."

"How can I ever thank you?" Nina pulled a hankie from her pocket and blew her nose.

Carol shook her head. "No need. I think I did it as much for me as anyone."

"For *you*?" Nina studied Carol's face. "I don't understand."

"I needed to make amends somehow, Nina. I'm so sorry for the way I treated you. Once I got over there and realized what life had been like for you, for your parents … the choice they made for you and Geoff and Hazel … well, I could see how much they sacrificed. Out of love."

"I understand why it was hard for you when we showed up." Nina smiled. "But thank you."

"There's more." Carol turned her gaze toward the ceiling. "I think somewhere deep inside, I desperately wanted to redeem myself because of what happened to my own brother and sister. I thought if I could just find Sully and bring him to you, it would make up for it. I'd be able to forgive myself."

Nina wasn't sure what to say. "And have you? Forgiven yourself?"

Carol let out a slow sigh and nodded. "I believe I have."

"You know what your parents would say, right?"

"Yeah. There was nothing to forgive. It was an accident."

"And they'd be right."

Carol smiled. "Thank you for saying that."

"So … what happens now? I'm due to board a ship for England in a few hours."

"I think the first order of business is to get you off the manifest for whatever ship you're booked on."

"CORB will not be happy with me, but I'm sure they'll understand once I explain."

"Once that's done, we need you to spend as much time with Sully as possible before I leave, so he's comfortable with you."

"You're leaving?"

"My instructions were to bring him to Canada, place him in your care, and then get back as fast as possible. I'm so glad I don't have to travel all the way to Manitoba. You wouldn't believe the work that's left to do over there."

Nina looked up to see David and Sully returning hand-in-hand, each holding a donut in their free hand. "So… are you and David… you know?"

Carol began laughing. "Me and David?" Then she laughed harder. "Oh, you silly goose. Don't you know how crazy he is about you? Besides, I've got a fella waiting for me back in Liverpool. An American named Roger."

"Another reason to hurry back."

"Exactly."

Sully released David's hand and ran to Carol, holding up his donut. "Look what I got!"

David pulled a paper bag from his pocket and held it out to Nina. "Breakfast's on me."

"Thanks." Nina pulled out one and handed the bag with one remaining donut to Carol.

"You're welcome. And I don't believe we've had a proper hello." David held the rest of his donut between his teeth while he pulled Nina to her feet.

Laughing, she wrapped her arms around his neck. It was really him, and he was really hers.

"Now don't you be getting my hair all sticky with that donut," he teased, removing his wedge cap and running a hand through his crew cut. "You don't want to ruin perfection."

Sully turned his sticky face toward Carol. "Does David love my big schwester?"

Carol nodded. "I think so, but why don't you ask him yourself?"

Before Sully could ask, David responded with a resounding, "Yes! Your big sister is the sweetest, smartest, most beautiful woman I ever met, Sully." He turned and gazed directly into Nina's eyes. "And I love her very much."

Nina to Carol

August 15, 1945
Cedar Bluff, Manitoba
Dear Carol,

By now you'll probably have heard how closely we missed the series of explosions at the Bedford Magazine in Halifax—just days after you departed back to England and after David, Sully, and I boarded the train for Manitoba. We saw pictures in the newspapers. It looked horrendous! Only one life lost, but one too many of course.

David succeeded in getting us booked together rather than his originally scheduled trip with the other troops (although there were plenty of soldiers on our train too). This was a blessing because Sully missed you horribly, and at least David was somewhat familiar to him. By the time we reached Winnipeg, Sully had taken to me as well. It's been eye-opening for me, getting to know him. Some of the children that crossed with us five years ago weren't much older than he is now. He doesn't seem to have any memory of our parents, but I'm hoping that perhaps something will be "jogged loose" as time goes on and he's exposed to our memories of them.

I wish you could have seen the reunion. I know it's not accurate to call it that exactly—although it was certainly a reunion for Geoffrey, Hazel, and me. And for David and his family. Emma came with us from Winnipeg to Cedar Bluff and we were all met at the train by your parents and theirs. David and Emma went home with their family. Sully clung tightly to me, but Hazel managed to charm him very quickly, and by the first evening, he and Daniel behaved like lifelong pals too. I can already tell that when Daniel starts grade one in a couple of weeks, Sully will want to tag along. I'm glad he'll have Daniel to show him the ropes when his turn comes next year. Meanwhile, Geoffrey is already teaching Sully to catch a baseball.

What has the reaction there been to the bombing of Japan? We are all greatly relieved that the war is now truly and officially over yet horrified at the same time. Your mom said, "If man can cause that much destruction in so short a time, surely all mankind's days on this planet are numbered." She worries for our futures, having lived through so much. (And by "we" I mean our entire generation, everywhere. I consider myself one of the fortunate.)

Carol, I wish I had the words to express my gratitude for everything you did to find Sully and bring him over—and not only for his sake. You shared with me how healing it was for you. For myself, I've needed for a long time to learn that everything doesn't depend on me. That God places others in our lives to help us along our journeys, and sometimes that help comes from where we least expect it. I thank you from the bottom of my heart, and I know that you and I will grow as friends and sisters whether you return or we remain far apart.

Lastly, David and I are talking about marriage. It was wonderful to have the train trip to get reacquainted, but we've agreed there is no rush. For the next year at least, he will work with his dad and adjust to civilian life. I'll stay with your family while Sully adjusts and help out wherever I can. Then, when the time is right, we plan to marry and raise Sully together. Just between you and me, David has hinted that I might expect a ring by Christmas. Then we can start making plans for real … such as the one I already made to include Emma, Hazel, Irene, and you in my wedding party. I sure hope you're home by then.

Now please write back. I want to hear all about this fella you've met.

Love,
Nina

Chapter Thirty

Jean to Nina

January 1990

Mrs. Nina Cain
PO Box 55
Cedar Bluff, Manitoba

Dearest Nina,

I know you don't want to hear this, but you and I will have known each other for fifty years this fall! How is that possible? I'm so glad we've kept in touch. The trip Bruce and I made to Manitoba in '66 will remain one of my dearest memories. I can still picture you and your passel of oh-so-Canadian teenagers gathered around your dining table, celebrating your fortieth birthday with that massive chocolate cake. I think I returned home twenty pounds heavier from all your delicious, farm-fresh food. I always hoped you and David would be able to visit us here in PEI and enjoy some fresh seafood… and maybe, just maybe, this will be the year?

If you haven't heard, fiftieth reunions are being planned for CORB kids—there's one this month in London. But since several of us stayed in Canada (or returned, like I did), we're also hoping to hold one in Halifax in September. I'm on the committee, and we're working out some possible activities—a tour of Pier 21 will be top priority. We're looking at the weekend of September fifteenth and sixteenth. The eighteenth will be the fiftieth anniversary of the sinking of the *City of Benares*, so we could commemorate that as well. I've also written to Alice in England, hoping beyond hope that she might be able to fly over for it. Wouldn't it be grand for the three of us to be together again? Hazel and Geoffrey too, of course!

Bruce asked why I didn't just call you, but I knew you'd need some time to talk it over with your family. Please give me a call after you've had a chance to do that, and let's plan. We are thinking of selling our house at some point, but it won't be until next year at the earliest. With the kids all gone, there's plenty of space for anyone who wants to stay with us following the reunion (beforehand would work as well, although I'll be tied up with organizing—after would be better if that works for you. We'd love to give you a tour of this dear island that attracts so many tourists and has become our beloved home.)

So hoping you can attend,
Jean

Nina rested her head against her seat on the Air Canada DC-8 for the final leg of their journey, Toronto to Halifax, while David recited details like engine type, air speed, and range of the aircraft to anyone who would listen. His knee jiggled up and down, making him appear nervous to other passengers. Nina knew he was merely itching to see the cockpit or perhaps tell stories about his flying days. She'd heard them enough times she could tell them herself, but she didn't mind. Far better to listen to the stories than to be stuck married to a veteran who refused to talk about the war at all. Over the years, the results of such behavior seemed to have shown up everywhere—from alcoholism to abuse of loved ones to suicide. Nina felt grateful she'd married a man who spoke freely about both the good and painful memories. It was only in the past decade that the world of psychology stopped using terms like "shell shock" or "battle fatigue." Now, "Post Traumatic Stress Disorder" was recognized as an official mental disorder.

She had so much to be grateful for. While this reunion might be one of the only times other CORB kids had an opportunity to share their memories with others who understood, she'd always had her siblings nearby. Even after they all married and moved to other towns, they'd never lived more than a two-hour drive apart. Nina and David had hosted untold family gatherings on the original Cain farm, with lots of space for the cousins to run around and become great friends. How many times had Nina viewed the scene from her kitchen window and been swept with the conviction that her parents would be so pleased to see their children and their children's children all together? Even if it was in the middle of the Canadian prairie.

Behind her, Hazel and Geoffrey settled into their seats.

Nina craned her neck to turn around. "Don't forget to buckle up."

"Nina, please." Hazel rolled her eyes. "I'm fifty-seven years old."

Geoffrey merely laughed. "Some things never change, Sis. May as well embrace it." He made a point of displaying both ends of his seatbelt for Nina's approval before fastening them with a satisfying *click*.

"I know. She promised Mum and Dad she'd look out for us." Hazel winked and gave Nina a playful smile. "Love you, Sis."

"Love you too." Nina turned around and sighed. She'd tried to talk Sully into coming too, but he had little interest. Besides, at forty-nine, he was still working full-time as an audiologist and wouldn't want to use up limited vacation time on a sentimental journey that held little sentiment for him. With Doris Day's version of "Sentimental Journey" playing in the back of her mind and her hand resting in David's, Nina dozed.

"Nina!"

"I saw her first."

Nina twirled around, still disoriented from the flight and the unfamiliar Halifax airport. Toward her rushed two sixty-something women, one as stylish as a fashion model and the other stuck somewhere in the late seventies.

"It's Jean and Alice." Hazel recognized them immediately and waited while they both embraced Nina. Soon everyone was hugging everyone else, shaking hands, and exclaiming things like "You haven't changed a bit" even though they had, or "I'd recognize you anywhere" even though they wouldn't.

"When did you arrive, Alice?" Nina pulled her bag off the carousel and turned to follow Jean to her vehicle.

"Oh, I've been here a week already. Plenty of time to get reacquainted with Jean. I'm so glad you all came."

"And we're glad *you* came." Nina didn't admit she had worried there might not be enough to talk about after all these years. By the time they reached the exit, it was clear they would run out of time long before they were through exchanging stories.

Jean led them to the parking lot and then to a blue Ford van. "I've borrowed this from a friend, so we have plenty of room for all." She unlocked the doors and opened the back for luggage, which Geoffrey and David immediately began loading. "We've got it for the whole week."

Once everyone was strapped in, Jean drove to the very hotel Nina had stayed in when she almost returned to England with the other CORB evacuees forty-five years earlier, now called the Westin Nova Scotian and nicknamed Halifax's "Grande Dame."

"After the reunion ends," Jean explained, "it's about a four-hour drive to my place in PEI, including the ferry ride. I can't wait to show you my home."

The next two days passed in a blur as "CORBites" gathered, introduced themselves, told their stories, and reminisced. A tour of the now out-of-commission, deserted, and rather bleak Pier 21 brought heaviness to Nina's heart.

"This is tragic." She looked around the space, dubbed "Canada's Gateway," imagining how many thousands of immigrants had come through here. How many British Home Children, child evacuees, and war brides? How many troops departed from here during both world wars? "I mean, it's not like we're not still receiving lots of immigrants every year. Somehow arriving by air just seems less—" She couldn't seem to find a word for it.

"Dramatic?" Jean smiled.

"Maybe."

"Well, if it makes you feel better, I've heard rumors that a group of dedicated people are working toward making Pier 21 a national historic site. You know, to give visitors an authentic glimpse into Canadian history."

Nina nodded. "I hope that happens."

The tour of the train station helped lift her spirits. While rail travel had greatly declined, the place had changed little and was certainly still in use. Nina and David found the spot where they'd been reunited after the war. "Look." She grabbed Hazel's hand and looped her arm into Geoffrey's. "This is where I first met Sully."

"I remember being here as a kid, I think," Geoffrey looked around. "Although we passed through so many train stations, who's to say? What about you, Hazie?"

"No. I barely remember the ship, and that's probably because I was so sick. And you were always getting yourself into some sort of trouble.'

"True. I was." He put an arm around Nina. "I don't think it let up much when we got home, either."

"Home?" Nina smiled up at him.

"To the Wrights' home. Sorry I put you through all that, Sis. I don't think I've ever thanked you for looking out for us the way you did."

Nina returned his side hug.

At the banquet that night, they heard story after story as the former CORB children took turns sharing. Some stories were tragic—homesickness, being placed in unsuitable homes, being separated from siblings. Some had been passed to as many as five different homes during their stay. Some went home early. When Nina's turn came, she took a deep breath before speaking into the microphone.

"There are so many stories I could tell, it's difficult to choose. But tonight, I want to tell you about my big sister, Carol. You see, Carol never wanted her parents to take in us three Gabriel children—or any evacuees, for that matter. And who could blame her? Her young heart had been shattered by the loss of two younger siblings—for which she blamed herself—and at sixteen, she did not have the tools to deal with everything that was going on. I wish I'd understood then what I do now, but life doesn't work that way, does it? Though she did everything in her power to make our lives miserable, it wasn't until after she joined the Canadian Red Cross Corps and discovered for herself what we'd been living through back in England that her eyes were opened. She understood why we were here. Not only did she change her attitude towards my siblings and me, but she worked tirelessly—and succeeded—in locating our youngest brother, whom we'd never met, and bringing him back to Canada.

"You see, our parents died in a London bombing in 1944."

Gentle gasps were heard around the room. Some people offered sympathetic nods.

"Carol became my hero, my sister, and a dear friend. We lost her to breast cancer five years ago. She was sixty-one." Nina paused, pressing her lips together a moment. "I've learned that family bonds are not necessarily something that come with birth. Sometimes, they are learned. Sometimes they occur between the least likely of participants. But always, they must be fought for.

"I think I speak for my siblings too, when I say I am eternally grateful to the Wright family who made us their own, despite their grief and pain. None of us knows what our lives would have been like if we hadn't left England. But for myself, I can say with confidence, it's been a good life."

Nina returned to her table, where her companions were wiping their eyes. David took her hand and squeezed it tightly.

After the last story was shared, a brass plaque was unveiled on behalf of the CORB evacuees, expressing "Our unbounded gratitude" to Canada. Lastly, the group rose to sing first "God Save the Queen," followed by "O Canada." Most of the people present had become Canadian citizens, and they sang with enthusiasm. By the end of the first line, "Our home and native land," Nina was fighting back tears. By the time they neared the end, "God keep our land glorious and free," she could hardly find a dry eye in the room.

Nina to her parents

July 30, 1990
Dear Mum and Dad,

This is only the second letter I've written you since you passed, and I'm fairly certain it will be my last. In the first one, I was so confused and filled with anger. A child still, not understanding how you could have sent us away, how you could have had another child, how God could have taken you from us, or how you could have lain so much responsibility on my young shoulders.

Now I'm a sixty-four-year-old grandmother, and my perspective has been completely reshaped by life. The reunion last month brought back so many memories—things I've been too busy to think about for years. Seeing the others and hearing their stories has made me nothing but grateful. I want you to know two things. First, I have completely forgiven you. Not that your choice truly requires forgiveness, for it was made in love. I know that now. I forgive to set my own heart free.

You would love my David. Oh, we've had our tough times for sure, but he's been a wonderful husband and father, and his family has truly become mine. Together we raised kids you'd be proud of too. Penny and Barbara are both teachers. David Junior is an excellent carpenter. Vince is a musician and teaches guitar from his home. Their spouses have fit into our family well and so far, they've presented us with five grandchildren—three boys, two girls.

Geoffrey ended up partnering with Jim in taking over the Wrights' farm. He and Rebecca have three sons, all married. One grandchild so far.

Hazel's the only one of us who returned to England, and that was only briefly, for her honeymoon in 1960. She became a nurse and married a dentist, so their two kids have great teeth. One is married. No grandkids.

How I wish you could see Sully now! He's brilliant. He's an audiologist, so passionate about helping children with hearing problems that he's made umpteen trips overseas, volunteering his time in developing countries. He is still single at forty-nine, but I think he'd make a terrific catch for the right woman. He says he has no time to go looking, so I suppose if it's going to happen, she'll need to come to him.

Sometimes I try to imagine how our lives would have turned out if you'd kept us home all those years ago. Sully was already on his way, though, of course, I didn't know it. So I suppose the same fate would have befallen you two, leaving us children floundering. Probably separated.

My second and bigger purpose for this letter is to say *thank you*, because I never really have. Once I became a mother myself, I began to understand what an impossible situation you were in. We do anything to protect our children, don't we? I get that now. I can't imagine how hard that was for you. I thank you from the bottom of my heart for making that difficult choice. For loving us enough to put our best interests before your own. Canada has been good to us and for us. I hope we and our descendants can be and do the same for her. You made the right decision.

Lovingly,
Nina

End Quotes

THE QUEEN'S LETTER OF THANKS SENT TO ALL HOST FAMILIES WHO ENTERTAINED CORB EVACUEES IN THE DOMINIONS

I wish to mark, by this personal message, my gratitude for the help and kindness which you have shown to the children who crossed the sea from the United Kingdom many months ago. Since the early days of the War, you have opened your doors to strangers and offered to share your home with them. In the kindness of your heart, you have accepted them as members of your own family, and I know that to this unselfish task, you and all your household have made many great sacrifices. By your generous sympathy, you have earned the true and lasting gratitude of those to whom you have given this hospitality, and by your understanding you have shown how strong is the bond uniting all those who cherish the same ideals.

Elizabeth

"Time might show that the disruptive effect upon the children, and the absence of parental control during the formative years, was a drawback which might leave a mark.

"Transfer of children of this age from the horrors of war, the restrictions on food, clothing and fuel, and the effects of the blackout, to the freedom of affection and friendship, may prove to be of incalculable benefit. These, and many other features of the scheme can only be assessed later."

—Marjorie Maxse, Director, Child Overseas Evacuation Board in 1944

Author's Note

There are so many fascinating aspects to the stories behind the British and Canadian governments' scheme for evacuating children to relative safety during World War II that I could only touch upon a few in this book. One area where I took liberties for the sake of the story was with the sinking of the *SS City of Benares*, the theme of my next novel. When Donna writes to Nina to tell her she's also coming to Canada, she would not have known which ship she'd sail on, when she would depart, or who her escort would be. All such information was kept secret until boarding time, for security reasons. If she had written to Nina after she boarded, the letter would have gone down with the ship. I wanted Nina to learn in this dramatic manner that her friend had been on board the *City of Benares*. None of the children aboard that ill-fated ship came from Middlesbrough.

Another area where I fudged was in bringing David home in July of 1945. It's highly unlikely that David would have been shipped back to Canada that early. Between the need for military help with post-war clean-up and the challenging logistics of getting all those soldiers home, some did not return until early 1946. Married men were generally discharged first.

The Canadian Museum of Immigration at Pier 21 in Halifax opened to the public in 1999, nine years after CORB's fiftieth reunion.

I love to hear from my readers!

Feel free to email me at terriejtodd@gmail.com or through my blog, www.terrietodd.blogspot.com where you can sign up for my newsletter. You can also find me on Facebook at www.facebook.com/terrie.todd.31 or Instagram: terrie.todd.31

Other Books by Terrie Todd

Fiction

The Silver Suitcase
Maggie's War
Bleak Landing
Rose Among Thornes
The Last Piece
Lilly's Promise
April's Promise

Releasing Fall 2025

Even If I Perish

Non-fiction

Out of My Mind: A Decade of Faith and Humor